Helensburgh Library

Argyll and Bute Libraries
34115 00471373 7

For John and Cathy
and
Luke and Evan

*'Every day sees humanity more victorious in
the struggle with space and time.'*

Gugliemo Marconi.

Book 1: The Marconi Paradigm

Book 1: The Marconi Paradigm

   1. Vatican, Pope Julias XVI.

   2. Rome, Priest Development quarter: Santiago.

   3. Cartergreen, Malachi.

   4. New Mecca: Prime Cleric.

   5. Darkland Fortress: Cole.

   6. Himalayas, 'Half Realm': Vaughan.

   7. Vatican: Santiago.

   8. Vatican prison: Rodrigo Gomez (The Surgeon).

   9. Himalayas, 'Half Realm': The Affinity.

   10. The Vatican Church of St. John: Pope Julias.

   11. New Mecca: Basset.

   12. Cartergreen: Misba Ranha.

   13. Darkland Fortress: Cole.

   14. Vatican: Meniux.

   15. Vatican: Santiago.

16. New Mecca: Basset.

17. Rome: Priest Development quarter: Anna.

18. New Mecca: Maria.

19. Clefton Green: Colonel William Carstairs.

20. Darkland: Santiago.

21. Clefton Green: Irkalla.

22. Vatican Prison: Vaughan.

23. Darkland: Cole.

24. Cartergreen: Malachi.

25. Himalayas, 'Half realm': Vaughan and Maria

26. New Mecca: Basset.

27. Darkland, City of Castor: Tel R Amir.

28. Vatican prison: Rodrigo Gomez (The Surgeon).

29. Rome, Priest Development Quarter: Meniux.

30: Darkland: Santiago:

31: Vatican: Pope Julias XVI.

32: Sub Marianas Trench: The Exile.

33. New Mecca: Prime Cleric.

34. New Mecca: Basset.

35. Talker Plains: Malachi.

36. Darkland, City of Castor: Cole.

37. Darkland, City of Castor: Santiago.

38. New Mecca: Basset.

39. Vatican: Meniux.

40. Himalayas, 'Half realm': Vaughan and Maria.

41. Talker Plains: Malachi.

42. Pre-meltdown City of Sappho: (Year 2177).

43. Darkland City of Castor: Cole.

44. Vatican: Pope Julias XVI.

45. Darkland City of Castor: Santiago.

46. Rome, Priest Development Quarter: Irkalla.

47. City of Sappho: Vaughan.

48. New Mecca: Basset.

49. Vatican: Malachi.

50. New Mecca: Maria.

51. Vatican: Pope Julias XVI.

52. Florence: Vaughan.

53. New Mecca: Basset.

54. The Vatican Church of St. John: Meniux.

55. Vatican Transit Device Room: Paula.

56. Himalayas, 'Half Realm': Vaughan.

Book 1:

1. Vatican, Pope Julias XVI.

The Holy Father's personal quarters had that musty smell you find in an elderly person's home. Not quite the smell of death, but a lingering background odour that wants to suck you in.

He sat at his desk having just completed the world Mass to an audience of two billion dedicated Christians. He spoke of the ongoing war with the Muslims. How through prayer and endeavour, new ground was gained in the fight for territory with few casualties. About how the field hospitals were caring for, and saving, countless injured fighters, and about the martyrs who had not been so lucky.

Since the Tellurian Nuclear Eradication Treaty Earth went back to basics. To never again see the level of genocide witnessed on that fateful day in 2201, Earth had embraced a new path to a supposed better future. All technology was banned by Muslims and Christians. In fact, the putting together of the Treaty was the most sedate 10 years that the planet could remember; both parties strived for a future that would be separate, but peaceful. Land divided up. Continents divided up.

The outlawing of technology was far easier than anticipated. Humanity had become reliant on it. A self-replicating dependence that was both efficient and fast. With this, came the ability for information to be disseminated immediately to millions, however, control of this information was nonexistent. Human selfish needs and inherent greed thrived using this medium and consumed itself. As soon as satellites and interwebsphere became inoperable, all the intelligent receiving devices followed suit.

The internal combustion engine was now the most technical thing on the planet except for the Tightbeem, itself controlled by a wing of the church rumoured to have direct access to the same section working within the Muslim camp. After the Tellurian Nuclear Eradication Treaty, twenty years of peace talks and blame-apportioning, the only thing either side could agree upon was that neither side would ever agree. Massive exoduses ensued with both religions congregating in the few habitable areas left. All other religions apart from Christianity and Islam were outlawed.

'Holy Father, may I say that was a beautiful touching sermon today.' Father Meniux was an incorrigible sycophant. He had flattered and manipulated his way to a comfortable job as Pope Julias' chief attender.

'Thank you Father Meniux. I think it went well.' Julias hated Father Meniux with a passion, and only tolerated him as he was easy to control: playing Meniux like a fiddle competently saved him having to conduct the rest of the orchestra. A few words to Meniux got things sorted out. The Holy Father only had to turn a partially blind eye to his chief attender's rather strange pastimes.

'I feel that God himself is speaking through you at times, Holy Father. Not even he could show more wisdom or compassion in his words.' Father Meniux bowed his head as he spoke.

'Father Meniux, I am but a fly compared to Our Lord. Yes, I try to preach his tenets, but in a bid to understand him, it's easy to miss what's right in front of you.' Pope Julias was a master of prattle. He could preach on Tightbeem for hours without really saying anything. Truly, a gift from God. 'My lunch now, if you please Father Meniux.'

Father Meniux left the chamber and sent in the serving girls. They carried two large trays of corn, some claret and fresh bread. Food was scarce, but you wouldn't think so looking at Pope Julias. Often Meniux was reminded of a dead horse he had seen once years ago: its body blown up to a ridiculous unnatural size as decomposition set in, and the gases tried to get out. He often thought how the Holy Father would pop like a balloon, just like the horse did.

Every lunchtime Pope Julias would devour enough corn for a small army. He dismissed the servers and sat to begin. After gorging himself, the Pope knelt down to pray for guidance and inspiration for his second of the day's world Masses. No sooner had he began when, in the corner, a casually dressed man in his twenties appeared in front of him. Astonished the Holy Father then heard the stranger speak: 'Holiest Father! My name is Vaughan.'

The young man confidently walked over to the sitting Pope Julias and leaned on his large desk. Pope Julias was still dumbstruck. 'Relax, Holy Father,' smiled Vaughan. 'May I have a minute of your time?'

2. Rome, Priest Development quarter: Santiago.

Santiago spilled most of the morning tea over his lap and was sure that God was saying his latest sermon needed a bit more work. He knew he was on to a telling off from his wife, Anna, for not sitting at the dining table, but he simply couldn't be bothered as he would be sitting in a torturous wooden chair all day at the Ministry.

His kitchen was small, yet functional (as was pretty much every room in the house), but he knew he was lucky to have a covered roof and thanked God daily for this good fortune.

From an early age Santiago was a dreamer. He always had grand ideas and plans which often landed him in trouble. More curious than mischievous, on countless occasions he had come a cropper. Once whilst cleaning the tabernacle in the church, which as a child he did before the service every day, he had the bright idea to try fitting inside. Santiago remembered thinking that if Christ was in there then he could fit too. The flimsy stand gave way as his legs got in, and the tabernacle toppled onto the old wooden floor face down, locking him inside. The 20 trapped minutes felt like days, and when freed by his father he was rewarded with a hard boot up the behind – but nothing more was ever said.

'Don't even try to cover up the mess you have made!' said a furious Anna, who spotted Santiago's vain attempt to disguise his clumsiness.

'Sorry darling!' Santiago lied. 'Get me a cloth, will you?'

'If you sat at the table, I'd not need to get you a cloth,' Anna scorned.

'Yeah yeah, very good. Now get me a cloth please.'

Santiago wiped his crotch and the old easy chair which had belonged to his dad, Marcus Rees. Drying it off, he thought of how much easier things had been before his father's death in the 2403 push. An anti-personnel mine exploded underneath the bandit (a small cart pulled by a rudimentary traction engine), Marcus was driving. Miraculously, Marcus Rees was saved by the drums of cooking oil being transported within the bandit, which softened the blast; but whilst lying unconscious, he was bitten in the arm by a snake. When he was rescued, it was assumed that the bite was damage caused by the explosion and, as conditions at the field hospital were antiquated, only a field dressing was applied. His father had often said more effort was made erecting temporary churches than helping the wounded; prayer certainly did not prevent Marcus from dying a slow, painful death from blood poisoning.

Santiago had only ever been told about the explosion, and dreamt of his father's heroic end whilst saving someone's life.

'You need to be more careful! That robe's to do you till Friday!' Anna moaned.

'I know Anna, just a bit nervous about this nonsense today. Why would the Holy Father want to see me?'

'Maybe they finally realise what a dedicated servant to Christ and the Fatherhood you are,' smirked Anna.

'Doubt it, I'm no different to everyone else in there,' Santiago replied, pretending he did not notice the sarcasm in her voice. 'I preach, I pray, and I write sermons which never get a second look.'

'Well maybe your last one caught someone's eye … like the conductress'. I've noticed her glancing your way. Do you fancy her, Santiago?' Knowing fine Santiago had eyes only for her, Anna still liked to pretend she was a little jealous from time to time

'No way, she's huge. She would eat me!' frowned Santiago.

'Has she ever come on to you?' Anna smiled as she put her arms around her clumsy husband.

'No, never. Where are you getting this from?' Santiago asked, knowing his wife was toying with him, but enjoying the pretence.

'I've just heard she uses some Junior Ministers for her own end, that's all.'

Anna kissed Santiago on the cheek and went over to rinse the cloth in the sink.

'Well I wouldn't go near,' said Santiago. 'Her breath stinks and she spits when she talks.'

Anna laughed. 'You couldn't stand that darling, and I know you only have eyes for me. What time are you meeting the Holy Father?'

'Three o'clock,' Santiago replied. 'He has asked me to bring the last Sunday's sermon.'

'Any idea why?' asked a perplexed Anna. 'What was it about?'

Santiago looked at the ceiling. 'I was just using it to draw comparisons between our life now and what life must have been like pre-unification. I drew on the old stories of how man used to use machines and artificial intelligences to do everything, but in doing so lost touch with himself and Christ. And now similarly, as we push to unite both halves of the world through Holy War, we need to remember that we do this for Christ and not to suit ourselves or our own ends.'

'Pretty much like all your other sermons then,' Anna giggled.

'Fuck off!' laughed Santiago.

'Seriously, was there anything in the sermon out with the written creed?' asked a more serious Anna.

'Like what?'

'I don't know, anything that could be interpreted as heresy or seen to undermine the Holy Father. Last thing you want is a penalty or worse.'

'No it was plain, boring. Just like all my other sermons,' Santiago said whilst grabbing his satchel and his father's bible.

'You will just need to wait and see then,' Anna said as she kissed her husband goodbye, not knowing it would be the last she saw him for some time.

3. Cartergreen, Malachi.

The siege of Cartergreen lasted four days. Defences were now at the breaking point and General Devlin knew this. He had been briefed by key Strongheart Commanders from all quarters. Protocol was clear. All information, maps, codebooks and itineraries had to be destroyed; every man, woman and child who could would now fight to the death.

Cartergreen was a small settlement but significant, in many respects, to the ongoing campaign. It lay at the foot of a large hill – the entrance to a long winding valley which had access to many key Christian settlements along the coast of what was, prior to the Meltdown, the West Coast of France. The area was rich in safe, workable, unpolluted land with clean water and easy access to the sea.

The General actually had many reinforcements to defend the area under 'all cost' instruction, but his decision-making had been flawed and his Muslim counterpart had read him like a book. Cleric Atarn secured all main roads into the settlement and had cut off the supply chain. He knew only time stood between him and a superb victory for the Muslims, which would prove crucial in the long term. The up-and-coming cleansing of Christian innocents was on his mind, but the rules of this new super war were clear on both sides. The 'No Prisoners Taken Ever' imperative with interrogation carried out 'in battlefield', and only on special circumstances would a prisoner be returned to the respective Holy City to have the pleasure of meeting a senior interrogator. Indeed, this was known to be the worst fate anyone on either side could suffer.

The settlement had many hideaway rooms, but most of these would be discovered and their occupants would suffer a swift (or not-so-swift) death. It was to one of these rooms that Malachi's mother was leading him by the hand after the general retreat – or, as more commonly called, the 'run for the hills'.

Malachi was twelve years old. He was small for his age, but what he lacked in height, he made up for with charm. His mother often called him 'a rascal', a perfect description of him. He had a slight frame and blondish hair. A handsome face, which looked older than his years, a look many children seemed to have. Excelling at school, his flair for anything relating to machinery or engineering was noticed by his masters, and he had been due to be sent to a larger group college before the siege began. His mother wished she had received the notice of this sooner as she knew what was likely to unfold.

'If dad was here he would have stopped this from happening!' Malachi spurted out breathlessly as his mother dragged him along.

'Maybe so darling, but he's not been here for a long time so we just need to get to a safe hideaway as soon as we can,' his mother replied.

'There are no safe places and you know it. Toby Carter said when they took Rochelle they killed everyone, even the babies.'

Malachi's mother hated young Toby Carter. He was a great-grandson of the village founder and a right little pain in the arse.

'What have I told you about listening to Toby Carter? Has ever a true word come out of that boy's mouth? No!' But Malachi's mother knew that, on this occasion, Toby *had* spoken the truth for the first time in his life.

They approached a warden and stopped beside him. He was busy trying to make out the message coming over a crackling short wave radio.

Order............ decision.......... .....uate .... apply..... ...... destroy......

The warden was trying his best to acknowledge the message but appeared to have no idea how to do so.

'You need to press the button on the side if you're speaking, Sir.' advised Malachi.

'Be quiet Malachi, the warden knows what he's doing!' rebuffed his mother.

'Clearly he doesn't,' argued Malachi.

'Okay son, which button do you mean?' sighed the warden to Malachi, desperation clear in his voice.

Malachi took the bulky radio and showed the warden how to send a signal, and then how to tune in manually to improve the signal he was receiving.

'Thanks son – you're a bright boy. They could do with the likes of you back at headquarters.'

Malachi's mother interrupted. 'Can you tell us where the nearest hideaway is?'

The warden paused and looked around. 'The Ostler's house. Do you know where that is?'

'Yes,' both Malachi and his mother replied.

'In the barn next to the huge anvil there is a trap door. That's your best bet. The Ostler is long dead and his family will be at the Tightbeem square with the rest of the town. Get there fast. I don't think there is much time.'

'Thanks so much and God bless you,' Malachi's mother shouted as she ran off towards the Ostler's house.

At Tightbeem square, the panic was evident. The 'run for the hills' alarm was still sounding as groups of women and children joined together in hope that someone would have an idea. No one did. The main road into Cartergreen was being bombarded on a scale beyond anything the settlement had witnessed so far. Any defenders had been killed or were long gone as the Muslims slowly advanced.

'The church! Run to the church!' one woman screamed. Another sat on the fountain's edge and breastfed her baby like nothing was happening.

'Run you fool! Find a hideaway,' a warden said to her.

'But I need to feed my baby,' replied the shell-shocked woman.

The Muslim-led troops were ruthless. Any man, woman or child they encountered was slaughtered without compassion. As had been Earth's history for millennia, the 'tit for tat' rules of selfishness and greed provided all the justification needed for this behaviour. 'It's for the greater good!'

A woman fled from a small house close to the main road, dragging an older woman who may have been her mother. Confused, they ran straight into a group of the settlement's assailants and were cut down like animals and kicked into the gutter. As the oncoming forces grew in number, any remaining Christian defenders vanished or were killed. The first major building to be sacked was the church. The Muslim war machine had a special way to deal with this 'corrupt' building; the sheltering men, women and children within learned how as the smoke and fire engulfed them.

Malachi and his mother cowered in the small, dugout hideaway. They heard the explosions and gunfire advancing.

'Malachi, I want you to promise me something,' whispered his mother. 'I want you to take any chance to get to safety with or without me – and I want you to know something about your father.'

'What about him?' Malachi replied.

'He's not like other men. He's special. That's why he's been gone. He could not go along with all the nonsense that has brought us to this point, and the authorities would not accept it. He is no longer in the front line,' admitted his mother.

'What do you mean? He's a hero! You told me he was a hero,' cried Malachi.

'A hero, of that there is no question. The stories you have been told about the death field are true. He was the only survivor, Christian or Muslim.'

'Then where is he?' pleaded Malachi.

'He's in prison, held within the Darkland fortress.'

'No, that's where traitors and cowards and thieves go. He would never be there,' Malachi whimpered.

'Son, you and I would not be here today if he wasn't. His acceptance of his fate was a trade-off for us.'

A gunshot, followed by laughter, rang in the barn. Malachi could hear a young man pleading for his life and a mother pleading for her son. Two further gunshots silenced them!

'Search this barn for hideaways then torch it,' barked whoever was in charge.

Malachi's mother held her son and put her finger to her mouth, signing him to be silent.

Footsteps above them grew closer, but they remained undetected. Malachi felt around the hideaway and crept under a ledge formed by natural slate. More gunfire sounded as an older man was discovered.

'Do your worst you devils and may God forgive you,' were the last words to come out of his mouth before he took his last breath.

'Look for trap doors, you idiots; there's always trap doors,' the leader commanded.

Malachi's mother knew this was it. Malachi sensed what was going to happen and looked at her eyes, wide and filled with tears. She kissed him and whispered, 'Hide under this ledge and make no sound.'

Malachi's mother covered what could be seen of Malachi with an old sack, then stood up and raised the trap door.

'Wow, a pretty one we have here.' A monstrous ghoul of a man cried. He ran over and pulled Malachi's mother out of the hole by the hair and flung her to the ground. Another burly man came over and kicked her in the stomach; she vomited as another tore off her dress.

'Do we have time for some fun with her, Commander?' asked the grotesque man, smirking.

The commander walked over towards Malachi's mother, pointed a pistol at her head and fired.

'No!' He replied.

The monster had a quick look in the hideaway but missed Malachi and closed the trap door.

'On second thought don't torch this building. We can use it for the horses and our field nurses.'

As it grew dark, Malachi lay still and whimpered. He was in no doubt what fate had become of his mother and with the news about his father, his life was turned upside down. Women's voices now filled the barn, sounding stern and unhappy. Malachi imagined his father bursting in to save him in scenarios where his mother was alive – anything to keep the awful reality of his predicament at bay. Lying still, he first heard a rustle then felt a piercing pain in his foot. He did his best to stifle a horrified cry: in the dim light, he could make out a snake in the hideaway. It recoiled and went into the corner.

He tried to settle himself and hide further in when light footsteps approached the hideaway. The trap door pulled up slowly and Malachi peeked out to confront a woman's face looking down. The lantern she carried shone in, revealing the snake and the badly hidden Malachi.

'Do not move, child,' the woman said kindly. Reaching for a well-used set of tongs resting by the anvil, she easily removed the snake. As she walked away with the serpent, Malachi thought he would have to make a run for it, but his legs would not move. As the snake venom worked its way through his body, Malachi became rigid.

The woman reappeared. Lifting Malachi from his hideaway, she took him towards a horse-drawn, gypsy-looking carriage. That was the last thing he remembered.

A day later Malachi regained consciousness. He was lying hidden in another hideaway, but this time, it was within the nurse's field hospital carriage. Opening his eyes, he saw the woman who had dealt with the snake.

'Do not be afraid, child. You are safe for now. My name is Misba Ranha. I am a nurse and have treated you for the snakebite. Be assured, if you try to flee, you will be killed. If you call out, you will be killed. If you scream, you will be killed. There are soldiers all around and they will carry out their duty. I beg you to be still and I will try to conceal you. What is your name?' Misba Ranha moved closer and offered a glass with water to Malachi.

'My name is Malachi. Your animal soldiers just killed my mother, I hate you all.' Malachi turned and knocked the glass from her hand.

'And you think the women and children of my Muslim villages are spared such a fate? Your mother would want you to survive. Don't be a fool child, drink when I tell you to.' Misba Ranha refilled and returned the glass, which Malachi accepted.

'You know my father will rescue me and you will all pay,' Malachi spurted out after gulping the water.

'Young Malachi, if your father was in this settlement he has suffered the same fate as your mother. You need to move on and think of your own survival,' Misba Ranha said gently.

'He wasn't in this village. He's a brave soldier on the front line and he will come for me. He's a hero.' Malachi knew this was a lie, but he had to grasp at something.

'A hero,' smiled Misba Ranha, 'that's very good. I think the world could do with some heroes don't you?'

'Don't laugh at me. He is a hero. He was the only man who survived the battle at the Deathfield,' Malachi boasted.

At that Misba Ranha's voice changed. 'Young Malachi, you mention the Deathfield. What is your father's name?'

'His name is Cole!'

Upon hearing the name Misba Ranha's face dropped; she turned and closed the hatch to Malachi's hideaway.

4. New Mecca: Prime Cleric.

Six Tightbeem Aid to the Chosen Services a day was taking its toll on the Prime Cleric. In his fifteenth year as Muslim Prime, he felt he was running out of ways to disseminate the word of Mohammad and the New Prophets.

Inspiration was his job. 'Inspiration of the mind, inspiration of the soul, and inspiration of the heart' was how his own father had tried to explain *his* role as Prime –presiding as the serving head of over three billion Muslims – when handing over the baton to another.

Since the 'Meltdown', as their ancestors called it, a free scholar family with a direct ancient lineage had been chosen to play this part. Saladin, the present Muslim Prime, could trace his family line back to the 18th century; his was one of the only pure, uncorrupted gene lines on Earth.

Saladin's father had reigned over a very successful time for the Muslim cause – an act he was finding hard to follow. News of various recent victories lifted Saladin's spirits, however, and his final Tightbeem of the day had certainly been the best. He felt at long last he may be coming to the 'Juncture': a point in time predicted hundreds of years earlier, which would be the epiphany of the new Muslim world.

The Juncture or 'tipping point', as the masses referred to it, would be a point of no return for the Christians. Using a combination of science and pseudo-science, scholars theorised that eventually – through faith, endeavour and the will of Allah – at some point Christian armies would be unable to recover sufficient ground to make a difference, no matter how hard they fought. It would be like closing out a one-sided game of chess. Through meditation, prayer and planning, the Prime Cleric was mentally preparing for this outcome; indeed, his key military advisors were indicating to him that the time was close.

Since the inexplicable battle at the 'Deathfield', both sides had been desperate to make the first positive step forward. A truce had been ordered and agreed upon after a private Tightbeem conversation between the Prime Cleric and Pope Julias. Neither Julias nor the Prime Cleric could offer an explanation to the events that took place that day.

The simultaneous slaughter and mutilation of between two and three thousand Muslim front-line assailants and an equal number of Christians would remain a mystery. Those first to visit the site of the slaughter told tales of bodies skewered together, forming gruesome double helical towers, rising from pools of dried blood and severed heads. Hundreds of these columns rose from the ground; many of those who witnessed this horror remained dumbstruck. Not one Muslim survived, but Saladin's senior advisors said there were rumours a Christian soldier had survived.

Further information revealed the man was a drunkard whose magical explanations made no sense.

Julias had given Saladin his word that he would maintain the truce for thirty days. On this occasion, his word had been true. Saladin's advisors suggested that Julias' eagerness for the truce was due to necessity rather than empathy; as the rest of the year's campaign unfolded, he was beginning to think this was true.

Saladin was not like Julias at all. Though both led millions, each had very different hearts. Saladin dreamed of days after the Juncture when the cleansing of innocents could stop and, through teaching and prayer, the world could eventually unite as one. On the other hand, Pope Julias said on more than one occasion that he would not rest until every Muslim soldier was taken care of.

Saladin sat in his private enclave and prepared for meditation. He found great peace during these moments and was always invigorated afterwards. As he began to submerge in and be subsumed by his faith, Saladin sensed that he was being watched. He opened his eyes and was dumbstruck by the sight of a round-faced Asian girl in her twenties, staring at him from the corner of the room. Dressed in shorts and a tee shirt, her smiling face possessed an avian quality. As the Prime bowed his head to pray for the girl – her fate was sealed by her very presence – she spoke.

'Prime Cleric, you're looking well today! Sorry to just appear like this. My name is Maria.'

The Prime Cleric looked over at her. 'Woman, you know the consequence of your presence here. What insanity has overtaken you? No woman has entered this palace for hundreds of years!'

'Well, all the more poignant my presence here should be for you Saladin,' Maria smiled in reply.

'How did you manage this, woman? You must have been very well disguised ... or are you in the service of Basset?'

'I know not of your "Basset" Prime Cleric, and my presence here is not to alarm you or bring you ill will. There is much I need to discuss with you. But first, you must accept my presence here, and believe me when I say to you, I needed no door to gain entry.' Maria walked over and attempted, unsuccessfully, to open the still-locked door.

'What are you trying to say? What did you say your name was again?' asked Saladin as he rose to approach her.

'My name is Maria; I guess you could say I am an envoy. As we speak, my friend is having the same conversation in the new Vatican with Pope Julias – but I sense things are not going as planned there,' smirked Maria.

'Are you an assassin Maria,' asked an unflustered Saladin, 'or do you come here with a death wish? Surely you know even your garb will bring about an ignominious end! How many have seen you enter here?'

'No one has seen me enter, Saladin, and I can leave undiscovered at my own will. The question I have is, do you wish me to leave or are you curious to find out the reason for my presence? I chose this time to come here as I knew our privacy would be guaranteed.'

Maria approached Saladin with her arms wide. 'Saladin, I know you are different from your father. I know of the unusual presence that surrounds the depth of your meditation. Will you let me say my piece?' pleaded Maria.

'Maria, Maria, Maria!' Saladin looked to the roof in exasperation. 'You have dealt me a poor hand. You know I would be in violation of everything that I stand for if I do not summon my guards right now.'

Maria gestured her hand towards the door. 'Prime Cleric, if that is what you want then I will open the door for you. I, however, would prefer for you to sit down and I will make us some tea,' Still pointing to the door with one hand and pantomiming sipping tea with the other, Maria smiled at the Prime Cleric. 'What's it to be?'

Saladin knew his curiosity would be his better. 'Okay! You have my attention – if only for a short while.'

5. Darkland Fortress: Cole.

From space, few things were visible on the remnants of a devastated Earth. Parts of the Great Wall of China could be seen, though the continent of Asia was all but uninhabitable. One could play 'join the dots' with numerous craters, caused not by meteors but by playing nuclear ping pong. A large part of the giant world metropolis, 'Sappho', was still visible but this was also contaminated.

Unmissable from orbit was the Darkland strip and, like the dot on an 'I', the Darkland Fortress stood at its head. Since the Meltdown few people could accurately relate the actual size of the strip, except the few scholars who spent their lives in its study. At maximum, it was over 300 kilometres wide and 900 long.

From space, the DNA wall that was the area's perimeter bent and curved to envelop the undulating land, shimmering like fish in the sea. The Darkland Fortress, which stood proudly at its head, had once been a hotel catering to rich thrill-seekers from all corners of the globe. Thousands would arrive daily, and often reside for several years waiting for their slot. During this time they would train with Darkland veterans, spending months learning about which weaponised, adapted mechanimal they would encounter. The adverturers' own bodies would also be adapted with motorised, impenetrable exoskeletons which incorporated the latest micro and neuro technology, enabling calls on satellite imaging and direct downloads from their allocated transit station. The whole endeavour was a multitrillion pound venture. Within the boundaries of the hotel were laboratories and cloning stations run by the finest minds on the planet.

The art of mech grafting was refined at Darkland over the course of a generation. Initially, animal DNA was cloned and grafted with intelligent materials, then shaped and coded to form the desired killing machine. The early attempts, though formidable-looking, proved incompetent; instead, the method of advanced DNA proxy epigenetic evolution was introduced: the manipulation of individual strands of DNA, each one's evolutionary potential mapped and categorised. At first taking several hours to map a single strand, the process was ultimately assumed by AIs and development increased exponentially.

Eventually holding all manner of fantastical beasts – all of which were adapted to provide superior armour and a wide range of mech-grafted, self-replicating weapon systems – the Darkland was advertised as '*Hell IS a place on Earth*'; an appropriate slogan (apart from the lack of fire and brimstone). No perimeter fence was needed to prevent access or egress as DNA compatibility would allow entry and exit exclusively within certain time periods. These were chosen and controlled by the 'dysfunctionists', whose genetic material had been altered to accommodate the

Darkland AI interface. This kept the monsters in, and the not-so-wealthy thrill-seekers out (attempting to cross between the gruesomely carved perimeter's markers would render any life-form catatonic).

After the Meltdown, the hotel was abandoned and technological advances ground to a halt. When the need for prisoner and citizen containment became necessary, the Christian hierarchy moved back in and modified the massive building to suit its own needs. Rooms were split to become cells, parks became exercise yards and viewing towers became watchtowers. As almost the entire fortress was surrounded by the Darkland strip, only one heavily guarded way in or out was required. The addition of a series of new checkpoints along this single path made the fortress inescapable.

Over the years many inmates attempted to run through the DNA wall whilst on exercise but everyone had suffered the same fate: losing consciousness and command of their bodily functions.

In holding cell 2022, Cole pinned a burly man by the neck against the cell door with one hand whilst ramming a second's head, he was holding by the hair, against a nearby metal locker. 'Listen, you pair of weasels, I warned you not to interfere with me!' Cole spoke with calmness as the two brigands gasped.

'We didn't realise mucker, we thought you were easy,' the gasped the second thug, bent double; at this Cole smashed his head into the locker so hard the door caved inwards, jamming the man's head within. Blood ran out onto the cell floor. Both hands now free, Cole engulfed the first brigand on either side of the head and pushed together like a vice.

'Easy you say? I mind my manners and my own business so I'm easy? Does this feel easy?' Cole's calm voice began to contain an element of agitation. 'You pair of lizards prey on the weak and have no honour.' The man's eyes began to roll in his head as a drop of blood dripped from his nose.

'Tell me when this stops feeling easy for you. Is it easy now? NOW?' Cole compressed his hands further and the man's skull cracked like an egg.

Cole stood back as the man slumped to the floor, then washed his hands in the small sink and lay down on the bunk.

The two had been transferred in with him the night before; after the initial threats and tirade about Cole's protection he had nodded along with them and then went off to sleep. He awoke in the morning and was forced to give the pair their early morning alarm call. The hatch in Cole's cell opened shortly after.

'Fuck Cole, what've you done now?' said the guard as he raised the alarm. Cole remained on his bed and did not reply. Eventually a team of guards pushed in past the body at the door.

'Are you going to give us any trouble? We are not in the mood for any more of your crap today,' said McCoy, the lead guardsmen – knowing full well Cole would comply.

'I'm good, no trouble from me McCoy; do you wish me to follow you, sir? You know you are wasting your time with the restraints,' Cole raised his hands to allow himself to be cuffed.

'Sorry, it's procedure,' McCoy said as he clipped the manacles together. This was not the first time McCoy dealt with Cole, and they had developed a mutual respect for one another.

The volume in the secure wing increased as Cole was led in between the guards along to the punishment zone. Prisoners screamed insults from their cells.

'Fuck you Cole not so tough now!'

'Hope they fucking fry you, you freak!'

'Bout time you got that freak show out of here!'

Cole was impervious to their taunts and shuffled along. He was average in height and barrel chested, making his arms stick out as if he was carrying a bag of grain under each when walking. Long, straggly hair framed a pointy chin at the foot of a worn out, tired face that had seen many troubles in its day. As they approached the punishment zone, a final taunt from a prisoner made Cole stop in his tracks.

'Hey Cole! Heard the Muslims made a real mess in Cartergreen. Rounded them all up and had a nice fire in the church.'

Cole paused for a second and McCoy saw an unfamiliar look on his face; then he continued on his way to the punishment zone. After Cole was stripped and ushered into the holding area, McCoy saw his moment and spoke to him. 'I saw the look on your face back there. Is there going to be trouble?'

'McCoy, you have been fair with me. Don't be working anywhere around me tomorrow. I'm leaving.'

McCoy gave Cole a sad look and shook his head as Cole went over and sat on the cold metal bench that would be his bed for the night.

6. Himalayas, 'Half Realm': Vaughan.

Vaughan slept like a log 15 kilometres in the air above the Himalayas, in an Infinity-created 'Half Realm'. As far as Vaughan could tell, he had taken human form identical to his previous incarnation shortly before death. Vaughan only had fleeting memories of his most recent attempt at a flesh-and-bone life, and most of these comprised a young woman's face and a barn. He had romantic ideas that she was his lover and soul mate, but the face in his memories was that of a passer-by who had tried reviving him after his heart had stopped beating.

This was the way of it for all eight billion conscious life forces inhabiting Earth since the dawn of man, either in the physical realm or in the ether. Each life force would have only a slight memory of its final moment in the physical realm, plus a few others. There was no karma involved in this process, good or bad; life forces would take their opportunity for another life when the chance arose. A life force that was unspeakably cruel in one lifetime could be angelic in the next.

The behaviour during physicality was dictated by epigenetics over which the life force had little control. At any one time, over two billion life forces would be in a non-physical state, half dwelling in Earth's reality, and half at the edge of the void – whilst the other six billion inhabited the bodies of every other man, woman and child on Earth. The homeless life forces would naturally congregate on and around the highest place on the planet so the Half Realm was created there.

Immediately, Vaughan knew this manifestation was different. An instant later, he was familiar with his new surroundings and of the technical workings of this Half Realm even though he understood its creation was instantaneous and recent. It was almost as if the Half-Realm's architects had downloaded its drawings and schematics directly into his conscious mind. Simply, it was a massive holding area joining two planes of reality.

However, the reality which Vaughan had previously considered (during non-physicality) to be the void, was now evidently so much more than that.

Vaughan now knew of the reason for its existence and he gradually understood the complexity of the entities that had created this Half Realm. As he opened his eyes, his mind opened too and everything was clear. He knew of his new purpose, of the danger he faced; Vaughan also now knew he could call on every memory of every one of his lifetimes if he chose to.

Also evident was that his latest existence would not start in a birth canal, but as a man in his late twenties, with an epigenetic gene environment matrix tailored to suit his mission. He wondered at his new form's potential. Absorbing everything like a sponge, he spoke for the first time to the entities.

'What can I call you?'

We are The Affinity
You are everything to us

At that, Vaughan's mind was subsumed by the entities and everything made sense. Rising from the bed, he stretched his legs and saw the girl he now knew as Maria also get up from the bed beside him. He walked over to her and as they embraced, he knew that this was the woman he had shared many lives with. He would not call her his soul mate; Maria was more like the missing part of his soul, the final piece in Vaughan's jigsaw.

They kissed once, held hands, and their minds joined – each fuelling the other. The link created meant they no longer need to speak to communicate. DNA codex potential strands within them, evolved millions of years in the future, provided this new ability and many others. Both had a bio arsenal at their disposal and technical expertise beyond anything ever seen on Earth, even before the meltdown.

But it was time to go. Vaughan closed his eyes and willed himself to the place on Earth he knew he must be. Instantly he appeared in the New Vatican for his lunch date with Pope Julias.

'Holiest Father, My name is Vaughan.' Vaughan confidently walked over to the sitting Pope Julias and leaned on his large desk. Pope Julias was still dumbstruck. 'Relax, Holy Father,' smiled Vaughan. 'May I have a minute of your time?"

Julias reached under the desk and sounded his personal alarm before Vaughan could stop him or say another word.

'Pope Julias, I was hoping we could talk some before you did that. Are you not curious as to my 'Christ like' appearance?'

'Do not speak Christ's name, demon! I have been warned of your arrival and will not be drawn in by your attempts to undermine me and my church.' At this, Pope Julias stood up abruptly and walked backwards into the corner holding his cross and muttering towards Vaughan.

'Really? A demon? Holiest Father, I promise you I'm as real as you are,' said Vaughan holding out his hand to Pope Julias.

Julias recoiled and held out his cross. 'Though I walk in the valley in the shadow of death, I will fear no evil.'

'You've got to be kidding me,' laughed Vaughan. 'Pope Julias, trust me when I say to you this is your first chance to hear me out and make a bigger difference to your flock than any Pope in history. Do not waste it.'

The sound of running in the outside corridor let Vaughan know his lunch date was over. He could leave now as he had arrived, or await the Vatican guard. He chose the latter and sat down on the end of Pope Julias' desk as the guards burst in. Holding pistols, the guards formed a neat line in front of him and ordered Vaughan to his knees.

'Holiest Father, are you okay?' said the man in command.

'Yes my son. This demon held no threat to me; but close your ears to his fabrications! Escort him immediately to a jail cell and fetch me Meniux.'

At this, a burly guard stepped forward and prepared to strike Vaughan on the face with his pistol. Vaughan thought this over and decided to slow things down a bit. He had been absorbing every detail of his surroundings since his arrival and was now at one with it.

Every atom in the room was now his to command to the quantum level. Vaughan isolated the groups of atoms that were attempting to assault him and ground them to a halt. He swithered whether or not to allow Pope Julias to witness this, but decided to stop him, if for no other reason than to end the tedious demon chat. Pope Julias and the guards now stood like mannequins at a museum. Vaughan rose and walked round to Julias's big desk; he took an ornate quill from its inkpot and wrote a short note. He folded the note and put it in Julias' pocket.

After some deliberation, Vaughan decided not to leave as quickly as he had arrived, realising the best path would be to remain inside the Vatican for the time being. Rather than doing anything that would appear miraculous, Vaughan decided upon a different course of action and knelt down where he had been previously, released his atomic proximity control, and allowed himself to be struck with the pistol and knocked unconscious.

7. Vatican: Santiago.

Sitting in a waiting area in the Vatican proper, Santiago's mind was working overtime about why he had been summoned. The waiting room was stately with wooden-covered walls and orderly lined niches, each containing some ancient artefact along with a small card detailing its history. Ordinarily, Santiago would have read each one but today his mind was elsewhere. As he glanced out of the large window into the courtyard, he saw a woman and a child tending the orange trees. Tugging at the woman's dress, the child gestured that she was hungry. Santiago smiled and said a quick prayer of blessing for the mother and daughter whom he would never meet.

He had passed through numerous checkpoints on the way here, the last of which was the 'Checkpoint of Faith' manned by Father Meniux. To Santiago this was a travesty. Of all the men of the cloth he had ever known, Meniux was the worst on many levels: a liar and a manipulator, he was not to be trusted. Santiago had had to bite his tongue as Meniux asked him the faith questions off a card with a scowl; they shared a less than harmonious history together.

They first met while Santiago was a serving Deacon in the Portuguese town of Alcobaca. Meniux, as a new priest, arrived to bolster the Provence. First impressions told Santiago he was dealing with a snake, a fact confirmed when he caught Meniux in a state of undress with a young girl after evening mass in his private vestry. Santiago was initially unsure what to do – being only a Deacon – but he found the will to verbally chastise Meniux and the following day reported him to the Archbishop. Days later Meniux was removed and sent to the back of beyond on a long sabbatical, only to re-surface many years later in Vatican City with a position of some power. After his arrival, Santiago's prospects in the church vanished. Seconded to various awful locations and often sent to field hospital duty for months at a time, he had no doubt who was behind these assignments.

In the waiting area a door opened and a young woman approached him. 'The Holy Father will see you now. Please refrain from entering into any dialogue with him unless he encourages you to do so,' with this she led Santiago through the door into the Popes private anteroom.

There was a large window in the room and a cool breeze with the scent of orange blossom wafted in. Pope Julias sat by the window with a leather bound book in hand and raised a glass of claret to his mouth. Julias pointed for Santiago to sit but continued to read from his book which, after several minutes, became quite unsettling. The woman had warned him not to enter into dialogue so he sat like a schoolboy waiting for the headmaster and looked around him. The room was filled wall to wall with books, hundreds of which were clearly pre-Meltdown. He saw works of Shakespeare, Tennyson and large encyclopaedias, which all looked ancient. Also held within a glass case to the side of the Pope's desk was the complete, old Codex Sinaiticus bible that Santiago had heard so much about. What he would give for a few hours to look through these books!

Abruptly, Pope Julias took to his feet and approached Santiago. 'Father Santiago, please forgive my rudeness since your arrival, but I had a need to complete a chapter of this book before I spoke to you. I felt it would perhaps make our conversation less one-sided. Did you bring the sermon you wrote from Sunday as instructed?'

'Yes Holy Father, I have it here,' Santiago handed the sermon to Julias. Julias took the paper and returned to his window seat to contemplate its detail. After a few minutes, he again addressed Santiago.

'Father, this sermon brings me much hope today. I find that in my role as Pontiff I am closer to God than I ever have been, but this closeness comes at a cost. Rarely do I get the chance to speak to an ordinary priest like you, who knows nothing of claret and papal conclaves, but who nonetheless still has a wonderful connection with God. Your parish is lucky to have you and I now understand why you came so highly recommended from Father Meniux.'

Santiago tried to conceal his astonishment at this and for the first time, realised that there perhaps was much more to this meeting than he had anticipated. Pope Julias leant over, placed the sermon on his desk and looked directly at Santiago.

'Father, we are speaking today during a time when our church and our very way of life are under attack on many fronts. Muslims assault us daily from the east, gaining ground by the hour, and our field hospitals talk of unexplainable disappearances. Soldiers dying in their beds go missing overnight, never to be seen again, with no evidence of how it happened. You will have heard of the massacre at the "Deathfield" in your own home country of Portugal.

'These happenings are not coincidental,' Julias continued, 'but are linked in some way we have yet to understand. You speak in your sermon of times before the Meltdown and I understand you have studied this period in depth. Is this correct?'

'Holy Father, I have studied as you say, but it has been more of a hobby rather than a vocation. I find I can draw inspiration from the period, which I sometimes include in my sermons – like in the one you read today. I am sure there are many others, far more qualified priests and historians, whom you could call upon should you wish.'

Julias looked perplexed and held his hand to his face. 'Yes Father, that is probably true; but what I require is a priest with no agenda. Someone who can advise me honestly, and offer an uncorrupted opinion on matters I feel are of the utmost importance. Has your pre-Meltdown studies included the use and manipulation of DNA?'

'Yes Holy Father. I have read extensively in this subject, but have found that there are many conflicting reports on the DNA evolution process of that period. The most compelling literature I have read on this was written by scholars from the giant city of Sappho. It was said that the president of Sappho at the time had more DNA altered strands than any human on Earth, including those who worked at the Darkland.'

'Now, how these DNA alterations benefitted their host is of much debate,' Santiago continued. 'Conservative scholars on the subject say increased mental capacity and longevity was the main aim, but there are those in the field who suggest near-superhuman abilities were available. Extrasensory perception and even actual real time manipulation have been spoken of – but my stance would be the truth lies somewhere down the middle.'

Santiago gulped and coughed a little after his explanation, prompting Pope Julias to offer him a drink of claret. Santiago rose, fixed himself a full glass full and gulped it down, hoping it would settle his nerves as much as cure his thirst.

'Father Santiago, already I feel inadequate in your company with regards to this subject. Could you explain to me what you mean by "real time manipulation"?'

Santiago took his seat then began. 'Well, some scholars speculate that after single strand DNA evolution was accomplished, certain covert areas within government took the process to a critical level. The entire genetic code of a human could be identified, allowing the future potential of each line to be mapped. Mutations caused by environmental or social factors over the course of millions of years would be identified and run through simulation devices, projecting multiple scenarios, until certain desirable effects took place to the host. These simulations were harmless, but showed any subject the pinnacle of their own evolutionary path.'

'Now, we know for certain that some people pre-Meltdown went through the process, the Darkland dysfunctionists being the most well-known example. From what I can gather, there is speculation that certain individuals gained the ability to manipulate time itself – or at least appeared to do so. I am unsure how this was achieved, but it was said they could control the surrounding environment to some extent.' Santiago rose and poured himself another glass of claret without waiting to be asked, and Pope Julias held his own glass out for a refill.

'Father Santiago, you have no idea how much our chat today has helped me. You cannot know the significance of the information you have given me and the impact it may have on the future of the Church. I would love to hear much more about this subject, but I need to carry out the final worldmass shortly.

'I would like you to stay within the city for the next few days,' Julias said. 'I will have word sent to your family and my aides will make you most comfortable. During this time you will be have unconditional access to all Vatican libraries and historical vaults. In return, I would like to call on you for advice. Is this acceptable for you?'

'Holy Father, it would be my honour to assist you in any way I can.'

8. Vatican prison: Rodrigo Gomez (The Surgeon).

The locker area within the Vatican prison had 24 tall wooden lockers. Twenty-three of these were allocated to guards and rota chiefs, and held their change of clothes and various other personal items. Often, a photograph of a loved one would appear as a locker door was opened or some beautiful nude woman would stare back.

Locker 24 belonged to Vatican interrogator Rodrigo Gomez. A gruesome reputation had gifted Rodrigo with a nickname: 'the surgeon', a name he dismissed, but rather liked. Instead of a family photo, what greeted Rodrigo as he opened his locker door was a picture of the Holy Father and a card with three words written boldly – 'devotion, diligence, and determination'. Rodrigo did not really live by this motto, but he liked his colleagues to have the impression he did. His job was special, and only an exceptional person could do the tasks and then go home to his family. Long ago Rodrigo settled his conscience on the matter; from day one, he proved to be skilled in the art of persuasion. Torture to Rodrigo was an art form: the human body a vessel to be manipulated and, especially, controlled.

At home, Rodrigo had a fat, domineering wife whom he detested; his only child, Amanda, was slowly turning into a carbon copy of her mother. Rodrigo found his true calling working alone in Interrogation Chamber 1, and often he would work on a subject for over 24 hours without interruption. His chamber was steel-lined and most of his torture devices were on display. He had found that the very sight of the finely polished steel would loosen the lips of most visitors, though this would rarely spare them the pleasure of seeing Rodrigo at his work.

Usually, Muslim men captured during battles were brought to Rodrigo; his mission was to obtain every piece of information from them and pass it on to the Vatican mission. On rare occasions when the delivered captive was a woman, he had difficulty concealing his delight (but the other guards were well aware of this fact). Rodrigo had a special wooden box of implements designed with the female body in mind, and this forced intimacy both stimulated him sexually and provided him with an outlet for his misogyny.

Today Rodrigo arrived in a chirpy mood, went into the prison complex security office and was greeted by the rota chief. 'You went too far with the boy from cell eight yesterday Rodrigo,' the lethargic guard coughed out as he handed Rodrigo the register.

'How do you mean, Smythe?'

'Well, the boy only went and smashed his own head so hard off the bed frame that he bled to death during the night. You must have put the fear of God into him, or else he had something he really wanted to hide.'

Rodrigo signed his name then replied 'Well, can you tell me why the fuck that was allowed to happen? When I returned him to his cell, he was securely restrained. What kind of fucking show are you guys running here?'

'Hey, don't start shouting at me Gomez. I've been here in security all night. Speak to the guard master if you want find out the story.' Smythe slid the glass window closed in Rodrigo's face and turned around in his chair.

'Idiot,' muttered Rodrigo as he proceeded down the corridor to the locker area.

As he changed, the locker room door opened and a tired-looking guard master entered. Rodrigo straightened his long white coat, walked towards him and began his tirade.

'Guard Master, I understand you have a taxing job. I understand you work long hours for little reward. I understand that a prisoner pleading throughout a nightshift to be released from his restraints may be hard. I also understand that you have more than one prisoner to deal with.'

'Bearing all that in mind, I would like to say this to you: the boy who smacked himself to death under your watch last night was only just beginning to reveal information that could be very important to the Vatican Mission. Now we will never know if his previous statements could have been confirmed under duress. Lives on the field may be lost because of your incompetence, so let me give you a word of advice.'

Rodrigo directed a piercing gaze at the man. 'Should the same thing ever happen again under your watch you, your wife and child will be paying me a visit in the interrogation chamber. Is that clear?'

The colour drained from the guards face, he lowered his head and muttered a reply.

'Sorry Guard Master! I did not hear you – do I make myself clear?'

'Yes Rodrigo, it will not happen again.'

'It fucking better not,' snapped Rodrigo as he pushed past the guard and made his way to the holding cells.

At the end of the holding cell corridor there was a cell with a larger door than the others, used to hold violent prisoners or inmates deemed serious enough to merit an escort of guards at all times. Rodrigo approached it as a team of Vatican guards, along with five prison officers, were coming out of the cell. The officer in charge locked the heavy door and turned to speak to the nearest Vatican guard when he noticed Rodrigo.

'Rodrigo, Father Meniux has given instructions that this prisoner be given the utmost priority.'

Rodrigo pushed past the guard, opened the viewing hatch and looked inside. A young man with a gash on the side of his head was lying unconscious on the bed. His hands and feet were secured and a gag was tied around his mouth, which Rodrigo knew was not normal procedure.

'Who is he? Is he from the front line?' Rodrigo closed over the hatch gently as he beckoned the guard to answer.

'Come on, quickly Guardsman. I've not got all day,' said Rodrigo, catching the eyes of the other guards to emphasise his impatience.

A Vatican guard stepped forward and addressed Rodrigo directly. 'Mr. Gomez, the prisoner was apprehended after gaining access to the Papal suite. We started an investigation into this and will be passing on our findings directly to Father Meniux as instructed. I suggest if you have any further questions you put them to him. Good day.'

With that, the Vatican guards and the relieved prison officers made their way along the cold corridor.

Rodrigo had another look in the cell, thinking that the cut on the man's head seemed to be much less severe; he noticed that the gag was now lying on the floor beside him. How this was possible he couldn't fathom, but Rodrigo had seen many weird things and strange behaviour exhibited by people in confinement; he gave it no more thought and turned to make his way to another interrogation chamber where he knew an old Muslim man was waiting for him.

As he approached the interrogation chamber he saw two guards coming towards him, dragging the old man in question. Rodrigo had previously concentrated two hours' worth of efforts exclusively on the old man's feet, and as the guards stopped beside him the old man spat towards Rodrigo. It landed on his shoulder.

'Let him stand. Release him.'

'But Mr. Gomez he is unable to stand.' The guard gestured to the man's swollen, bloody, nail-free feet.

'Do it now, Guardsman!'

When guards released the old man he wobbled and then crumpled into a heap on the floor. Rodrigo knelt down beside the old man and sneered. 'You see how with little effort I have disabled your feet, old man? Let's see you spit later without lips!' Rodrigo rose and asked the guard, 'Why is this prisoner not in my interrogation room? Who authorised this?'

'The order came from Father Meniux himself, Mr. Gomez. He awaits you in the room and gave orders for you to join him immediately.'

Rodrigo pushed past the old man and walked quickly to his interrogation room. As he entered, Father Meniux was there, sitting in his chair and holding a still-bloody pair of tablillas – clearly the cause of the old man's disablement.

'A nasty business this interrogation is,' said Meniux.

'Nasty but necessary Father,' replied Rodrigo.

'Can I offer you a drink Father Meniux?'

'No thanks, my son – unless you have some hidden claret?'

'Water or cardamom tea is the best I can do, I'm afraid.' Rodrigo walked into the small adjoining room to fetch cups. 'Two sugars as usual Father Meniux?'

Rodrigo asked as he took Father Meniux's usual cup from the drainer.

Father Meniux was a regular visitor to Interrogation Chamber 1 on Vatican business, and sometimes concerns of a personal variety. Rodrigo would alert Father Meniux when a young girl or child was to be interrogated; Father Meniux would make the initial contact under the guise of spirituality, but the truth was far more sinister.

Rodrigo was well aware of what went on. In return for his silence, he had an elevated position in the Vatican prison and powerful friends in high places.

'Rodrigo, I need to speak to you about the prisoner in the large holding cell.'

'I have already seen him, Father. Is it true he managed to gain entry to the Papal offices?'

'Not only to the Papal offices but to within a few feet of the Holy Father himself, though as yet we are unable to establish his intentions.'

'How could this have happened, Father?' replied Rodrigo.

'We are not sure. as yet,' Father Meniux took the cup offered to him from Rodrigo and took a sip. 'All we know is he was in the company of the Holy Father for several minutes before the Vatican guards apprehended him. The Holy Father was shaken but unharmed.'

'So you think it was *not* an assassination attempt? A few minutes alone would be ample time for an assassin to carry out his work.'

'This is true, Rodrigo and another reason for my visit. This prisoner has to be dealt with delicately – that is a quote directly from the Holy Father. You must ascertain how he gained entry to the Papal offices, then accessed the Pope's private quarters.

'We need to know his intentions and you will have all resources available to you for this interrogation,' Meniux continued. 'All other prisoner work will have to be put on hold, and I would like to be present during the first verbal interview with him. I trust you feel up for the job Rodrigo?'

'Father Meniux, I will not disappoint you. I have a few new techniques of persuasion which I would think may loosen the young man's tongue.'

'I need not know of your methods Rodrigo, only your results.'

9. Himalayas, 'Half Realm': The Affinity.

The Affinity picked up the first radio transmission from Gugliemo Marconi almost five hundred years after it was made. Since that instant, less than a femto second had passed in real Earth time before they had arrived, inhabited the space between every atom on the planet, and then created the 'Half Realm' kilometres above the Himalayas.

They subsequently withdrew from atomic space with a new understanding of events and created Vaughn and Maria. In order to communicate with the two newly-made envoys, The Affinity chose to form humanoid-shaped bodies, though most of their being constantly flitted between the Half Realm and the greater universe. Their language, if you could call it that, was always a communication of feelings and experiences, developed over trillions of years. The Affinity knew this would be inadequate and incomprehensible to the people of Earth, so they now attempted to adapt to the rudimentary form of language used by humans.

> *My grief rips me apart.*
> *My pain eats at my being.*
> *How can this be?*
>
> *We developed as the universe grew old.*
> *We matured and cast aside our ails.*

All we became was nonchalant.
The detritus of our development is to blame.

The Exile is real?

Yes it is real!

In the compressed environment of neutron stars we deposited our failings.
Strewn universally.
How can this be?

It was calculated as a possibility.
Should we end this universal construct?

The pain would be unimaginable.
Each consciousness has the potential to be us.
To be a part of us.

We could progress them all?
Move them into Affinity?

We cannot be direct.
But we can give them a road.

The Exile is the cause.
Can we save The Exile?

We will try.
He has developed mankind.
Their history reveals this.
His failed models are evident to us.

Do not underestimate him.
His plan to date has succeeded.
We are here.

But why?
For revenge?
Why allow this pain?
Why create dependency on pseudo-science?

It's part of His plan.
Every critical alteration in humanity.
Moulded by him.
I detect DNA manipulation throughout time here.

I see it also.
From Palaeolithic times.
Pre-Greek Minoan.
The same altered DNA patterns.
Archimedes.
Christ.
Mohammad.

Newton.
Harrison.
Marconi.
Einstein.
Fujiyama.
All players in His lengthy game.

None of which could have known.
None could see the agenda.

Let's play His game.
Let's break His code.
Let's change this.

Do we ask too much of the envoys?
Do they risk the real death?
I die at the thought.

They know what's at stake.
We can guide but not interject.
The Exile will be revealed.

Then he is non-atomic?

Yes he is beyond that state.
He is like us.
He is a part of us.

He is our family.

10. The Vatican Church of St. John: Pope Julias.

'The child has spoken of you Holy Father, during her seizures.'

'You did well to alert me of her change. She has been in my mind.'

Pope Julias beckoned Father Chadwin to rise. 'This is no time for ceremony, Father. Please take me to her immediately.'

Father Chadwin turned and walked into a nearby niche inside the church, opening a door obscured by a daunting statue of Saint Thomas Aquinas. Pope Julias followed Chadwin up a tight spiral staircase and out into an upper corridor. He smelled cooking nearby and heard voices and laughter, but ignored this and moved alongside Father Chadwin.

'How long have you tended for the girl now Father Chadwin?'

'Three years Holy Father, since she was seven and had the event.'

'And do you think the stigmata are getting worse?'

'I do, Holy Father. The visions and dreams are more frequent than ever, and she often loses consciousness.'

'And what of the girl's mother, Father Chadwin: the woman with the foot facing the wrong way?'

'Sadly, she has died Holy Father. She was never the same after the girl's first seizure.'

Father Chadwin stopped in the corridor, blessed himself, then took an old key from his vestment and opened the door. Inside a slight, mousy haired young girl in a beautiful yellow flowered dress sat at the window, next to a table filled with fresh fruit.

'Liliana, I have brought a very important visitor to see you.'

Liliana turned round and stared at Pope Julias. 'He's the man in my dreams. The man I told you about, Father Chadwin.'

'This is Pope Julias, the Head of our Church. He has some questions to ask you.'

Liliana walked towards the Pontiff and Julias could see the bloodstained bandages on her wrists and feet. 'I prefer this one to the other priest you bring. He looks at me funny. He's not a good man. This Pope can be a good man.'

'Liliana this is the Holy Father of our Church. Please show him some respect and....'

Pope Julias interrupted Chadwin before he could finish.

'Yes girl, I could be a good man and I want you to help me be that man. You say you have seen me in your dreams, can you tell me about that?'

'I can draw you a picture if you like.'

'That would be great Liliana.'

Excited, Liliana removed some crayons from a drawer, sat at the table and began to draw. After some time, she handed Pope Julias the drawing.

'Now that's a great drawing Liliana. Can you explain it to me child?'

'Okay silly.' Liliana took the picture back. 'That is the man in the cage who scares you. That other man is a doctor – I think – and he tries to kill the man in the cage with a shiny silver knife, and that's you in your house.'

'So Liliana, what are the black and red round scribbles at the end?' asked Pope Julias.

'Oh, that's you. When the doctor tries to kill the man in the cage your house falls down on you and you die.'

'Well Liliana, I don't want that to happen, I've got too much important work to do. I see another thing in your drawing: the letter "V" above the bit where my house falls on me. I can tell you are very clever, because my house is called the Vatican.'

'Would you like to play noughts and crosses with me? I will beat you easy.' Liliana took a fresh piece of paper from the drawer, put it over the drawing and began to draw a grid.

'I wish I could child, but I need to go now. Thanks so much for your help and your beautiful drawing.' Julias turned back to Father Chadwin. 'I think Liliana needs a special treat tonight, Father Chadwin, for all her hard work. Get the cooks to make her favourite dinner.'

Pope Julias walked over to where Liliana was sitting, kissed her on the head and said a prayer for her. As he touched her, Liliana felt like water was running down her face but instead drops of blood from her forehead landed on the paper. Pope Julias stepped back and alerted Father Chadwin, who quickly came over and wiped the girl's forehead with a towel.

'Father Chadwin, I think I will leave you to tend for Liliana and go now. Thank you for your time.'

Pope Julias walked back out through the door, much more quickly than he had entered, as Father Chadwin continued to reassure Liliana.

'There, there, child it's ok, no need to panic. I think Pope Julias really loved your drawing.'

'It will be ruined Father Chadwin. There is blood everywhere.'

'Yes, but your noughts and crosses paper has saved it. See!'

Father Chadwin lifted the blood soaked paper that covered the drawing. But some of the blood had soaked through and, as he looked closer, he noticed the bloodstain formed a word next to the 'V'.

'Do you see that child? Next to the letter "V" that you wrote. Is that your doing?'

'Father Chadwin, I don't write well and I'm still learning to read. What does it say?'

'It says "Vaughn", Liliana!'

11. New Mecca: Basset.

The corridors within the main enclave of New Mecca were wide enough for five or six people to walk side by side. Constructed with sandstone, the walls were painted terracotta and decorated with various hanging tapestries. There was always a smell and a sense of spice, caused partly by the burning incense lamps hung periodically along the walls. Adding to this was the aroma emanating from ventilation ducts running from the kitchens, floors below, up through the cavities to the rooftops.

After the Meltdown, much consideration had gone into the construction of New Mecca; no other post-Meltdown building had such delicate woodwork and detail on doors and window frames. On the highest floor, the Prime Cleric's quarters included the Tightbeem ante room and sleeping area. This floor was luxurious and heavily guarded; only a handful of people had ever entered the main prayer room. This was where Basset, the chief attender to the Prime Cleric, was heading today.

Basset was a young man in his late twenties who possessed wisdom beyond his years. He had bargained, bribed, manipulated and intimidated his way into the most influential job within New Mecca (with the exception of the Prime Cleric himself).

Basset's bloodline was nothing special his father had been a soldier and his mother a keen gardener and homoeopathist. As a child, he often enjoyed helping her brew remedies from all sorts of plants. He had cultivated this skill and still maintained it as a hobby to this day, but his intelligence enabled Basset to rise from a lowly political propaganda assistant to his current position as one of the most powerful and feared figures in the Muslim world.

Today, as he walked through the various security cordons, he was delighted with himself and looking forward to delivering his good news to the Prime Cleric. There were also some delicate matters to discuss and he was mulling over scenarios of how and when to broach the subjects.

Basset had a network of subordinates, whom each in turn had their own network of underlings and all worked from the same dictate. 'Information collection' was imperative and accurate transfer of this data back up the tree to Basset was vital. Each section of the new Muslim world had head clerics, and every one retained chief recorders who wrote, photographed and kept exact, accurate diaries of every Muslim day. This information was transferred on a weekly basis back to to the various real time analysis sections in New Mecca who had been trained to filter out the nonsense. They in turn passed all relevant data onto the New World Clerics, who were really only concerned with identifying likely signs of the Muslim world reaching the point of

'Juncture'. Finally, Basset himself would receive the cream of the information barrel.

The few people who were close to Basset were wary of him. He was pleasant and amiable to everyone, but those well acquainted knew better than to underestimate him. He was a strict fundamentalist adhering to the new modern Islamic dictates and expected others to do so.

His extensive personal library contained many works which were hundreds of years old, and he had digested every one of them. Basset believed firmly in the ongoing battle and was convinced his side boasted the moral, political and religious high ground. He knocked on the door to the Prime Cleric's quarters and heard movement inside, and then a voice through the door.

'Please enter, Basset.'

Basset opened the huge door and went into the room. 'Prime Cleric, I trust you are well today and feel up to receiving some good news.' Basset smiled as he walked over and took a seat. He adjusted the folder of paper on his knee and made himself comfortable.

'Basset, I think only a fool would not want to receive good news. Perhaps yours will be a remedy for an old man's ails.'

'The news is threefold and I will save the best for last,' Basset began. 'There have been events taking place throughout our lands that have been flagged by our various information gatherers. Reading between the lines, it seems that magical, even supernatural occurrences are taking place. One or two of these reports would be disregarded, but the recordings of these incidents have been in the hundreds.'

Basset opened the folder on his lap and started to read from it. 'Our field hospitals have reported instances of casualties near to death making miraculous recoveries overnight. There are reports of amputees in the field waking with healthy limbs restored. I had one account of a child horrifically injured in a mortar strike, only to be returned to its mother completely healthy the following day. The doctors and medics can offer no explanation, but the rumour mill is turning and our people are attributing these events to the onset of the "Juncture".' Basset paused to rise and pour himself some water.

'This news is both thrilling and worrying for me Basset. I think it is too soon to judge whether or not these events are a result of us nearing the 'tipping point', even though my life has been devoted to this. I have....' the Prime Cleric paused to consider his next few words. 'I have had inspiration, shall we say, that has made me think twice about a lot of things. But please, carry on with your report.'

'Well, the next thing of note I must raise with you, is the report on the killings at the Deathfield. The stories of what happened that day have spread like wildfire among our people, particularly on the front lines. I think it would be prudent to release an official explanation as to the events that day, and, perhaps, include it in the monthly people's Tightbeem.'

'And what would you suggest we say, Basset? We are no closer to knowing what happened that day.'

'I have prepared a short passage that should cover the event, but have omitted from the report the gruesome fate of the bodies. Hopefully, this will quell any gossip on the matter,' said Basset. 'I have also assigned extra resources to the investigation after confirmation of a survivor in the Christian ranks; my informants have indicated that the survivor, known by the name of Cole, was immediately imprisoned in the Darkland fortress by Papal decree. We have a contact within the fortress and are endeavouring to find out more about the soldier, and about what happened.'

'As ever Basset, you seem to have every base covered. I do not know how I would function without you.'

'Prime Cleric, I do not require praise. I do my job to the best of my ability and take pride in it.'

'Well Basset, your diligence allows me to concentrate on more spiritual matters so, for that, I am thankful. But I digress – tell me your third piece of news.'

Basset closed over his folder, placed it on the floor at the side of his chair, and stood to begin.

'Prime Cleric, after digesting all the latest intel I am also of the opinion that we are nearing the tipping point. I am not convinced that the 'Juncture' as prophesied will happen; for example, I'm sure the earth will not open and engulf the Christians and all their corrupt churches, but I do think the metaphor used by the prophets is pertinent to our situation today. Our front line forces have successfully taken Cartergreen. The cleansing is complete, and we now hold the port and all key supply routes in and out.'

'What I am saying, Prime Cleric, is we have now reached the point where we can inflict the killing blow on the Christians. The Vatican proper is cut off on all sides and the Christian forces are in disarray. The portents all indicate the time to end this, to force our final victory, is now.' Basset looked ecstatic as he finished and returned to his seat. 'Prime Cleric, at your command I will mobilise the bulk of our forces to march on the Vatican proper. I have already put procedures in place to disseminate the order.'

'Basset, I can see this news from your point of view, which,, on the face of it, magnificent,' Saladin said. 'I am sure your clinical planning has put everything in place, but I would like to take some time to consider this final step. There are other variables that I and only I have to consider before making this decision, and I trust you will have patience on this matter.'

Basset looked perplexed and further implored the Prime Cleric. 'Perhaps I have been inadequate in portraying the situation to you, Prime Cleric. It is clear to me and all our key military advisors that the time is now. You need only say the word. I fail to see what issue should prolong this decision. Please, forgive me if I speak out of turn.'

Thinking he heard movement, Basset turned suddenly towards an ornate screen separating the room;

but seeing nothing, he returned his gaze to the Prime Cleric.

'Basset, I appreciate and hold you in higher regard your frankness. But my decision on this matter is final. I will continue to assess the situation and would like your reports daily from now on.'

Basset nodded but was astonished at what he was hearing. The Prime Cleric had never taken such an interest in these matters, and this was the first time he had overruled his chief attender.

'Prime Cleric, may I say one more thing for you to consider?'

'Carry on Basset, of course you can.'

'I am no war monger, as you know. My desire for this action comes from wanting the war to end, for our soldiers to stop dying on the field. I long for the day when our children can grow and be taught without fear or prejudice. This is what I dream of, Prime Cleric, and that dream is at our fingertips. Should we let this opportunity slip through our fingers, I will have failed you and our people.' With that, Basset rose and left the room without saying another word.

The Prime Cleric looked over to the screened partition and Maria stepped out from behind.

'Did you hear all that Maria?'

'Yes Prime Cleric, I did.'

12. Cartergreen: Misba Ranha.

The town of Cartergreen was unrecognisable after the Muslim onslaught. Most of the wooden structures had been razed to the ground, with the exception of those deemed to be useful. The church was burnt out and the collapsed roof still smouldered, sending wisps of smoke into the sky above. The 'cleansing' had been thorough and now the Muslim women were clearing the streets of bodies and burning the corpses to prevent disease. The senior Muslim command centre was established at the Tightbeem square, and the electrical supplies and generators were soon utilised to provide the necessary temporary working headquarters. Large areas were now being cleared to allow building of accommodation units for the Muslim regiments continually arriving.

Misba Ranha was relieved to have been spared the aftermath of the cleansing operation. The indignity of the operation laid a heavy burden and the memories of the fires gave her nightmares. After setting up a field hospital unit in the barn where she found Malachi, she was busy day and night treating the Muslim casualties. This suited her as it allowed her to keep close to the young boy of whom she was growing fond.

After his initial tirades, the boy slept for two days without interruption, Misba Ranha thought this may have been caused by exhaustion combined with shock. She went in to see him in his concealed room as often as possible; following some long conversations, she was sure Malachi fully understood his predicament. She had not really given much long-term thought to the situation, but for now, she just wanted to keep the boy safe and hide his presence from her husband, Bal. Bal was a few years older than Misba Ranha and they had been together since she was thirteen. The arranged marriage was loveless, from day one. She had become desensitised to his physical and mental abuse over the last twenty years. Bal was a dolt and a brute of a man; but as he had grown older and weary from the campaign, the rapes became less frequent.

Misba Ranha's physical abuse, however, recently grew worse as Malachi had overheard since his arrival. Misba Ranha warned the boy to be silent when Bal was in the carriage; on each occasion when he had heard her sobbing and pleading for her husband to stop, Malachi had also whimpered into his blanket.

In their usual daily ritual, Misba Ranha prepared food and knocked on the false wall to let Malachi know it was safe to come out. 'Quickly Malachi, I have made you some food.' Misba Ranha handed Malachi a plate with some bread and meat stew. 'Eat it up quickly now, before Bal returns.'

'Thank you Misba Ranha, I am hungry.' Malachi took the plate and began to scoff it down.

'Young Malachi, there has been talk that we will be setting up a more permanent hospital in Cartergreen. If this happens, I think we will need to find you a better place to hide.'

Malachi looked up from his plate and shook his head.

'I don't think so, Misba Ranha. You have been kind to me and I know I owe you my life, but I need to leave here. I need to find my father.'

'Malachi, we have spoken of this You're too young to survive on your own. You will be captured and cut down. There are sentries and checkpoints around the village now and it would be impossible for you to slip through.'

'You could come with me, Misba Ranha,' Malachi said. 'You should. I can see the bruises on your arms and neck. Your husband is an evil man. You could drive your carriage through the checkpoints and then we could go away into the hills and be safe till my father finds us. We could do it.'

Misba Ranha pulled down the sleeves of her blouse to cover the marks on her arms and looked dejected. 'Please little one, do not speak of Bal in that way. For all his faults, he is a good man who is dedicated to doing his duty.'

'What about his duty to you?' Malachi scorned. 'My father would never lift a finger to my mother. He's a monster and you know it. If my father was here he would stop Bal.'

Misba Ranha looked perplexed and replied, 'Malachi, your father is not coming here. I am the only hope you have. Do not make this more difficult than it needs to be. There may come a time when an opportunity arises that allows you to flee, but until then please just do as I say.'

She paused, and then continued with great intensity. 'You must remain undetected. Do not under any circumstance make your presence known to Bal. He will kill you without a second thought. Your life means nothing to him. Will you do this for me?'

Before Malachi could reply, they both heard the sound of footsteps approaching.

'Quick my child, take your food and return. I will close the hatch behind you.'

Malachi scarpered into the hideaway and adjusted his eyes to the darkness as the hatch was closed behind him.

'Who were you talking to you slattern?'

'Bal it's you, I made your dinner. I was just talking to myself as I tidied the kitchen. How has your day been?'

Bal looked around suspiciously then settled on the armchair. 'Just bring me my fucking dinner, will you! My day's been a misery.'

Misba Ranha knew better than to argue and brought Bal over his plate of food.

'Am I not getting a drink with this garbage?'

'Yes, hold on, I will bring it over.' Misba Ranha was shaking slightly as she handed Bal his cup – and was also embarrassed because she knew Malachi could hear every word.

Bal gulped from his cup then flung it onto the carriage floor. 'That was fucking vile. No Has no one ever showed you how to make a decent drink? I don't know how I put up with you. You're fucking hopeless.'

'Maybe if I had some proper provisions to work with, it would be better,' protested Misba Ranha. 'I've been doing my best.'

Angrily, Bal sat forward in his chair then replied. 'Well, maybe if you tried to look after me like you do those injured bastards, I wouldn't need to complain.'

'No chance of you not complaining.'

Misba Ranha knew her mistake as soon as she opened her mouth. Bal immediately rose and struck her on the side of the head; she crumpled to the floor.

'Fucking bitch. Don't get lippy with me. After everything I do for you. Fucking slut. I will teach you to answer back.'

Bal grabbed Misba Ranha by the hair and forced her face down onto the carriage floor. He pulled up her dress and unbuttoned himself. 'Let's see how you like this, slut.'

Inside the hideaway tears filled Malachi's eyes but he made no sound. The boy knew he should burst out and try to help Misba Ranha, but in truth he was so scared he again covered his ears and buried his face in the blanket.

Malachi knew his father would be ashamed, but the boy trembled at the thought of being exposed and suffering at the hands of Bal. He promised himself next time, he would be brave. Brave like his father.

13. Darkland Fortress: Cole.

Cole sat upright on the cold metal bench all through the night. Though naked and damp from the hosing he received upon arriving, he did not seem bothered and no guard had observed him shivering.

As the first morning sun crept in through the cellblock's upper windows, Cole came to life. He stood and basked in the sun for a moment, then walked over and gave the cell door a push. He then did the same with each wall of the massive cage, as if testing for weakness. Next, the guard observed Cole crouching in the middle of the cage, lowering his head into his body. As the guard moved closer, he heard a groan coming from Cole and noticed the defined muscles on his arms and legs were tensed and shaking. As the guard readied to raise the alarm, Cole sprung into the air; the manacles on his wrists and ankles flew off, scattering around the cell. Cole landed like a cat and stared directly at the guard. His face was emotionless as he walked over, pulled the steel toilet out of the ground and flung it in the guard's direction. Water sprayed everywhere yet Cole stood in the middle of the cage naked staring impassively.

'Now would be a good time to raise the alarm,' Cole said as he stood. He then raised his hands in the air and stared above as if summoning some ancient deity. The guard hit the alarm button and ran to the barred entrance to wait for support. As he turned, he saw the spraying water from the toilet pipework becoming less random; it began to take shape, forming a spiral around Cole's feet. The water made rope-like strands that began to look more solid, and as they rose around Cole, he lowered his arms to reach into the viscous coils. The astonished guard gaped as Cole manipulated and spun the water coil, quickly releasing it whip-like against the metal bars of his prison. The bars bent slightly but did not break.

Finally, the reinforcements arrived. Piling into the room, they were dumbstruck by the spectacle. The commander of the guards, without warning, fired his pistol at Cole. The coil of water absorbed and then immediately directed the bullet back into the forehead of the guard, who fell like a rag doll onto the floor.

Cole then raised his hand into the beam of sunlight that came from the slotted window and retracted it with a clenched fist; for an instant, it seemed to glow. He buried his fist within the coil of water, where it sparkled as if thousands of fireflies were trapped inside, before punching both hands towards the waiting, astonished guards. The water vortex hit the men like a sledgehammer; they crashed against the wall and fell to the floor like sodden rats.

Alone, Cole was now able to fully concentrate on the atomic manipulation he desired. He utilised every element and force around him, drawing energy from the sunlight, the water's movement and even gravity. To him, every moving water droplet was stationary and every atom contained within was there for him to command; he grasped them as easily as if picking an apple from a tree. He combined these forces where necessary, and added forces and secondary influences where required until the end of the water rope became impossibly thin, invisible to the naked eye. Cole, however, could see and control this new filament weapon, the likes of which had not been seen since before the Meltdown.

He walked toward the bars and with a slight movement of his fingers the metal disintegrated. He stopped to rob some clothes from a similarly-sized guard and again crouched on the floor. This time, his concentration and focus was aimed at the building's main wall, which was over four feet wide and made with reinforced concrete. Seconds later, after a push from his hand, a large section of the wall fell outwards down onto the exercise yard.

Cole could not switch this ability on and off, but had meditated all night to produce it. Now, as he leapt down from the wall, fully sixty feet into the exercise yard, he was operating at his optimum level. As the watchtower machine gun opened fire upon him, the swirling filament weapon enveloped Cole's body and each bullet dropped to the ground at his feet. Cole walked on calmly and the prisoners in the yard ran for the prison block door, climbing over the large section of wall which lay on the unfortunate inmates below. As he moved, Cole summoned all the potential energy from his surroundings and utilised every object's height and mass and surrounding gravity. He focused and brought all this energy towards himself to assist in his end game.

The DNA wall was impenetrable, but Cole possessed knowledge of its workings and could see its fields moving and adjusting to his presence. The wall looked to Cole like a living wall of skin, moving and contorting to the actions and forces placed upon it. The wall had detected Cole's energy manipulation and was bolstering itself as a result. Cole was glad he had caught its attention. The watchtower guards looked on as Cole approached the wall, waiting for the inevitable.

Reaching within 20 feet of the boundary, something stopped Cole in his tracks. He turned round abruptly and looked upwards; he could see an elliptical haze in the air. Normal atomic conditions no longer applied here and the ellipse grew darker. Now even the guards could notice, but only Cole knew of its meaning and was aware of the fate in store for everyone in its proximity.

Cole spoke under his breath: 'So you find me once again, Scolopendra.'

With that, Cole began to sprint towards the wall. He abandoned the filament weapon and all other atomic manipulations and concentrated on the DNA wall. Behind him, the ellipse was now jet-black and forty feet wide, and a blood-curdling shriek came from within. Bringing all his focused energy together, Cole directed it to the area most bolstered by the DNA wall's rationality. As he neared, he gave a final push with both arms. The wall, in a futile attempt to prevent its own breach, became its own enemy. In struggling to negate the bombardment of energy, the DNA wall became super-solid for a moment and its structure fell within normal physical boundaries. Cole identified this and instantly withdrew his energy assault. The resulting energy imbalance caused the DNA wall to collapse into itself for a second; seeing his opportunity, Cole ran straight through into the Darkland. As the wall closed behind him the unearthly shriek and the screams of the bystanders became silent.

One hundred and one kilometres to the east of Cole's point of entry into the Darkland, the small city of Castor was an hour into its dormant cycle. Tel R Amir's neuro inhibitors took control of his synaptic functions, rousing him from REM sleep. A trigger flag he had not seen for over 200 years was blinking in his cerebral enhancer. He rose from his bed and went over to a humming communication panel, signalling an incoming transmission. Tel R Amir's voice activated the console, and a severely mech-grafted face greeted him.

'Tel, did you get that flag?'

'Yes Cubo, I did.'

'What does it mean Tel? Is it what I think?'

'Yes Cubo. It means a dysfunctionist has entered the Darkland. The DNA wall has been breached for the first time in 245 years. We may just have a ticket out of here.'

14. Vatican: Meniux.

Meniux had never seen Pope Julias look so disheartened. Julias lifted his head from his hands and tried to compose himself.

'Father, forgive me; I just cannot make sense of what I am hearing. Tell me again about the incident at the Darkland fortress.'

'Holy Father, first let me say that due to its nature, I corroborated this report before bringing it to you. Even though it sounds unbelievable, I am assured of its accuracy,' said Meniux.

'Basically, during the shift change this morning at the Darkland fortress, the relief guards were greeted with unexplainable carnage. The official report I received says every guard and prisoner in the Darkland fortress was found dead; 60 staff and 1,341 inmates. Another gruesome formation, similar to those found during the aftermath of the Deathfield massacre, were constructed in the largest exercise yard, only this one was even more horrendous if that could be possible.' Meniux took a deep breath. 'Our top academics have investigated the structure; they maintain it's a model of the DNA double helix – only one that is 55 feet tall and 5 feet wide. The structure is made completely from the heads of the unfortunates in the prison.'

Pope Julias couldn't contain himself and tears filled his eyes.

'Father Meniux, what devilry is this that comes upon us? It seems that our battle to free our planet from Muslim tyranny may not be the key struggle we must win.'

'Pope Julias, what do you mean?'

'I mean, Meniux, Satan himself may be acting on their behalf. I think we need to evaluate our position worldwide.'

'Pope Julias, let me evaluate it for you. Since the siege of Cartergreen, we have been expecting a direct assault down towards the Vatican proper and, as you know, have put measures in place to thwart such an attack. As yet nothing has transpired and the reason for this is beyond us. Saladin knows this is his chance and perhaps may believe, wrongly, his beloved Juncture moment is upon him.

'We are still confident that our subterfuge regarding Cartergreen has gone undetected,' Meniux continued, 'and await his troops marching directly into the lion's mouth. But the longer time passes without this happening, the more chance there is that we have been foiled – and that the loss of life at Cartergreen was in vain.'

Meniux paused, then finished his thoughts. 'Regarding the Darkland prison situation, I am at a loss, but feel that somehow the prisoner who made his way into your quarters may have some answers. In the next hour, Rodrigo will begin an interrogation which I will observe.'

Pope Julias went into his desk and removed a sheet of paper with a child's drawing on it.

'Father Meniux I visited the stigmata child, Liliana, yesterday.'

Julias handed the drawing to Meniux who studied it. 'I watched her draw this picture with my own eyes, but to my shame I left when she had an episode. Father Chadwin brought the picture to me later, after a rather miraculous event took place.'

Pope Julias went on and explained the whole scenario to Father Meniux in detail.

'You see Father Meniux, at first I wrongly assumed the "V" stood for Vatican, but the blood from Liliana's blessed head formed the word "Vaughn", which is the name of the prisoner you spoke of. Now I think it would be prudent if we defer Vaughn's introduction to Rodrigo for the moment, just in case this is a portent of significance.'

'I agree Holy Father; as ever you are thoughtful and wise. There is just one other matter I would discuss with you regarding the episode at the Darkland fortress. There was one inmate missing from the manifest; his body could not be found anywhere and he was not in his cell like the others.'

'Father Meniux, I'm confused. You spoke of the gruesome formation in the exercise yard. Were all of the bodies not outside of their cells?'

'No Holy Father. I am sorry that I never made myself clear; each inmate's body remained in its cell except for the group that must have been on exercise during whatever happened. My sources say the heads were removed and the wounds cauterised, with the bodies lying on the bunks with folded arms.'

'More and more bizarre this turn of events becomes, Father Meniux; but please go on.'

'Yes, anyway, there was a prisoner whose name was on the manifest but who was missing altogether. No body! No head! Also, there was no evidence of any of the checkpoints being compromised, so the inmate in question was either involved in some way with the massacre or just disappeared.'

Pope Julias looked perplexed for a moment, and then offered his reply.

'Let me guess Father Meniux: the inmate in question was the same one who survived the Deathfield massacre?'

'Yes Holy Father, that is correct. Now the question is, did this prisoner in some way carry out both atrocities, or is he connected in some way? There is one theory that a creature beyond our imagination may have escaped the DNA wall; a throwback from before the Meltdown,' said Meniux. 'Another theory involves the missing prisoner. This man, Cole, was originally from the village of Cartergreen. A rota guard has been questioned and revealed that, the night before the incident, Cole was made aware of the village's siege. Now should this Cole wish to return with the misguided notion of saving his family, then he would have a 900 kilometre journey – or a 300 kilometre journey if he found a way to go through the Darkland.'

'Father Meniux, surely that would be madness on the prisoner's part. Who knows what monstrosities from the bygone era of greed remain in there?'

'I agree Holy Father. But if he managed to escape, I think it is in our interest to attempt to apprehend this Cole and find out what he knows. He seems to be the key in many aspects of the puzzle before us.'

'Father Meniux, are you suggesting we use the transit device and imprison a regiment within the Darkland, in the mad hope that they may or may not come across this Cole vagabond, and may or may not find an exit that no other has – for hundreds of years! As you know, the use of the device has been outlawed, and we do not even know for sure that the Darkland was its final destination. The technology is beyond us.'

'Pope Julias, I agree this is too risky a venture with only a fool's chance of success. So I suggest we use the device to send just one person. Someone who, if he is there, knows enough about the Darkland to maybe be of some help and could bring this Cole to us.'

'This is too much to ask of a scholar, Meniux. Any academic would refuse to go, and rightly so.'

'That is true Holy Father. Perhaps we could instruct an appropriate priest with the relevant skills to take the mission under the threat of excommunication.'

Pope Julias shook his head and looked at Father Meniux. 'You mean to send in Father Santiago, don't you Father Meniux? I hope there is no hidden agenda behind this. Do you and he have a history?'

'Holy Father, there is no agenda except that to prevent any further damage to our Church. I see this as a small sacrifice that may make a difference … or not.'

Pope Julias stood up and walked over to the open window. Picking up the sermon that Father Santiago had given him, he turned back to Father Meniux. 'Okay, make it so. But ensure his wife is well taken care of should he not return.'

'Holy Father, I will personally make certain she is looked after.'

15. Vatican: Santiago.

For more than fifteen hours, Santiago had been in the Vatican lower vaults studying all manner of books, manuscripts and artefacts, many from pre-Meltdown Earth. He was working through the inventory and singling out any relevant pieces which corresponded in some way to his recent conversation with Pope Julias, but some unrelated information was too interesting to pass over. The archive was catalogued alphabetically with no regard to dates, a rather frustrating way to organise such treasures; Santiago was sure he could do a much better job given the chance.

So far, he had reached the letter 'C' and was looking in a narrow aisle for a copy of Chaucer's *Canterbury Tales* from the 15th century, (if the manifest was to be believed). Surely a book nearly one thousand years old would be falling to bits – but he came across a gilt box bearing a name card. After inspecting the writing and carving on the box he began to think it could be genuine. As he brushed the dust away from his ancient package, the attendant who had helped him find several items throughout the day approached.

'Father Santiago, could you come with me to the silent room next door? There is a volume there which I have been instructed to tell you to read without delay.'

'Yes sir, that's no problem. Let me just return this to its rightful place.'

Santiago placed the box back on its shelf and contemplated what Chaucer would think of this new world: whether or not he would still have been as critical of the Church today? An idea for a sermon was in the making. He smiled to himself and thought how Anna would laugh at the notion and tell him he was an old bore. 'Tell me sir,' he said to the attendant, 'who has given you this instruction? What's this all about?'

'The request came directly from Father Meniux, and he delivered the volume himself.'

The smile left Santiago's face immediately and he followed the attendant somewhat reluctantly. The attendant opened the door to the silent room and handed Santiago a bell.

'Please, ring this when you are finished and I will come back along and unlock the door for you.'

With that, Santiago went inside the room; the door was closed and locked behind him. Walking around the table sitting in the middle of the room, he pulled out the lone chair tucked underneath and sat down. He inspected the volume sitting on the table, which was entitled:

'Transition and Caldetic Interloping'
Compiled by Deitron Lee and Faith Le Boer

Santiago opened the book. The first two pages were 'intentionally blank'. The following two contained a system of strange ciphers which sparkled and changed colour as he moved his head; at the bottom of those pages, a footnote declared 'Suitable for retinal absorption', which meant nothing to Santiago.

The next page began with the heading 'Background' and Santiago finally began to read:

This documentation will ensure a written hard copy record of the Transition device and the Caldetic interloping interface. Direct neural downloads are available for functionaries with level 1.4 clearance and above. Further schematics, system programs and Caldetic data can be accessed in the paired volumes noted in Appendix B.

All development and introduction rights are owned by T.R.A Associates.

Summary testing and confirmation dialogues have accepted a true 'Fissure link' dedicated to the primary Transition device and becoming active on 23.03.2177

One-way direct transition between the allocated locations has been accepted and will be monitored by primary 'AI Calvin' and secondary 'AI X5'. All transition participants will be guaranteed full cerebral download and character storage options. The Transition device is safeguarded to be incompatible with the Hidden AI.

Fissure pre-envelopment will be instantaneous and final transition between agreed points will be AI manipulated. This static device will not pair with any other fissure device unless AI-approved Caldetic interloping has been established.

Santiago re-read the page and was no closer to understanding what was before him. Clearly, this document pertained to some pre-Meltdown device but the terminology was beyond him. As he turned the page, he heard approaching footsteps and then the key unlocking the door.

'Father Santiago, how are you enjoying the light reading I passed down for you?'

Santiago did his best to be respectful in case the attendant was within earshot but retorted in kind. 'Yes Father Meniux, I nearly dozed off there. What exactly is this book?'

'Father Santiago you disappoint me. I was told you're an expert on all things pre-Meltdown, and that was the reason the Holy Father has chosen you for such an important and unique sabbatical.'

With the door fully closed now, Santiago felt a little more at ease. This was the first time he had been truly alone with Meniux since the incident at Alcobaca and he wasn't going to miss him, 'What sabbatical? There has been no mention of this to me. Is this one of your games Meniux?'

'He has left me the pleasure of providing the first brief on the matter, Santiago.'

'Well, I just hope it's a sabbatical similar to the one you got sent on after Portugal. You seemed to return from that having landed well on your feet.'

'Now now Santiago, let's not be petty. That was a long time ago.'

'A long time ago, maybe, but I think you still have the same heart Father. Now don't waste any more of my time; tell me what this is all about.'

Father Meniux began his pompous speech and was clearly enjoying every moment as he slowly paced back and forth. 'The Holy Father has selected you for a "mission", shall we say, that is both perilous and critical to the future of our Church. I'm sure you have heard of the massacre at the Deathfield; well, a similar event has taken place within the Darkland prison, rendering every inhabitant dead.

'Now I don't want to alarm you,' Meniux continued, 'but in all likelihood you will suffer the same fate as those unfortunate souls. However, your Martyrdom will be praised and your memory will be venerated – especially by me. I have personally promised the Holy Father that I will care for your lovely wife, should the grief of your passing prove too much to bear.'

Santiago jumped out of his chair and pushed Meniux against the wall. 'Father Meniux, I swear should you so much as breathe near my wife you will pay. You snake.'

'Calm down Father Santiago,' Meniux managed to say as he pushed his assailant away. 'Please try and keep your feelings in check. I would advise you to listen to me if you want to have any chance of returning.'

With difficulty, Santiago settled himself. 'Okay, Meniux, go on.'

'There was a survivor from the Deathfield and a survivor from the massacre at the prison. Bizarrely enough, it was the same person: a man named Cole. Your task is simple – journey into the Darkland strip, find Cole, find a way back out and bring him to us. Easy.'

'Meniux, what madness are you talking about?' But as he spoke, Santiago glanced down at the document he had just been reading – for it all began to make sense.

'Ha-ha, Santiago, I see the cogs turning in your head as we speak,' said Meniux, noticing the direction of his gaze. 'Yes, we have a way into the Darkland. Unfortunately, it's a one way trip using a device we don't understand, nor know how to control. From what we can gather, the Transition device could send you to any place with a receiver, but as it stands you can only go to the last place where the bus stopped. This, lucky for us and you, is the Darkland strip.

'Now, we haven't utilised the device for some years as the forced repatriation of certain troublesome characters became frowned upon, but for you we are going to make an exception. We believe Cole has information that could swing the war in our favour; so regardless of my pleasure at your predicament, it actually would be useful if you could return with him.'

'So has this man, Cole, used the device to travel into the Darkland?' Santiago asked.

'No. We are unsure how he has managed to enter, but have intelligence that he has.'

Santiago slammed his fist on the table. 'This is nonsense! There is no way he could have crossed the barrier. No one ever has. This is a suicide mission constructed by you. I refuse.'

'Father Santiago, Pope Julias wishes to speak to you after you have fully digested the volume on the table. He wants to discuss it with you and give you a blessing for your campaign. I'm sure after you speak to him, you will see I'm just the messenger and a bystander in this game. Your own Sermon the other week has sealed your fate, not me.'

Father Santiago put his elbows on the table and shook his head. 'Go away Meniux, I need to read this.'

'Good day to you, then. The Holy Father will see you one hour from now. I suggest you write a short letter for your wife – which may not include anything we have discussed. The Holy Father will be providing your key directives as well as a Papal summons, which you will present to Cole should you meet him, so be prepared.'

Father Meniux rang the bell to leave. Before proceeding to leave, he turned and said, 'Father Santiago, it seems your sabbatical will be nothing like mine after all.'

After the door shut, Santiago closed the volume and began writing a letter to his wife.

16. New Mecca: Basset.

Since the meeting with the Prime Cleric, Basset had been in a state of rage. He played the meeting over and over again in his head and could find no way to explain Saladin's reaction. His initially feeling had been that he had not made the case strongly enough, but further reflection and meditation on the matter convinced him that this was not the case. Saladin, Basset knew, had always been more liberal than his father – the previous Muslim Prime – but his recent decision seemed an act of cowardice, whose implications could seriously undermine the Muslim cause and the continuation Islamic council.

Basset's subsequent daily reports to Saladin became matter of fact and frosty, and he perceived that the Prime Cleric's mind was elsewhere. Further reports, he decided, would be more spiritual than factual – which seemed to be Saladin's preference. Hard facts appeared to mean less than feelings and instinct, a choice Basset felt was imprudent.

Information was the backbone of the Islamic state. The gathering and dissemination of this data was the key. Keeping the Prime Cleric out of the information loop would be the first step in a plan preventing this incorrigible act of cowardice from causing serious damage. Today, Basset would first speak to the operations advisor in the Tightbeem consul building, where he would kick a stone over a ledge that would hopefully end up becoming a landslide which would bury Saladin. Misinformation, Basset decided, would be sharper than any assassin's blade.

The ops advisor waiting for Basset's arrival had clearly tidied his office only in the last five minutes. As Basset entered, a folder the man placed on top of other folders on a cabinet slid off, and paper was strewn everywhere.

'Basset, I'm so sorry, how foolish of me.'

'Let me help you,' said Basset, as reaching down to collect the papers.

'I know you are busy so I won't keep you long.' Basset handed the papers to the ops manager and took a seat at his desk. 'What I want to speak to you about today must be kept in the strictest confidence. Now I'm sure my reputation precedes me, so am I assured to have your word on this matter? Forgive me – I do not know your name.'

'It's Raza. My name is Raza and yes, Basset, you have my word.'

'Thank you, Raza. It's like this: the Prime Cleric has an illness that is causing him to lose focus during Tightbeem sessions, and larger life as a whole. The deterioration is slow but becoming more evident. Our finest doctors have managed to identify the problem and curtail it to a certain extent, but the medications have side effects. The Prime Cleric is often sleepy and forgetful; I have noticed a change in him. As you can imagine, my heart is heavy and I am doing everything I can to reduce the pressure on the Prime Cleric.'

Raza shook his head, astonished. 'Basset, I must say, these last few weeks I have found his preaching's to be inspirational. How can this be true?'

'I'm afraid I must burden you with another secret, Raza. All the most recent Tightbeems have been scripted by me. While not unprecedented, my worry is the Prime Cleric's insistence on ad-libbing the first and final Tightbeems of the day. This is not the time for the populace to be anything other than supremely confident in the Prime Cleric.'

'I fully understand, Basset. How can I be of help?'

'I would like you to change The Tightbeem schedule. I will provide the appropriate signatures and our explanation will be that the Tightbeem has developed a technical issue. You are in a position to carry this out Raza? Am I correct?'

'I can change the command nature of the Tightbeem to whatever you specify, but with all due respect, I think you underestimate the number of operatives involved in the Tightbeem's maintenance. It will be very difficult for me to convince them of a problem, when no problem exists.'

Basset was sure Raza had no idea he was being played, and the rumours that would spread due to the misconceived ruse would be exactly what Basset was hoping for.

'Raza, I have every faith in your leadership and delegation skills. I will mention nothing to the Prime Cleric. He will give his Tightbeem speeches each day as usual, but the first and final of these will not be transmitted. Is that clear?'

'As you wish, Basset. I will also do my best to stifle any awkward inquiries.'

'I'm sure you will Raza, I'm sure you will.'

Basset rose and walked to the door. 'And Raza, this office. It's like a pigsty.'

On his way back towards the main quarter of New Mecca, Basset planned to make a detour to the records and archive building. Over the last week, he had noticed two used cups and plates in the Prime Cleric's chamber and to his knowledge there had been no planned visits. The daily entry log would show everyone who had been in the building this week, and that was as good a place to start as any.

17. Rome: Priest Development quarter: Anna.

Anna was employed in the parish headquarters for medical logistics. Working twelve-hour days, she had hardly had time to miss Santiago since his visit to the Vatican. However, she was still preoccupied with him after receiving his letter that morning. Anna sat in the staff canteen on the lunch break and took the letter out of her bag to read again.

Dearest Anna,

A situation has arisen that has placed me in an impossible predicament. I am unable to give you details at this moment, but I need to let you know that I may not be able to return home for some time, nor can you visit me.

Everything was going so well up until today. I have studied books over 1,000 years old, written by the finest wordsmiths in mankind's history. I was given the opportunity to gain access to areas in the Vatican that I could only have dreamed of. I have been visiting the Holy Father daily, and our discussions had become less formal and almost friendly in nature. He was keen to learn about my studies and knowledge of epigenetics, and I did my best to oblige him.

I wish I could tell you more, but I do not have much time. One thing I must say: I think a 'wolf in sheep's clothing' may be behind this.

> *I trust you will understand what I mean; do
> not trust or be alone with the wolf under any
> circumstances. I must go now, but rest assured,
> you will be in my thoughts until I return. Be
> safe and be happy with my blessing.*
> *Love, S.*

What could this mean? Would she be able to contact someone to find out more? Anna hardly ate a bite of her lunch; she folded the letter back into its envelope and put it away. The next four hours at her desk seemed like an eternity. When she walked out of the building gates, she headed home in the rain, walking briskly through the muddy streets, avoiding the well-known potholes on her familiar route. When she arrived at her house, she saw two palace guards standing abreast her front door and went into a panic. Anna ran towards them as her eyes filled up, and she called for Santiago. The nearest guard held up his hand to calm her.

'Steady, woman, we are not bringing you news of death. We are merely here on escort duties. You have a visitor.' The guard stood aside and gestured for Anna to enter her house.

As she walked in, Anna saw a priest's cape on the hanger and thought for a moment that maybe Santiago had returned after all. She entered the room and found Father Meniux sitting on Santiago's father's old armchair.

'Anna, you're in quite a state, is everything okay?'

Rendered speechless, Anna could not believe her eyes.

'Let me take your coat Anna, you're soaked through.' Meniux stood and reached to unbutton Anna's sodden jacket.

'I can get it myself,' Anna said scornfully, stepping backward away from Meniux.

'Okay, I was only trying to help. Please, take a seat; I have something I need to discuss with you.'

Anna sat down and folded her arms and legs. Not looking Meniux in the eye, she replied, 'Go on.'

'I trust you have received correspondence from Santiago?'

'Yes, I have.'

'Well, you will be aware that your husband is currently helping the Holy Father with a very important problem. The problem is so complicated that he may be away for a very long time. Now, I have taken it upon myself to see that you are looked after during his absence.'

'I can look after myself, thank you.'

'Oh, I'm sure you can Anna, but I have pledged myself to do this and I intend to do so to the best of my abilities. There is, however, another variable that you should be aware of. Although the details of your husband's errand are secret, I would like you to know that I will do everything I can to ensure his safe and prompt return.'

'Can you tell me, Father Meniux, is he safe at the moment?'

'For now, yes, he is safe, but I will not lie to you. He may be faced with some dangerous trials. I could possibly help alleviate these dangers, if I am convinced that it was the correct course of action.'

Meniux smiled over at Anna, who still could not look at him.

'What do you mean by that Father Meniux?'

'What I mean, Anna, is that if you allow me to ease your burden, you can take the opportunity to convince me to help you and Santiago. Don't you see? We have a situation where, through my obligation towards you, you can indirectly help your husband? You do want to help your husband, don't you, Anna?'

'Of course I do, but I don't think I like what you're inferring.'

'I'm not inferring anything, Anna, merely stating a fact. You have it within your power to help your husband, who, believe me, will require all the help he can get. The choice you have is whether you love him enough to do so. Do you love him enough to give yourself up to help him?'

Anna broke down in tears and Meniux went over and sat beside her. 'Anna, Anna, there is no need to cry.' Meniux put his arm around her shoulders and placed his hand on her thigh. 'Don't upset yourself over this, just think of what an honourable thing you are doing.'

Anna continued to sob as Meniux slowly slid his hand further up her leg and under her skirt.

'What is wrong with accepting affection while you are in a time of despair? Just let yourself go and you will enjoy it.'

Anna suddenly pushed Meniux away and stood up. 'Get out! Get out of my house, you beast, I will never so much as touching you. Go on, get out now!'

Standing up, Father Meniux grabbed her shoulders and pushed her back onto the chair, pinning her down. 'I forgot to mention, Anna: as well as improve your husband's chances of returning to you, I can also reduce them. Have a think about that and bear it in mind when you come to your decision. I will leave you now to contemplate. I'll return in three days' time without my escort, when I trust I will be shown a bit more hospitality.'

Meniux released Anna and ran his open hand down her face gently, then turned and stepped into the hall, lifting his cape from the coat hook as he passed. 'Have a lovely evening. Oh and one other thing: please, be careful now that Santiago is away. There have been reports of a wolf loose in these parts.' Meniux laughed and stepped out of the door.

In despair, Anna and fell onto the floor, crying uncontrollably. Finally managing to gather herself, she went into the kitchen and poured a glass of water.

Meniux had obviously read Santiago's letter and was holding all the cards. Should she do this? Could she do this? Was what Meniux said true? Could he help Santiago, and, more important, would he if she did what he asked?

She thought of Meniux's return and what it would involve; then she ran to the sink and vomited.

18. New Mecca: Maria.

Since her arrival in the Prime Cleric's private enclave, Maria had flitted in and out of atomic space at regular intervals. Though witnessing her performing the feat numerous times, the Prime Cleric was always startled at her sudden appearances. Today, she arrived shortly after Basset had given his daily brief. The Prime Cleric had a cup of tea waiting for her, which he nearly knocked over when turning to find her sitting on his desk. 'Maria, is there not some way you can give me some warning of your arrival? You're going to give this old man a heart attack.'

'I'm sorry Saladin. Do you not feel a slight change in the room temperature before I arrive?'

'Can't say I've noticed, Maria. Anyway, here you go,' said Saladin, handing the tea to her. They both took a seat then Saladin continued, 'let's continue where you left off yesterday. Tell me more about The Affinity and their claims. Are you saying they profess to be gods unknown to us, or our own gods with different names?'

'They claim no "god qualities", Prime Cleric, and the idea of all-powerful deities is preposterous to them.'

'So what is your point, Maria?'

'Prime Cleric, the whole thing is difficult; I will try and be plain with my explanation. The Affinities have always existed. Initially, they were one entity, but over time (if you could call it time) they have become a pair. During their existence, they witnessed the creation and demise of countless universes and have played a part in the development of them all.'

'They have seen the evolution of many wonderful worlds with fantastic life forms and have watched them come and go. Earth is the one and only occasion where they have witnessed the development of a life form possessing consciousness. To The Affinity this is all the more remarkable as humans on Earth are still atomic, rather than non-atomic in structure like themselves.' Maria paused and took a sip of the tea.

'You mean they have a non-physical form?'

'Yes, but they can choose any form they wish. They also know Earth's history in the greatest detail and that history pain and bloodshed has brought them only despair.'

'Say I choose to believe you, Maria: what then do these entities demand?'

'Prime Cleric, they have no demands, only love. Total love for every human soul on the planet, dead or alive.'

'You say dead or alive,' Saladin repeated. 'By that, are you saying there is indeed an afterlife?'

'Not in the way you would like to believe, Prime Cleric, but it is a fact that there are a set number of life forces on the planet, an amount which has remained pretty much the same over Earth's history. The Affinity is now tied to every single soul and in each they see themselves; over time, each soul could potentially become permanently non-atomic. But their first goal is to stop the bloodshed.'

'Ok Maria. This all sounds fantastic and let's just assume for a minute it's true. The problem is that mankind has embraced the religions of our world, and people have died and will continue to die for their beliefs. No amount of talk or magical appearances will make them change their mind. How does The Affinity propose to change things if they will not interfere or force a change?'

'Prime Cleric, to force any change would be abhorrent to The Affinity. They have spent an eternity – in our terms – perfecting their existence. Shedding any part of that to force a change, could cause a lack of compassion. The very existence and creation of this universe and others, offers The Affinity a medium in which they can develop. Direct control by them is unthinkable and could jeopardise that.'

'Well, again I ask you, how can anything change?'

'That's where I come in. I'm human like you, and until now, have had six incarnations on Earth. Thanks to The Affinity I can now remember every single life: every word I spoke, every person I met. The Affinity made available my future incarnations and their genetic benefits, which is one of the reasons I can be "elsewhere" as I choose.'

'So, although they cannot and will not interfere, they want you to do their dirty work, is that it?'

'Far from it Prime Cleric; my job is to try and convince you to do it for me.' Maria smiled broadly at Saladin.

'It may take you a long time to convince me, my dear, but I promise I will listen to everything you have to say. You certainly have me intrigued.'

'I appreciate that, Saladin. My focus right now must be that to convince you to call a ceasefire and put a stop to the killing.' Maria took a deep breath, and continued with her revelations. 'The Affinity has been using certain bodiless souls to help heal and cure those caught up in your Holy War. You may have heard talk of this.'

'Yes, it has been reported to me. Our elders have an entirely different explanation for the events. My question is, how did this happen? If it's all some kind of mistake that's unheard of throughout time, how has it happened at all? What changed?'

'The simple answer to that would raise more questions, so I will further describe the nature of The Affinity, which in itself will explain a lot.'

Gathering her thoughts, Maria continued. 'The Affinity has developed over vast periods of time, during which they became a pair and tried continually to perfect themselves. Now, throughout this process, any part of their expanding nature that they found had the potential to jeopardise their bid for perfection and total compassion was disregarded. These non-atomic glitches in their beings were deposited deep within neutron stars.

'The Affinity always knew that there could be a potential scenario where the spurned personality glitches could somehow bond together and create a new entity. They called this entity "The Exile". They believe The Exile is behind the evolution of mankind and the establishment of consciousness.'

'Does this Exile inhabit our planet?' asked Saladin.

'Not in the regular sense. He must maintain a non-atomic structure like The Affinity or his presence, so far elusive, would be evident to them immediately. What they *have* detected is manipulation of the human genome throughout your history. It seems that mankind has been steered in a particular direction by this entity, which itself lacks empathy and love, rendering its very nature imperfect.'

'And so this Exile, according to you, is responsible for human consciousness. Is that what you're saying?'

'Yes, that's it exactly, though it's been playing a lengthy game with mankind and has no problem with your suffering. We suspect The Exile has its own agenda with an end game that is unknown to us.'

The Prime Cleric stood up and walked over to the bookshelf to stretch his legs. 'Maria, let me have some time to think about what you said, then come back later and join me for some supper. Your stories are fantastic, but I need to digest them.

'In the meantime, I would like you do something for me that might help to convincing me – and would also make me very happy. Before the Meltdown there was a city called Sappho, which grew from a market town to the largest metropolis on the planet.'

'I know about Sappho,' said Maria with a smile.

'Okay. That's good. In the centre of the city there was a giant library and inside was an ancient Koran that was sacred to us. After the Meltdown, the city was locked down and its inhabitants perished; it's a toxic wasteland now. If you truly can be anywhere on the planet in an instant, would you be able to get this Koran for me?' Saladin looked at Maria and noticed she appeared perfectly still, like a statue, just for an instant.

'Okay, Saladin I need to go. I'm looking forward to seeing you later. The Koran you're after is in your desk drawer.'

Before Saladin could answer, Maria was gone.

19. Clefton Green: Colonel William Carstairs.

Heavy rain had turned Clefton Green into a swamp. The ongoing arrival of the Christian war machine had cut deep ruts into the ground, and the former village green now looked like a ploughed field. Beyond the ridge of the low-lying surrounding hills to the east, a large Muslim army awaited the order to advance. Daily they prepared their vehicles, briefed their troops on strategy and sent scouts to try and glean any knowledge that would provide even the slightest advantage.

Cleric Atarn, fresh from his victory at Cartergreen, was desperate for the order to advance. As far as he was concerned, they had gained momentum and had the impetus to deliver another clinical, killer blow.

Back in Clefton Green, Colonel William Carstairs also did not enjoy the waiting game and called a meeting with his key staff. News had arrived from the Papacy: he had been given the green light to proceed as he saw fit.

At 51 William was not too old to be a colonel, but he felt that he should have achieved the rank sooner. Spearheading many campaigns and leading various garrisons to victory over the three years served in this position, he had earned a reputation for being a no-nonsense leader who got results. William knew the forthcoming endeavour would be the most demanding, not to mention risky, but he was buzzing with adrenaline at the thought. As a leader who placed his faith on tactics, he had read extensively about the exploits of famous generals from Genghis Khan and Caesar to Napoleon and Rommel. In more recent history he had drawn inspiration from Caberni's blitzkrieg type tactics during the Meltdown.

As he walked to meet with his key staff, William knew exactly what his plan was. A direct offensive under the cover of darkness would be his opening – and only – gambit. He often preferred daylight assaults playing with flanking and pincer movements which the landscape on this occasion suited, but he also knew that this is exactly what the Muslims would be expecting (if they anticipated an assault at all).

Three hours later, at dusk, preparations were complete. William broke his army into their six home regiments, each containing around 800 men. His instructions were to march the troops and heavy artillery three kilometres to the brow of the hill, with each regiment making a stand half a kilometre apart. From the top, they would begin shelling and drive forward, with each regiment to fan back together so that upon reaching the Muslim encampment, a battering ram of nearly five thousand men would lay waste to their confused enemies.

He knew this assault was important – maybe the most important of his life. William just hoped that he had stressed that point effectively to the head of each regiment. If timed to perfection, 10 to 15 minutes into the assault, the sun would rise and by that time, the damage would be done.

As night fell, the regiments waited silently for the order to proceed. William Carstairs tramped through the mud, climbed into the seat of his basic jeep type vehicle and gave the signal to advance. The regiments slowly moved out, breaking step to reduce noise and fanning outwards up the hill. Those on foot found the going heavy and often slipped and fell. As they got higher up, the ground stiffened and soon they were making good pace.

After two hours, the first of the regiments reached the hill ridge, the first designated assembly location. Soon after the others followed and were dotted just over the summit of the hill like bunting.

Several small scouts groups from each regiment were now sent ahead with the best radios to report back, and give the go-ahead to proceed. It was these groups who initially witnessed the disturbance. The first and last radio message reported that 'a localised electrical storm has appeared overhead.' Soon, every regiment could see this event, as could the night sentries in the Muslim camp. The silvery ellipse in the sky grew bigger, and lights and flashes could be seen within. Next, a pounding shriek was heard; as each pulse reached the ears of soldiers in both camps, they felt themselves becoming immobilised.

William Carstairs struggled to raise his hands to cover his ears. As he forced his hands upward, his control over his body was lost and he too became immobile. From the ellipse, the cause of the event began to show itself. The distance made it impossible for William to gauge the abomination's size. Initially what looked to be a thick, black, scaled tail section appeared, followed by a pair of spidery legs. Each leg joint had a metallic look, with slime dripping from the articulation. William looked on as many more of these sections, each joined to the other, appeared out of the ellipse with ever-increasing speed. As the first section reached the ground, the creature continued to pour out of the sky like a rope being lowered from a window. Eventually, the end of the rope came into view and the pulsing sound ceased. William found he was now able to move his head; however, he had lost all feeling and connection to the rest of his immobilised body.

Looking up, he saw the head of the giant, centipede-like creature falling down from the sky and then, gently, it was on the ground. William could do nothing but scream, as did almost every immobilised person around him. Helplessly, they turned and looked at one other, whilst some of the standing soldiers collapsed facedown into the mud. What William saw as the creature fell from the sky was unexplainable and gruesome. The entity's hundreds of legged sections, now visible, led to an enormous multi-faceted head. Each facet contained a monstrous face of its own, with bulging eyes and a terrifying, salivating mouth piece.

Once fully on the ground, the body formed into an outward spiral with the grotesque head square centre. As the spiral became complete, the pulsing began again and everyone's head movement was again prevented. William watched as the creature began to undulate from the centre outwards like a snake; as each part of the wave moved along its body, the articulated sections separated and sped away in all directions.

Soon, many of these awkward bipeds were making their way towards the closest of William's regiment. As one came closer, he could see that the segment was larger than he had thought and actually stood as tall as a horse. Running along with an awkward gait, a putrid slime dripped from its legs and its body rocked back and forward like a swing. Eventually, William could make out another facet on the underbelly of the creature with bulging eyes and an awful mouth piece.

The first soldier it approached was lying on his back. The segment straddled him and the second it did so, the movement returned to the soldiers head. Screaming for help, he turned his head from side to side in vain. The segment's legs appeared to get smaller as it lowered its underbelly down towards the soldier's skull; the last thing the poor man saw was its many popping eyes looking down impassively. Quickly, it extended itself and moved on, leaving the decapitated body in the mud.

Hundreds of segments now overran the area. From his elevated position in the jeep, William had the impression of a swarm of insects consuming everything in their path.

Within minutes, William realised that his time had come. A segment approached and then elevated over his jeep until the facet was looking down at him. Closer inspection revealed that the segment was both organic and mechanical in nature, and that the slime was more like a lubricant.

Why was this his final thought?

The creature lowered its belly down towards him. Knowing he could do nothing, William closed his eyes and waited for the inevitable. The mouthpiece engulfed his head he felt warmness in his neck and he knew the end was here.

Seconds passed. Somehow still conscious, William opened his eyes and saw nothing but darkness. His neck was numb, his face tingled and he felt nips below his eyes. Then wet, foul-smelling feelers forced their way up his nose and into his mouth.

William's mind was no longer his to control. He felt like he was spinning, then images appeared in his consciousness, as if he had entered someone else's dream – but only for an instant. Suddenly he could see as if he was an eye at the end of each of the four feelers. He watched as they searched through his brain and inspected every minute area with amazing speed until each of the four feelers had found its goal. The feelers now increased their focus until each tiny part was viewed microscopically and then on an atomic level. Once achieved, the feelers identified and absorbed the space between each and every atom.

Colonel William Carstairs knew his consciousness was no longer within his severed head. Somehow, his entire awareness was contained within the now-withdrawn feelers that had searched it out.

The giant headpiece now began to emanate a chilling shriek and started to convulse. The uppermost mouthpiece opened and with each seizure, a putrid brown sludge spurted out until a pile had formed on the grass in front of it. Large antenna-like feelers reached out from the head and began to form smaller balls with the sludge pile.

The shriek seemed to be a call for the segments to return. As they sped back, each approached the next with belly spun up so the mouthpiece could join together with an awaiting proboscis from the segment in front. Soon, the monster was complete once more and, as the last piece and tail reformed, each mouthpiece on the multifaceted head began to wretch out a waterfall of human heads.

The large feelers took each head and quickly began to form its masterpiece. Growing in width and height, the gruesome tower was soon fifteen metres wide and rising into the air. The creature moved upwards in the space created within the double helix that it was forming and continued its work. As the sun rose, the creature put the final heads in place. As it did so, the localised electrical storm returned and the ellipse outside of normal time and space returned. As the disturbance engulfed the top of the awful double helix, the creature shot upward spirally through the helix into the void, and was gone.

20. Darkland: Santiago.

The first thing that struck Santiago about the fissure chamber was the change from old to new as you entered. The door to the room was in an old, oak-panelled corridor with a high ceiling and ornate carving. But past the door was a positive pressure lock with a formed glass-and-plastic door. On entry to the cubicle Santiago caught first sight of the chamber, which was like nothing he had ever seen in his life.

The wall seemed alive and displayed hundreds of similar chambers, which were obviously dotted all over the planet. Beside each chamber display numbers and ciphers rolled and changed, as if continually calculating and analysing data. There was a large sloping desk with runes and figures which seemed to float in mid-air above it, but as Santiago focused on them he realised he could see through what must be the holograms he'd read about. As the other positive pressure door opened to allow him access, he walked through with the enthusiastic technician, Paula, who would be operating the device. Santiago thought she was utterly delightful.

'You seem more excited about this than I am, Paula.'

Paula was small, curvy and not at all glamorous. But what she lacked in traditional beauty, she made up for with charisma. Giggling, she took Santiago by the arm. 'You don't understand what this means for me, Santiago. I took over running the device after the last steward was transferred. One week later, they stopped using the device and for the last four years I've just been responsible for keeping it ticking over, which really just means coming in every day and looking at it.' Paula laughed and let Santiago go. 'You will be my first subject and opportunity to see the fissure device operating.'

'Paula, I assume you are aware of the one-way nature of the device and its destination?'

'Of course I am. But as a scholar on the Darkland, I trust you are as excited to go there as I am to send you on your way?' Paula asked with a quizzical look on her face.

'My dear, I also know a lot about volcanoes but wouldn't want to jump in one of them.' Santiago laughed, grateful for Paula's bubbly nature putting him at ease.

Paula grinned and walked over to the large desk. 'Right, okay, let me just change the delivery point to the centre of Mount Vesuvius and you can be on your way.'

'Maybe that would be a blessing Paula, if true,' said Santiago.

Paula ran her hand through one of the hologram ciphers on the desk and another transparent screen appeared in front of her. 'Santiago, this is the control manifold for the fissure device. From here I can activate the Caldetic interloping interface to re-open the last known fissure link. Now, all the parameters were set for this transfer over a hundred years ago by AIs, as I'm sure you know; since we are unable to calibrate a new destination, we have only used it to go on this one-way trip.

'We have identified most of the receiving platforms shown on the walls around you,' Paula continued, 'and each one has been fortified and guarded. The Church fabricated a story that the buildings contain holy icons.'

'So, as you've never had anyone return, how do you know they get there safely? Into the Darkland, I mean?'

Paula turned, walked over to the liquid-seeming wall and pointed. 'Good question. Do you see that receiving platform right in the middle of the wall, with the cipher that looks like two serpents wrapped round a sword?'

'The caduceus cipher, you mean?' Santiago replied.

'Clever boy. Yes, that one: it is the platform within the Darkland. Each time we've used it, the person has appeared on that platform and walked right out the door without delay, often after being asked to signal back answers to questions about the transfer – but not doing so.'

'Well, I suppose that's a relief knowing I won't be immediately disintegrated into a million bits.'

Paula returned to the large desk. 'I trust you are familiar with the five zones within the Darkland, Santiago?'

'Yes, I am.'

When developed, the Darkland was manipulated to produce five different environments, allowing the thrill-seekers to experience combat and survival in different taxing terrains: a densely wooded jungle section; an icescape section; a desert area; a lake area; and at the centre, a deserted metropolis section. Santiago knew all this, having studied the Darkland in depth.

'Do you know which section the arrival platform is in, Paula?'

'Unfortunately we do not, but our best guess is that the metropolis section would be most likely. As you can see, though, we have supplied you with the equipment and clothing suitable for all areas. There are also some weapons and medical supplies in the rucksack, which I have already put into the interloping chamber. Do you have any questions?'

'I have millions, but I don't think I will bother. Let's get this over with.'

Santiago walked over to the chamber door, paused and turned to Paula. She followed him, stopping to collect a box from the floor beside the large desk.

'Good luck Father, and I think you will be needing this.' Paula opened the box and handed Santiago a pistol different from any he had encountered: gold and silver with no perceivable trigger, but possessing the traditional handgrip and barrel shape.

'This pistol is called a Frenzy,' explained Paula. 'We have established that these were issued to everyone who entered the Darkland and can only be used when within its boundaries. Every time we activate the device, one pops up on the big glass desk. Can I ask you to press the bottom of the hand grip whilst holding it with your other hand?'

Santiago did as he was asked and felt a sudden sting in his hand. 'Ouch, what was that?'

'I'm sorry; the Frenzy is pairing with you. It's taken a sample of your blood and analysed your DNA. Now only you will be able to operate it. The documents we have indicate that within the Darkland you will be able to use the Frenzy not just as a pistol, but as a means of creating fire, for example.'

Paula continued her explanation. 'The Frenzy can be altered to become all manner of weapons, and can remotely operate all types of electrical devices or override operating systems. The documents even claim that the Frenzy can learn to open locks. Of course, we have never witnessed this or been able to confirm it, but it appears that the pistol will explain its functions to you on arrival.'

Santiago passed the weapon to his other hand and watched as the small cut on his palm healed in front of his eyes. The weapon had also become warm and felt as though it was attracted to his hand, almost magnetic to his skin.

'Well Paula, I think I am ready. Do you have any other surprises for me before I go?'

'Just this,' replied Paula as she stood on her toes and kissed Santiago on the cheek. 'Good luck Father Santiago, I will pray for you.'

Santiago stepped into the open-topped chamber. There was a silver body shape on the floor, the outline of which was raised up an inch; he fitted himself within it as instructed earlier. Paula placed the rest of his paraphernalia onto a similar square section on the floor, then turned and left, closing the door behind her.

Santiago heard her shout from outside.

'Are you okay, Father?'

'Yes!' Santiago shouted back.

'Right then, on the count of three. One ... two ... three.'

Santiago saw a yellow glow appear on the surface of the metal perimeter; it grew taller and successfully enclosed him.

'Caldetic interloping achieved Father. This is it,' he heard – and then his heart stopped.

Santiago's mind was outside the chamber though his body remained inside, but only for an instant. He felt his consciousness being dragged back to his body and, watching from above, he saw himself disintegrate and gradually disappear only to reform again. This continued over and over: his body being dismantled and rebuilt until it suddenly stopped. His body was whole again and he was able to look out of his own eyes. The yellow envelope fizzled out as he stood up quickly,

Suddenly an automated voice spoke: '*You have thirty seconds to leave the platform before Caldetic disintegration continues. You have thirty seconds to leave the platform before Caldetic disintegration continues.*'

'So that was the reason everyone in the past had made a sharp exit from the platform,' Santiago thought.

He picked up his rucksack, felt in his belt for the Frenzy pistol walked to the door and gave a thumbs-up gesture for Paula.

As he opened the door, Santiago looked around and instantly knew that the expert's destination 'best guess' couldn't have been more wrong.

21. Clefton Green: Irkalla.

A party of Christian medics were the first to arrive at Clefton Green after the massacre. What they encountered was unspeakable. The gruesome double helix towered over the killing fields: a macabre statement that unnatural forces, beyond the Christian and Muslim capabilities, was at work.

Word soon filtered back to the Vatican and New Mecca, and an immediate cessation of hostilities was announced to allow both sides to collect their dead. Bad news was difficult to contain, however; soon, normal soldiers and wives, mothers and children were hearing stories of fantastical beasts, of how Satan was rising to make the world his own, and how a new Antichrist was in Rome. The Tightbeem's masses on both sides were doing little to quench the populace's thirst for news and the constant reference to 'unexplained events' only added fuel to the already blazing fire.

Several days into the Clefton Green clean-up a discovery was made by a priest who stumbled across a concealed bunker in the woods. The priest raised the alarm and the usual care was taken for booby traps, which were common. On first inspection the bunker appeared empty, but the priest, on an unknown whim, called for total silence. A scraping was heard. Soon a trap door was discovered and a woman was found chained within. Although restrained for at least three days since the massacre, the woman showed no signs of hunger or thirst. She was slim with dirty blonde hair and a dolichocephalic head, which gave her an almost wolf-like quality.

The priest was anxious to release her, but the soldier in charge was not.

'Father something is not quite right here. Let's not release her too soon.'

'Nonsense sergeant; the woman is chained, what should we fear?'

The woman listened intently and then interjected, 'Priest, maybe you should listen to your sergeant. Can't you see a slight woman like myself poses a serious threat?'

The woman laughed, and the priest became unsettled.

'Father, please, let's question her first before we release her,' repeated the soldier.

'Sergeant you know the protocol; she must be interrogated in the Vatican.'

'Okay. Well, I have some questions first. Woman, do you have a weapon concealed?'

'I do not.'

'What is your name, woman? And why have you been restrained?' asked the priest.

'My name is Irkalla and I'm restrained because no one was willing to release me. Are you willing to release me, Priest, with free will and without coercion from me?'

The sergeant was even more unsettled by the woman's remark and interrupted again. 'What kind of statement is that? Woman why do you not look hungry or thirsty, and how have you survived the massacre?'

'What massacre do you speak of, Sergeant? I have been incarcerated in this prison for days. I know of no massacre, though I do hope my captor has faced a horrible end.'

Now the priest was becoming impatient. 'Sergeant, I insist you release the woman now; she poses us no threat. We can return her to the Vatican, where a proper interrogation can be carried out and where she will be well looked after.'

The woman smiled. 'Yes Father, I have heard the hospitality of your Vatican interrogators is second to none. I look forward to a night or two as their guest. So I ask again, do you choose to release me with free will and without coercion? Please answer.'

'Sergeant, this woman is rambling. I think she may be dehydrated; fetch her some water.'

At this the woman began to make a guttural noise, which grew louder in volume and became a roar.

'Arrrrrggggh. Fucking priest! Do you choose to release me of your free will and without coercion? Answer me, you fucking faggot.'

The priest and the sergeant stepped back in shock and quickly left the bunker. Outside, they regained their composure and spoke once more. 'What the hell was that all about?' the sergeant said.

The priest blessed himself and replied, 'Sergeant, I think this woman may be deranged. Maybe her time in captivity has driven her to mania, or perhaps she is restrained for that reason. Regardless, I want you to go in with a few of your guards and release her. I will give her a blessing first.'

The priest returned to the bunker where the woman was sitting staring at her hands. Without looking up she spoke again. 'What's it to be, Priest? Have you the balls to answer my question?'

'I do my child. Of course I will release you, but first I will say a blessing for you.'

The priest held out his hands to the woman, 'Remind me of your name.'

'My name is Irkalla, Father Michael.'

The priest pulled his hands back quickly and asked, 'How do you know my name?'

'The sergeant called you Michael when you first came in.'

The priest hesitated then gave his hand to Irkalla once more and began his blessing. *'Father, help us today and bring love to your child Irkalla. May she be welcomed into your salvation and find peace in her heart.'*

Father Michael tried to release Irkalla's hand but she would not let go. She glared at father Michael and snarled, 'You've made your pledge Priest, now let me say mine. Get these chains off me right fucking now and say a prayer for yourself before you get what's coming to you.'

Irkalla let go; Father Michael called in the sergeant who released the woman, and put her in the hands of an escort back to the Vatican.

Later that evening, Father Michael was preparing for bed in his temporary accommodation when a young girl burst in holding a small wooden doll.

'Quickly Father, come quickly, it's my mother!'

Father Michael pulled on his cape and followed the girl out of the tent and down a steep hill, away from the main campsite, into a small abandoned hamlet with a few dilapidated houses.

'In here.' She said approaching one of the houses, 'Quick, follow me.'

Father Michael followed the girl into a ramshackle house, felt an arm wrap round his neck and was forced to the ground. When he looked up at his assailant, he saw it was the sergeant from earlier in the day. 'You should have listened to her,' he said.

Father Michael looked for the young girl but she was nowhere to be seen. Standing facing the wall was a woman holding a small wooden doll, and from the clothes she was wearing he knew it was Irkalla. She turned round and looked at the priest. 'You have no idea, do you Priest, the games I play?'

'Why? Why would you do this, Sergeant? Have you lost your mind?' blurted out Father Michael.

'No Father, more like I've found it,' the sergeant replied.

Irkalla approached and Father Michael began to pray.

'Father, look after me today and forgive these lost souls.'

Irkalla signalled the soldier to pull Father Michael to his feet and came nose to nose with him. She grabbed his head, tilted it to the side, and forced her lips against his. Father Michael felt her tongue enter his mouth and beyond; in an instant his mind was lost to her. Seconds later, Irkalla released him and he fell to the ground.

'Get up Priest.'

Father Michael opened his eyes, looked up and smiled. He stood up and, without a word, turned and calmly walked out of the door followed by the sergeant.

22. Vatican Prison: Vaughan.

Shifting about at night from his cell to all corners of the Vatican had familiarised Vaughan with its layout. He had left minute time markers everywhere, which was a new ability he had just perfected: He only had to find a vantage point and observe the scene before him. The inanimate materials he could ignore, he would only have to return to the 'set point' for an instant any time in the future to see everything that had happened at that location. Vaughan found this new skill most useful, especially for gathering information on Pope Julias and his wretched assistant. He was disturbed with the playback he was receiving from Interrogation Chamber 1, and couldn't understand Rodrigo's lack of empathy. He was looking forward to their introduction.

Having reviewed all of Pope Julias's recent conversations, he was now certain he had to approach his mission from a completely different angle. That Pope Julias thought he was some kind of demon from a bygone age didn't help, but Vaughan was intrigued as to his comment when they first met: 'I've been warned of your coming'. He could only imagine it related to the stigmata girl he had heard about, but had yet to locate. He would have to get to the bottom of this phenomenon that he now knew had no foundation.

Again he thought the stigmata must be an epigenetic manipulation, but the more he saw and discovered, the more he was beginning to understand the scale of the game in play. Yes, for The Affinity, mankind's history was a blink of the eye; but Vaughan himself was human. To conceive the lengths that The Exile had gone to over thousands of years – manipulating and guiding mankind in a particular way – was an accomplishment. The question was why did The Exile go to all that trouble? What was its end game?

Vaughan sat in his cell and replayed the last day's events in Pope Julias's private quarters, stopping at the moment the pope had found his note:

> *Pope Julias, I can assure you I'm no demon. I can answer every question you have ever had about your faith. Don't trust Meniux!*

Vaughn watched as a quizzical look appeared on Julias's face as he mouthed the words and searched the other pockets of his robes to no avail. Next, Pope Julias crumpled the piece of paper, placed it in his basket and rang his bell for an attender.

A young woman duly arrived and bowed before the Pontiff.

'How may I help you today Holy Father?' The girl kept her head lowered as she spoke, then looked up and smiled.

'Can you summon Father Meniux, my dear? Tell him I have need for his council.'

'Holy Father, Father Meniux informed me earlier that he would not be back for an hour or so.'

'Just typical! Do you know where he has gone?'

'Yes Holy Father, he took two guards and said he had an important errand to run in the priests' developmental quarter.'

'He did, did he? Well, if you can inform him on his return to come to me immediately.' Pope Julias paused to think before continuing. 'On second thought, bring me the guards who accompanied him first and mention none of this to Father Meniux.'

'Yes Holy Father, I will organise it as soon as they return.' The attender girl nodded, turned and left quickly.

None of the conversations Pope Julias had had made much sense to Vaughn, but he could see that Julias was unhappy about something, and he hoped his note had maybe struck a chord.

Reviews of other time markers showed the chaos caused in a few instances by his actions. Vaughan realised that he would need to be a bit more careful when it came to 'miraculous interference'. (Several younger detainees and a child had been processed through to the holding cells, awaiting their turn with Rodrigo. Vaughan had shifted them as a unit directly into a Muslim caravan train, which was relocating away from the war zones.)

Vaughan was aware of many such refugee trains fleeing from both sides of the war, but he was uncertain as to their motivation. He was aware that both religions based their foundations on miraculous events, complete with prophets and visionaries who claimed direct contact with deities. However, as soon as a few verifiable miracles occurred, like the cures in the field hospitals, the masses were easily spooked. No greater evidence was there of this than the rise of cults once again pledging their allegiance to darker, more sinister deities. This turn of events would need to be addressed. Vaughan closed his eyes and in an instant, informed The Affinity and Maria that they would have to commune to discuss this.

Vaughan returned his main body to his holding cell, as he knew some food would be coming soon. Sitting on his bunk, he could just make out whispering voices outside in the corridor. This caught his attention: even during the night, rarely did anyone attempt to have a discreet conversation. Vaughan focused his attention on the cellblock and slowed down relevant time to enable himself to have a look outside without being noticed. He shifted outside his cell into the corridor and saw three guards standing mid-conversation but frozen like a tailor's dummies. Rodrigo Gomez was also entering through a door at the far end of the row of cells, and in front of him were two guards escorting a manacled woman.

Moving past the living statues, Vaughan walked through the corridor and headed along to have a look in the folder that Rodrigo was holding. He squeezed past the guards and the woman, and gently removed the folder from Rodrigo's hand. The folder contained no more than a shift timetable alteration and some applications for leave of absence. He put the papers back in the folder and put it back in Rodrigo's hand. As he turned to return to his cell, he realised that he was no longer in control of his atomic manipulation and began to panic. He turned round and the woman being escorted abruptly looked up at him as the others remained still:

'Don't you know it's rude to spy, human!' She hissed.

Vaughan was shocked and tried to shift out the Vatican, as far away from the woman as he could, but he found the area of his mind required to do so was vacant and asleep.

'What's the matter little envoy, do you not want to play?'

Vaughan now was paralysed and felt his body being raised from the floor. As he hung there, he felt the life being sucked out of him. Darkness overcame him, but he held on. He knew he had to.

The woman's face now appeared to be contorted and gnarled; she spat out and hissed a mixture of voices and guttural noises. As the sounds reached Vaughn's ears, he felt himself being invaded. He vomited and wretched and still, his body hung in the air. Desperate, Vaughan used all of his effort to raise his head slightly. He saw the time marker he had left in the corridor and with a blink, activated it. The woman turned towards it for a second and the non-atomic marker was obliterated, but as she returned her gaze Vaughan was gone.

The woman shrieked then was silent. The scene returned to normal and continued as if nothing had happened.

'Guards, ensure the woman is hosed down before you bring her to my chamber for interrogation. There is a putrid stink from her.' Rodrigo waved his hand in front of his face as he squeezed past the guards and the woman.

The guards jostled the woman forward; the older of the two removed a bunch of keys from his pocket and opened a cell door.

'Right Irkalla, you can wait in here till we get the shower ready for you.' The other guard kicked her in the back into the cell.

'Steady on you idiot, there is no need for that,' the elder guard chastised.

'She's Muslim scum, of course there's need for that.'

Irkalla looked up at the violent guard from where she had fallen and smiled at him.

23. Darkland: Cole.

Cole's entry point to the Darkland, though only yards from the old official access site into the metropolis section, saw him shifted almost 250 kilometres into the heart of the Darkland's desert section. The shift was rapid and as he came to his senses, face down in the sand, he had a killer headache and a raging thirst. He sat up and looked around to get his bearings. Although 200 years has passed since he had last been inside the Darkland, as far as Cole could see nothing much had changed.

He rose to his feet and saw the citadel gate marker and its beacon blinking 50 to 80 kilometres to the south, and knew this was where he would be heading. All that stood between him and getting there were kilometres of shifting sand, windstorms and who knows what adapted creatures which had survived over the years. Cole felt and rubbed the skin in his elbow, extending his arm back and forth. After some time doing this, he could feel a small lump under the skin, no bigger than a grain of rice. He manipulated the lump as close to the surface as possible, then nipped the skin with his nails, drawing blood and removing the lump at the same time. He placed the gored skin and blood onto the palm of his hand and spat what little saliva he could muster onto the lump. Cole felt a familiar heat as the lump absorbed the skin, blood and saliva and increased in size exponentially. Seconds later his Frenzy, fully formed and gleaming, instantly linked with his synapses.

'Long time Cole. What year is it?'

Without the need to verbalise, Cole replied, '2424.'

'Over 200 years. Have I missed much?'

'Plenty, Hep.'

Without any prompting, the Frenzy began to divert moisture from the air, through itself and directly into Cole to rehydrate him. Each Frenzy contained an AI which would pair with its owner for life. These AIs possessed self-evolving personalities, each named after a character from ancient Greek mythology. Cole's AI was called Hephaestus – 'Hep' for short – after the blacksmith who made the weapons for the Gods, and was the first operating Frenzy ever constructed. It had assisted in the development of all further Frenzies and many other weapons, but chose to keep a few design peculiarities to itself and had never become totally subservient (as was the design protocol with all the others). This was partly a decision made by Cole, who liked the equal partnership relationship, as opposed to master and servant.

'You feel a bit different, Cole. You have a bit of excess weight round your middle. What's happened to the number one dysfunctionist to make him let himself go like this? Let me guess: women problems?'

Cole smirked as he replied, 'Hep, the world as you remember it has changed dramatically. Once you fully hydrate me, you can run a synaptic overlay and get yourself up to speed with the new, post-Meltdown world.'

Cole lay on his back and closed his eyes.

An hour later he opened them again.

'Cole, what a balls-up! So there is no functioning tech outwith the Darkland strip still operational?'

'None.'

'And this Scolopendra creature that's been haunting you. What do you think is going on with that?'

'No idea Hep. At first I thought the creature had escaped from in here, but it has atomic manipulation skills well beyond anything we ever saw. Well beyond our capabilities even at our peak.'

'It makes no sense, Cole. Someone or something from Sappho must have survived. Maybe the radioactivity has caused further epigenetic changes to some already well-fucked up organism?'

'Who knows Hep; the only thing I know for sure is it can't get in here, so we are safe for now.'

Cole stood up and started to walk through the sand in the direction of the citadel gate marker. On arrival he would merge into the jungle zone, which he would use as a shortcut over to the other side of the Darkland, and with the help of Hephaestus, make his exit.

After an hour's walk and much discussion, Hep dropped an alert marker directly into Cole's frontal cortex.

Cole stopped and crouched down, looking in the direction Hep had indicated. A metal orb with faded markings rolled through the dunes directly towards them.

'Hep, do you recognise what kind of tech this is?'

'It's like nothing I've seen. Its material structure and construction are similar to the prison subsets that were used for safe prisoner and mech-animal transport, but nothing this size was ever constructed.'

'Keep your presence hidden, Hep. Do you detect an AI in control?'

'Not an AI as such, but it is certainly more than a machine. There is a personality inside it.' Hep paused, then advised: 'Cole, you should dig in before it gets closer.'

'I agree,' Cole replied and then the giant orb stopped in its tracks, and a yellow glow enveloped it. Cole recognised the familiar defence grid and knew to expect trouble. Beneath his feet, Cole suddenly felt the ground begin to shake and the sand beneath him started to move. Cole lay down perfectly still and allowed himself to be carried towards the orb by the shifting dune. The sand fell away altogether beneath him and a metallic plate rose from the ground. Diamond shaped and translucent, Cole could see through it to the waiting group of Dissectors beneath.

Cole had encountered Dissectors many times in the past, but had never known them to work in groups; this revelation was not good news. Dissectors were hybrid mechanical insects. Like massive beetles, they had an armoured exoskeleton and ferocious mandibles.

Fully erect they were over eight feet tall, and had always been the alpha predator in the desert zone.

'This isn't good Hep. I'm still tired and dehydrated and in no state to use my usual defences. Any ideas?'

'Do you want me to try and join with the orb? Probably better in there than out here. I'm sure we would stand a chance with one Dissector, but I've identified nearly fifty below us.'

'Yes, try and link.'

Hep disarmed his shield facility and became detectable to the orb.

'Good day Hephaestus, I am Gobin. I'm afraid you and your host appear to be in a predicament. Why don't you run down here and sign yourself over to me and my ownership before you both get devoured? I can give you my word you will be treated well as you are prepared for sale. What do you say?'

Cole replied before Hep could. 'Gobin, how about before I get devoured, I run down, deactivate your protective shield, then melt my fucking name in your processing hub with my Frenzy?'

'Now, now, no need to be like that. I see we may have got off on the wrong foot. Your rank and age were not clear to me d-Cole, and until you spoke, I had no reason to treat you with regard. Please approach now, and I will provide you with sanctuary.'

Cole slid off the top of the translucent sheet as it began to delaminate and the Dissector mandibles forced their way out. The Dissectors snapped at each other and jostled to be first out; the largest prevailed and squeezed itself out to begin its pursuit of Cole.

'Hep we need a bit of help, or I don't think we will reach the orb.'

The Frenzy grew warmer in Cole's hand and became liquid. It spiralled up his arm and reformed on his shoulder. Shaped like a duck's mouth, it began to project tiny spiked missiles at the lead Dissector. As Cole struggled through the deepening sand, the creature was gaining ground, but soon a missile made contact and a small explosion shattered a piece of the Dissector's exoskeleton. The other pursuing Dissectors detected the breach immediately and pounced on the lead dissector, proceeding to rip it to bits. The delay allowed Cole to reach the orb; he flung himself towards it and merged through to the inside of the chamber.

'Gobin, can I stand my Frenzy down or is there going to be trouble?'

'd-Cole have no fear, my pledge is good.'

Cole looked around; he saw various mech-animals restrained in small cells and within liquid containment. Upside-down and held in a St. Andrews cross position was another tall human. The restrained man looked up and appealed to Cole with his eyes, for his mouth was covered with a flexible polymer band.

'Gobin I want you to release this human. I must speak with an insider, regardless of his crime or worth to you.'

'd-Cole he is no insider; I found him six kilometres east of the fissure chamber this morning.'

'What have you found out about him Gobin? Is he a hunter?'

'No Cole, he said he was here on a mission to find you.'

24. Cartergreen: Malachi.

The sound of horses being harnessed woke Malachi from his sleep. Though always dark in the hideaway, he could tell it was still night time from the noise of the insects and the cold. Misba Ranha had tried to make his bed as comfortable and warm as possible, but its location was such that the floor and walls didn't really provide much insulation from the frigid nights.

Malachi sat up and listened closely to find out what was going on. He could hear Misba Ranha was settling the horses and walking around outside; he was pretty sure she was alone. Next, he heard the caravan door opening and his voice being called.

'Young Malachi, young Malachi, are you awake?'

Malachi clambered to his knees, pushed open the hidden panel and stuck his head out into the warmer kitchen area.

'Yes Misba Ranha, I am awake. I could hear you outside with the horses. What's going on?'

'Bal has instructed me to prepare the horses and get the caravan ready. We have been told to proceed to another location to provide medical support. A place called Clefton Green. Have you heard of it?'

'Yes, it is a bigger town than Cartergreen, about five days walk from here.'

'There has been some kind of incident there, young Malachi. A temporary truce has been announced, so we are taking this time to reposition ourselves and send help to the areas that need it.'

'Why do you prepare the horses so late? Why not wait till the sun is up?'

'I am only following Bal's instructions, my child. I agree that would make more sense; travelling in the dark has its own risks. Come now, I want you to eat some of this food before we go, as Bal will be with us for the next two days and I will be unable to tend to you.'

'I do not need attending to, Misba Ranha. In fact, this could be the chance I need to make my way back to my own people. Of course, I am forever in your debt for all you have done.'

'We will see, young man. Meanwhile, quickly, I want you to eat this.'

Malachi went over and sat, scoffing the plateful of food Misba Ranha had prepared for him. He wolfed down as much bread as he could and washed it down with water.

'My mother used to make me bread just like this. You are a lot like her. She used to say that her bread was made by God, and that she only took it out the oven for Him.'

Misba Ranha laughed and smiled at Malachi. 'That is funny. I think I would have liked your mother, though I would argue my God makes the bread a bit better than yours.'

She pinched off a corner of Malachi's bread and scoffed it.

'Mmmm, so tasty. The best bread ever.'

Malachi laughed and put his arms around his plate, playfully guarding it from Misba Ranha.

'Okay Malachi, if your stomach is full return to your hideaway. Bal will return soon and I need to clear your plate.'

Malachi did as he was asked and shortly after heard Bal's heavy shoes climbing the wooden steps into the caravan. From the uneven sound of the heavy footfall, Malachi could tell he was drunk.

'Hey bitch, where are you?'

'I'm in the bunk Bal, trying to sleep before the journey.'

'Get up, you lazy slattern. I've not stopped all day and want some food. I can smell bread; get me some and bring my wine too.'

Misba Ranha got up and busied herself making Bal's supper as he slouched on the cushioned bench.

'Here you go Bal. What time do we leave? I've prepared and harnessed the horses.'

Malachi wasn't sure what happened next, but he heard a loud thud and Misba Ranha cried out in pain.

'You bitch! I'm fucking sick of you!' Malachi could hear Misba Ranha pleading.

'Bal, stop, why are you doing this?'

And with every further thud he heard Misba Ranha cry out.

'Stop Bal. Please stop!'

'I will stop when you learn your lesson, you whore!'

Malachi could hear more punching and kicking, and something inside him broke. His eyes were not filled with tears like on other occasions, but rather a controlled rage was within him. He pushed open his hidden panel and looked outside; Bal stood with his back to him, kicking Misba Ranha as she lay curled up on the floor.

'Fucking bitch, are you going to try to stop being such a stupid whore?'

Malachi stood up and lifted a large knife from the small kitchen table. Bal heard the movement and turned around to face Malachi.

'What have we here? Who the fuck are you?'

Bal stopped his assault, turned and lunged towards Malachi, who quickly stepped to the side and used Bal's momentum to trip the man, as his father had shown him; Bal fell facedown onto the floor. As Bal rolled over and grappled with the table for balance, it fell over – but he was still able to get onto his knees. Misba Ranha now called to Malachi, 'Run child, run!'

Bal's face was red with fury, 'I'm going to kill you, you Christian scum. How fucking dare you ...'

Then Bal was silent. Misba Ranha climbed to her knees and looked over; Malachi was sitting on top of Bal's chest. As he turned to look at Misba Ranha, she saw past him to the large knife which was buried deep into Bal's neck.

Covered in blood, Malachi stood up crying, 'I'm sorry Misba Ranha. I'm sorry.'

Misba Ranha climbed to her feet and embraced Malachi, settling him.

'No young Malachi, don't be sorry. What you did was a brave thing. He was an evil man, but he was all I knew.'

Sobbing, Misba Ranha held Malachi tight and patted his back.

'You are bleeding Misba Ranha,' said Malachi wiping blood from her face.

'Never mind about me child. Is he dead?'

Misba Ranha looked at the large pool of blood on the floor and her question was answered. Malachi's knife had severed Bal's artery and killed him instantly.

'Malachi, we must act quickly. Help me with Bal's body. We need to hide it before morning. We'll drag it to the hideaway, where I discovered you.'

Malachi and Misba Ranha managed to pull Bal out of the caravan and along the stable floor to the trap door. As Malachi bundled Bal into the hole, he thought of the snake that bit him and wondered if it was still down there. He hoped it was. Misba Ranha cleaned the trail of blood with dust and straw and began to scrub inside the caravan. As she cleaned a voice called from outside the stable. 'Bal. Get a move on. The medical caravan has left; you're last. What's keeping you? Are you fucking drunk again?'

Misba Ranha stuck her head out the window and replied, 'We are coming, Guardsman. Bal has taken ill, so I will be taking the reins.'

'Okay, well, hurry up woman.'

Malachi looked at Misba Ranha and his situation finally took hold of him. He began to cry uncontrollably.

'Young Malachi, I need you to be strong for me now.'

Malachi wept and buried his head in Misba Ranha's chest. Sobbing, he whimpered his reply, 'I'm so sorry. I'm so sorry. I murdered your husband. I'm so sorry.'

'Malachi, you need to stop this.'

'But I'm a murderer.'

'You are nothing of the sort,' replied Misba Ranha. 'You are brave, and had you not stopped Bal, I'm sure he would have killed me tonight.'

'Now pull yourself together. This could be our chance. We are late for the caravan train, so we may have an opportunity to slip away if we can get out of here with you undetected. I want you to lie in my bed and cover yourself, and if anyone comes into the caravan groan and curse like you are unwell. Do you understand?'

With effort, Malachi stopped crying and took a deep breath. 'Yes Misba Ranha, I understand. I won't let you down. Ever again.'

Misba Ranha saw the difference in Malachi's face as he replied, and knew the child she had discovered had changed forever.

25. Himalayas, 'Half realm': Vaughan and Maria.

In the Himalayas, the Half Realm was alive with consciousnesses when Vaughan and Maria arrived. Both tapped into the various scenarios being played before them. Each the work of a displaced, recently-deceased personality or a consciousness returned from the edge of the atomic void. They could see families' grief and happiness and other mixed emotions, all striving to be heard. The presence of The Affinity could be felt all around, reassuring every awareness, providing order to their individual melees.

Vaughan and Maria slipped out of actual time and bonded together. They absorbed each other's presence and became a single event. They relived every moment of their new experiences together, and discovered each other in ways beyond intimacy and sexuality. Their encounters moulded new ideas and opinions, and they knew it was imperative to speak and convey these feelings to The Affinity, from their individual and shared perspectives.

As they returned to real time, The Affinity absorbed and then moved the pair instantly by a lake that shimmered with a green liquid; the sky was unknown to them.

Approaching the lake, Vaughan and Maria spoke as one.

'Where have you brought us?'

You are beyond your place of origin. Beyond its mortal perimeter.

'Have you subsumed our experiences?'

Yes.

'What of Irkalla?'

She terrified you?

'Yes, she did. Is she The Exile?'

Not as we have predicted.

'We don't understand.'

We have traced her presence. She has been previously venerated by your humanity.

'Then she is not The Exile?'

Her existence is spectacular.

'In what way?'

She cannot exist.

'She exists alright.'

Perhaps that is so. We feel intrigued. We cannot feel like that without the danger of regression. We think she is like a weapon.

'Wielded by whom?'

A weapon wielded by solitude, unhappiness, and revenge.

'Can we return to our mission?'

You must return.

'How can we defeat her?'

By understanding her.

Immediately, Vaughan and Maria were no longer before the lake, but back on Earth in ancient

Mesopotamia, 4,500 years before the birth of Christ. They stood at the entrance to a temple, along with hundreds of worshipers outside its doorway, kneeling and chanting. The envoys realised they could not be seen and were mere spectators at a previous event in time; as they waited the large, golden temple doors began to open.

A masked woman emerged holding a newborn baby, still covered in blood, at her side like a doll. She flung the baby into the waiting crowd, who proceeded to rip the infant to bits. The envoys were horrified and watched as the woman turned around, removed her mask, and made her way back into the temple. As she did, she stopped and looked straight to where the envoys were viewing from; she smiled at them then moved on. The Affinity immediately returned the envoys to the Half Realm and spoke to them.

She was aware of you both?

'Yes, she looked straight at us.'

We cannot explain this.

'But you surely are omnipotent.'

No, much here is beyond us.

'How can we prevail? Surely past events are fixed? How could she see us?'

Yes, in every parameter that is the case. But what you saw defies all thought. She knew you were present, or she knew you were going to be present, some 7000 years later.

'And you say she is not The Exile.'

No, she is not The Exile.

'What is she then?'

As we progressed and developed and became two, we believe The Exile has done the same.

'Then she is The Exile?'

No, The Exile is far more like us.

'What then?'

To The Exile, she is its child.
To humanity, she is God.

26. New Mecca: Basset.

'So you say the Prime Cleric has had no visitors to his private quarters this week, except for me?'

'That is correct, Basset.'

Basset leaned over the reception counter at the New Mecca administration centre and held out his hand to the clerk. 'Can you show me the logbook please?'

'Certainly, here you go,' said the clerk, handing the book over the counter.

Basset placed the large folder on the desk and studied the details.

'And you're sure there is no way an appointment could have been overlooked. Maybe a last-minute meeting of some type?'

'Basset, our logbook keeper is studious, as you will see from the detail in all his entries. I can assure you there is no mistake. He is over in the library at the moment, but I can send for him if you wish.'

'That won't be necessary. Thanks for your help.'

Basset handed the log back to the clerk, turned, and made his way out of the building into the square. The heavy rain was cold, so Basset walked briskly along through the sheltered walkway back to his office. He pondered his next move as he prepared some coffee.

The lack of details in the log diary had caused his nagging doubts over the Prime Cleric to become a serious worry. Three times now, he had witnessed two used cups and plates in Saladin's private quarters. The system of access and egress to the Prime Cleric was well controlled for security reasons, so if the protocols had been circumvented, the Prime Cleric must be involved. What and who was he hiding?

'Perhaps an unexpected visit by me is in order,' he thought as he finished off his tea. 'He is never to be disturbed after his midday Tightbeem, so that will be my moment.'

Basset took the opportunity to read his most recent intelligence breakdown from the war fronts and tried to make sense of the Clefton Green incident. He knew the importance of his role, and this new event was elevating his prominence to a new level.

Mid-day came and went, and Basset made his way over to the Prime Cleric's private quarters. Not one checkpoint guard questioned him, which was unacceptable regardless of who he was; he would address that security issue soon enough. As he entered the private enclave, he stopped and moved to the door on tip toes. He listened and was sure he could hear voices. Holding his breath, Basset put his head to the door and heard more discussion. Then an unfamiliar voice said quietly but clearly:

'We have company.'

Hearing this, Basset opened the door quickly and stormed in. The Prime Cleric rose to his feet and faced Basset.

'What is the meaning of this, Basset?'

Basset stood at the door and looked around. He ran over and looked behind the Prime Cleric's desk and cabinet until it was clear there was no one hiding.

'Who were you talking to, Prime Cleric?'

'Maybe I was muttering to myself, Basset, but that's none of your business and is no reason for your behaviour. I think you are perhaps getting ideas above your station and do not understand who is in command. How dare you enter my private quarters without appointment and then without making your presence known before entering. I could have you locked up for this.'

Basset looked at the table. Seeing only one cup, he realized he would have to eat humble pie on this occasion.

'Prime Cleric, please forgive me. As I approached I heard a strange voice and thought that perhaps there was an intruder, as I knew you had no appointments. I evaluated the situation and concluded my best course of action would be to barge in unannounced, because if there was an intruder, this would surprise and startle him. Please, accept my deepest apologies and believe my ill-considered actions were only taken with your interest at heart. I hope I didn't startle you too much?'

'Nevertheless,' Saladin said after a moment, 'can you explain why you would turn up at my private quarters without an appointment?'

Before Basset could answer, two guards ran into the room.

'Is there a problem Prime Cleric? We heard raised voices.' The lead guard placed himself between Basset and the Prime Cleric.

Basset raised his hand and attempted to play the incident down. 'Guards, there has been a misunderstanding. You can return to your stations now. There is no trouble.'

The lead guard turned to Saladin. 'Is this correct Prime Cleric?'

'Yes guards, thanks for your concern, but there is no problem. Mr. Basset was just leaving. Please show him the way.'

Basset felt belittled at this comment, but could do or say nothing at this point other than accede to the Prime Cleric's wishes. 'My apologies again, Prime Cleric. I will see you tomorrow at our usual appointment time.

Before any further ushering could take place, Basset quick stepped out of the quarters and made his way through the corridors back to his office, slamming doors as he went. He entered his office, closed the door behind him and sat down on his guest chair. 'What the fuck is going on? I heard a voice. A woman's voice.'

Basset played and replayed the event over in his head. 'This makes no sense. There must be a hidden door in the Prime Cleric's office. A panic room, perhaps?' He spoke aloud to settle himself. 'But why would I not know about it? Maybe it's a secret passed from Prime Cleric to Prime Cleric. But from hearing the voice, to me entering was only seconds. How could someone move so quickly?'

Basset poured himself a drink of water and tried to calm down.

'I must get to the bottom of this. I will arrange a public event to draw the old bastard away from his enclave and then search it. I will need to create a ruse for the head of security, but that shouldn't be too much trouble.' Basset gulped down the last of his water and quietly spoke to himself, 'Saladin, your days are numbered.'

27. Darkland, City of Castor: Tel R Amir.

The skyline of the Darkland's metropolis area would now be unrecognisable to any visitor from before the Meltdown. Though built to provide a terrain to simulate urban warfare, the crumbling buildings and burnt-out tower blocks were long gone. As raw materials were the prime commodity in the Darkland, the whole metropolis area had been flattened and rebuilt, and every element contained there had been removed and refined.

The new city that took its place was named Castor. It was a quarter of the size of the original, but towered three times as high into the sky. When the AIs and the satellites died, a hundred or so thrill tourists, technicians and dysfunctionists became trapped in the Darkland; these had multiplied to several thousand.

Fortunately some of the finest minds on Earth were within the Darkland at the time, and their skills and expertise had seen the small community flourish against the odds. The constant threat from the mechanically altered killing machines, which many of these individuals had designed, had proved an immediate, but controllable problem. A smaller DNA wall was constructed to surround Castor, which gave the city a reprieve from constant assaults. Similar local AIs had been developed to control the wall, the city and its man-made yearly cycle; but until an exit or connection to the outside could be made, the inhabitants of the Darkland would remain trapped, victims of their own foolproof security measures.

The need to provide day and night cycles and weather changes became evident after 10 to 15 years, when younger inhabitants began to exhibit bouts of mental illness. A simulated year was accomplished by reproducing the exact weather patterns of the planet's 365-day cycle at the latitude and longitude of Lisbon, pre-Meltdown. Even the stars in the sky were visible, and the leap year was considered. This soon settled the occupants and allowed them to concentrate on their goal of escape.

After many years, younger groups of the populace began to revolt against the society's need to continually focus all efforts on the exit goal. They favoured further development of what they saw as their home. But the elders only saw this as naiveté and held a mock 'future' referendum. Every person who voted to cease the exit goal was severed from the communal neural link and banished out into the wilderness. Though the elder's decision was a harsh and unpopular, those who objected faced the same expulsion, so not many stuck their heads above the parapet.

The driving force behind the decision was also the self-appointed, so-called Chief Elder of State: Tél R Amir. He was the oldest man alive in the Darkland and had played a key role in its development from the beginning. Prior to the Meltdown, Tel R Amir had undergone extensive epigenetic DNA evolutionary therapy, and his immediate increased mental capacity propelled him in the scientific community. He individually proposed the idea and development of the fissure link. Caldetic interloping and the impenetrable nature of the DNA wall had been his masterpiece. His remit had been to consider every possible scenario to prevent the escape of the terrifying, adapted Darkland creatures; his diligence on solving the problem had trapped him inside since the Meltdown.

Tel R Amir had exhausted every possible avenue of escape, but would not give up on his quest. The society that had emerged under his rule was an effectively functioning but unusual social construct. Ability, worthiness and usefulness to the common escape goal were what gave an individual his standing within the group. This 'common escape goal' was the new deity on every individual's mind, and the path to this achievement began to take on an almost spiritual position in their lives. The search for a successful exodus offset many standardly-accepted ethics in the search for its realisation, and some of the elder's decisions taken over the years did not sit well with many of Castors citizens' sense of morality.

Since the recent DNA wall breach, Tel R Amir had implemented every scenario that the city elders painstakingly devised for such an occurrence. As had always been the main plan, every piece of AI controlled technology initially dropped everything and focused all processing power to locate the welcome intruder. Wingless micro drones were already scanning the desert section and beyond, and although the increased activity would draw the attention of the outcasts, the probability of their interference being detrimental to the larger matter of escape was calculated as negligible.

So far, all Castor's efforts had been fruitless; but Tel R Amir was not disheartened. He knew of only one dysfunctionist who could breach the wall from outside in such a way, and the individual in question would not be easily manipulated (if they could locate him at all). Local AIs had been crunching variables about the wall breach and all known information on 'd-Cole'; where information was scarce, best possible data was supplemented with actual facts. No concrete explanation existed as to why he dysfunctionist had entered in such a manner; when asked, the super-developed AIs, which owned unimaginable processing power, postulated: 'He was desperate'.

As no information had passed into the Darkland for two centuries, and the last known outside message had announced the onset of the nuclear holocaust, the trapped society had proceeded under the assumption that externally, something must be truly amiss. Why else would no one attempt to come in and get them? Hope of rescue receded and had almost vanished after a hundred years or so, but Cole's recent incursion at least confirmed that there was still some life on the outside.

Tel R Amir himself looked extremely different from when the exit door closed to the Darkland long ago. Previously he had been severely mechanically adapted, but new organic techniques had been developed which allowed many of his earlier modifications to now go unnoticed. The genetic material for this type of body work was scarce. Death from old age was a thing of the past, and only those who died through accidents could provide the carbon-based genetic material required. Being the most useful person in the Darkland had its perks, though; over the years, Tel R Amir had had his fill.

His assistant Cubo was not so fortunate, but Tel R Amir had promised his own adaptation would come sooner rather than later. Cubo was, in fact, running into the Chief Elder's command centre with news from a rover module.

'Tel, a low-level AI simulacrum had sent in an "under duress" signal from the desert zone. The signal was terminated after a fraction of a second so we have ruled out dissectors or outcast interference. The tech to jam a free unit's duress signal is not known to be available outside the city, and why would the outcasts bother with that kind of hardware development? The Local AIs speculate an 83 percent likelihood the disruption has something to do with d-Cole. We await your instructions.'

Immediately, Tel R Amir replied. 'Fuck Cubo, why wait? Prime a Bastion and let's go.'

'It's already primed, sir.' Cubo smiled, turned his awkward body, and made for the exit.

The Bastion was a vehicle, again loosely developed from the same technology that gave the DNA wall solidity. This time, however, the envelopment was controlled neurally by any authorised individual and its parameters contained only enough variables to allow flight, movement, ascent and descent. When not in use the Bastions grouped together, and the low-level operation AIs bonded and learned from each other. In the 20 years since their development, several Bastions developed quite unique personalities but the hard wired protocols remained. Any disposition that grew too big was returned for material harvest. Many people saw this as a crime and maintained the Bastions had earned the right for proper acknowledgment, as was the case with more advanced Local AIs.

The Bastion lowering onto Cubo and Tel R Amir looked like an upside down wine glass. Tel R Amir had been responsible for more Bastions being returned to material harvest than anyone else, so the AI personality within knew to watch what it said.

'How long will it take to reach your notified coordinates?'

The Bastion rose into the air as Tel R Amir spoke, and replied with a young female voice.

'One minute, eight seconds.'

'Good. On arrival remain 150 feet above ground and conceal with a lower blind.'

'Yes sir.'

No feeling of movement could be detected; almost immediately they were in position above a well-used rover module.

'Cubo, try a direct interface with the module.'

'Sorry Tel R Amir, we are blocked out completely.'

'Bastion, can you boost our attempt to call to the module below?'

'I can try sir.'

Seconds later the Bastion replied, 'I have formed a spliced network with the module's sensory centre. I cannot make contact, but I can show you what it sees inside its shell. Would that be of use?'

Cubo had already pasted the command to proceed before Tel R Amir could reply, and a vision appeared directly within their neural enhancers in real time.

'It's him Cubo. It's him!' Tel R Amir stood up and punched the air. 'It's d-Cole. I knew it would be him. I knew it!'

'I fail to see why d-Cole is so much better than the other dysfunctionists,' Said Cubo. 'What makes him so special?'

'Amongst the dysfunctionists, d-Cole has had more hours in the five combat zones than anyone. No other person even came close. He also never sustained any mind deterioration, from which so many others suffered. But the main reason I'm so excited is that out of all dysfunctionists, d-Cole's evolutionary DNA map produced a genome anomaly seen only once.'

'What was it, Tel R Amir? I have never heard of this anomaly.'

'It's very existence was denied, but he's here and it's true all the same: d-Cole has the ability to remap his own DNA at will, with no outside stimulus. He bonds with his environments and uses them to his advantage.

He's a walking weapon. I just need to convince him to become part of my arsenal.'

28. Vatican prison: Rodrigo Gomez (The Surgeon).

Overnight, two more internees had disappeared from the Vatican prison and Rodrigo Gomez was fuming with rage. Ordinarily, the night watch guard would be in big trouble; but due to the frequency of these peculiar happenings, Rodrigo knew he was probably not to blame.

'At what time do you check all the cells, Guardsman?'

'Every hour on the hour, from 20:00 till 08:00.'

'And when did you notice the prisoners missing?'

'On my 03:00 inspection, they were both gone, Rodrigo. As you can see, I logged it and raised an incident report immediately.'

'I can see that you imbecile, but that's not helping me get to the bottom of this. Did you hear anything or see anything? Anything at all that might be of use to me.'

'No Rodrigo, everything of relevance is in my report. Good day.'

The guard angrily flung his report onto Rodrigo's desk, turned and left before Rodrigo could say another thing. He thought twice about calling the guard back and giving him a verbal lambasting, but knew he would be wasting his breath. The guard knew as much as him … which together wasn't much.

Recently, several Christian internees had been raving about the return of the Antichrist and the rise of the fallen angel. They had been captured while performing black Mass rituals, which was becoming an all-too-familiar situation as society grasped for answers to unanswerable questions. Rodrigo pondered the situation; perhaps Satan was making a comeback and that was who was making the prisoners disappear. Why though would Satan want a couple of Muslim lowlifes? It made no sense. No, there had to be a rational explanation; most likely, a sympathetic guardsman.

He went over to his in-tray and looked for the day's 'schedule of atonement'. This was the aptly named document that told Rodrigo the order in which he was going to torture his prisoners; to him 'schedule of atonement' had more class. Rodrigo opened the schedule to the first page and read. It referred to a woman prisoner, named only Irkalla, who had been discovered chained underground after the slaughter at Clefton Green. Preliminary interviews during transit had indicated that she had a schizophrenic personality. His main objective was to ascertain why she was being held captive by the Muslims, and whether or not she could divulge any Muslim field information.

'Same crap, different day,' thought Rodrigo.

He could hear footsteps and voices outside his interrogation chamber and knew that the day's relief guards would be escorting the woman to him.

They knocked and entered. Held in between them was the woman, Irkalla.

'Guards, you know the procedure. Undress the woman and restrain her on the table, then you may leave.'

Irkalla looked at Rodrigo and smiled.

'If you untie my hands, I will gladly undress and jump onto your table, sir, without incident.'

Rodrigo looked at the wary guards then replied, 'I can see we are going to have a mutual understanding, Irkalla. Guards, untie her.'

For Rodrigo, this was unusual. Women usually broke down and became hysterical at the sight of the interrogation chamber, never mind offer to undress and be of help. The guards untied her hands and true to her word, Irkalla began to undress. As she removed her top a guard burst out, 'What the fuck?'

Rodrigo looked for the source of the guard's reaction and saw both Irkalla's breasts had at some time previously been cut away – hacked away, in fact. The scarring was uneven and as he looked closer, he saw every inch of her back and arms were also covered in scars. This woman has been mauled, thought Rodrigo, but he held his tongue.

Irkalla climbed onto the table and placed her arms and legs at the securing points: arms above head and legs held apart. This position was by design, as Rodrigo had discovered the increased vulnerability often helped with his cause.

After Irkalla was restrained, Rodrigo spoke. 'Okay, Guards, you may leave us.'

The guards avoided the glare of Irkalla and left hurriedly. Rodrigo pulled his chair over to beside Irkalla and began slowly.

'Irkalla, there are certain things that, for the good of the Church, I need to find out from you. Now, I'm not saying that this is going to be an enjoyable process, but if you are open with me from the start then it will be over quicker.'

Rodrigo ran his hand lightly up and down Irkalla's body, brushing in between her legs as he went.

'Do you think you can be totally honest with me?'

'May I call you Rodrigo?' Irkalla replied.

'Yes, indeed.'

'Okay Rodrigo, before we go any further, I am giving you the option to stop what you are about to do freely and without coercion. What do you say?'

'Irkalla I wish it was as easy as that, but I'm afraid I can't.'

'I ask you again, I am giving you the option to stop what you are about to do freely and without coercion. What do you say?'

'Ehhh when you put it like that, ehhh, no!' Rodrigo laughed, stood up, and walked over to a closed drawer. He opened it and removed an implement that looked like a fishing hook, but was 30 inches long. As he returned to Irkalla, he felt a bit dizzy and like he was losing his footing; he reached for the chair, sat down and a few seconds later was okay.

'Are you okay Rodrigo? You looked a bit pale there.'

'I'm fine Irkalla, it's not me you need to worry about. Now, what I'm about to do is a demonstration of the control I have over you at this moment. The reason I am going to do this is because you must accept that if I choose, I can make you suffer beyond your worst nightmares. Now if you accept your position quickly, your time with me may be less painful.'

Rodrigo leaned over Irkalla's body and with one hand, he held her right foot. He took the point of the hook he had, and quickly used it to pull each nail off Irkalla's toes. He felt some movement in her legs, but she did not cry out.

'You are a strong woman, Irkalla.'

'Rodrigo, before we go any further, you say this is for the good of your Church. Exactly whose Church do you mean?'

'I mean the Church of Jesus Christ; our Saviour.'

'And this Saviour condones your actions?'

'For the greater good, I'm sure he would Irkalla. But you do not ask the questions, understand?'

With that, Rodrigo leaned over and removed the remaining toenails from the other foot. Again, he felt some movement but no cries of pain.

'Irkalla firstly, are you in the service of the Muslim cause?' he asked.

'Do you like my breasts, Rodrigo? I noticed your hands over my body, but you avoided my breasts. Do they disgust you?'

'I told you, you do not ask the questions.'

Rodrigo now pierced the end of Irkalla's big toe, like a fisherman puts a worm on a hook. He proceeded to do this with every one of the toes and now a lot of blood was beginning to be spilled. Rodrigo leaned over, took some sawdust from a bucket beside the table, and rubbed it all over her feet which stemmed the bleeding slightly.

'You never answered me Rodrigo, do my breasts disgust you? Shall I tell you what happened to them?'

'Well, that was going to be a question I was going to ask you, so yes, tell me.'

'I bit them off with my own teeth and fed them to my favourite children.'

Rodrigo looked at her scarred chest and shivered.

'Irkalla, this is not proceeding to my liking. I'm afraid I need to step things up a bit.'

'Why, Rodrigo? Do you feel you want to assert your position of dominance? Like you can't do with your wife?'

'Something like that.' Rodrigo smiled back.

'Oh, I see, you just get a kick out of this?'

'Perhaps, Irkalla, perhaps.'

Rodrigo now used the hook to pierce under Irkalla's kneecap. As he did this, he pulled upwards, shattering and removing most of the patella. He really felt the legs twitch, and thought now she may not be so smart. The multiple signs of previous torture on her body explained how she was able to have a high verbal pain threshold, but the jerking of the limbs didn't lie. He now knew she was in pain. Serious pain!

'Tell me, why were you chained underground when our soldiers discovered you?'

'That would probably be because since time began, I've always had a sense of the dramatic.'

'You're not answering my question. Why were you chained?'

'It's theatre Rodrigo. It's all theatre.'

Rodrigo had had enough and gouged out more bone and cartilage from the bleeding knees.

'This would be easier if you gave me straight answers, woman,' thought Rodrigo. He was beginning to become frustrated and was starting to feel dizzy again, but tried to ignore it.

'Tell mem Irkalla, why did they feel you had to be chained up? If you do not answer me straight I will move on up in between your legs,' he threatened.

'I was waiting for that. It's always about the pussy. Every time.'

Rodrigo now had had enough. 'Very well, you asked for this.'

Rodrigo took the hook and savagely gored between the legs. Blood spurted out all over his hand and now he could feel the body convulsing, yet he continued to drive the hook in and out and around the genital area. When another, more serious dizzy spell took hold, though, he stopped his assault.

'What's the matter Rodrigo? You seem a little lightheaded,'

'Shut up, woman!'

'But I know what's wrong with you.'

'Fuck off, Irkalla.' Rodrigo was now beginning to feel really unsteady.

'You're feeling dizzy due to blood loss.'

'What the fuck are you talking about?'

Rodrigo's dizziness left him in a flash and was replaced with seething pain from the waist down. He glanced down to see the cause and saw *his* naked legs strapped apart on the table. *His* mutilated legs and genitals bleeding profusely; and in his unrestrained hands, he was holding the bloody hooked implement.

He screamed, 'Help, Guards, help! Fuck, fuck!'

Twisting his head up, Rodrigo saw Irkalla sitting beside him. She stood up, leaned over and said, 'What a mess you have made of yourself. You fuckin' disgust me, Jesus worshiper.'

With a frightening smile, she continued. 'Let me tell you this as you slowly bleed to death. Your fat wife and daughter are suffering the same fate as you, at the hands of the "imbecile" guard you spoke to this morning. Also let me confirm to you, Jesus your Saviour is not waiting at the other side for you. That soul is working as a cook in a Muslim field kitchen; it is female and loves cats. Do you like cats, Rodrigo?'

Rodrigo continued to scream for help, but then lay back on the table.

'That's it Rodrigo, lie your head down. I'm going to get you to do some self surgery on that smug face of yours; but this time, I'm going to let you fully appreciate it.'

29. Rome, Priest Development Quarter: Meniux.

True to his word, after three days Father Meniux travelled back to the priest development quarter to the home of Santiago and, more importantly for Meniux, his wife Anna. He had managed to secure the transport for his journey by calling in a favour with a regiment support officer, who turned a blind eye and allowed him to take a Bandit cart from the support warehouse. Meniux knew this journey could not be logged or catalogued. The distance was too far to be taken on foot without being noticed, so the covered seating design of the Bandit allowed him to travel incognito.

Controlling the traction engine that gave the Bandit its power, he nestled the large leather priest's satchel between his legs and thought about his plan for Anna. He had brought along the usual restraints, but hoped his usual manipulation would be all that was required.

He was convinced Santiago would never return, and good riddance as far as he was concerned. He had admired Anna the first time he had met her all those years ago in Alcobaca cathedral, before he was forced to make his sharp exit; indeed, he often thought of her whilst another vulnerable woman or child was under his control. Today was going to be extra special. In fact, he planned to make this a regular thing; eventually moving Anna closer to the Vatican.

The Bandit's suspension did its best to even out the very uneven road as he steered between the numerous potholes and avoided the open drains. As he turned into the development quarter, the street became quieter and Meniux felt more at ease. Moving along, he noticed a woman standing at the side of the road beside a billboard. She was looking in his direction and smiling, so he bowed his head into his collar and moved on. A kilometre or so further on he spied the same woman again up ahead, this time sitting on a bench staring at him. Confused, Meniux shook his head and thought he must be imagining things.

A couple of kilometres later he rounded the corner to the accommodation area, where Santiago and Anna lived. Once again he saw the woman, but this time she stood in the middle of the road. As he approached, he could see she was carrying a child's doll in her left hand.

'Get out of the way you crazy woman,' Meniux shouted from the carriage as he approached. The woman took no notice and held her ground. Meniux tried to steer the vehicle around her, but she moved from side to side to block him, continually smiling in his direction.

'I'm not going to say this again, woman. Can you please get out of my way? I'm on an important errand for the Church.'

The woman's eyes opened wide, and next a bellow of laughter came out of her mouth.

'An important errand for warped pleasure, you mean,' the woman shouted. When Meniux was so close he had to stop driving, the woman walked around the cart section and climbed aboard.

'Move on Meniux, and I suggest you do not go near the woman Anna today, as Pope Julias has detailed two guards to her protection. Protection, that is, specifically from you.'

Meniux's heart sank, his stomach turned, and he felt like he was going to throw up. 'What? What do you mean? Who are you?'

'Never mind who I am. I'm telling you to turn around now, and start making your way back to the Vatican. We will talk on the way.'

Meniux looked at the woman, who was still holding the doll, and turned the Bandit around as she instructed. The woman sat silently waving at the occasional priest or passer-by; each one of them seemed to bow their head in reverence towards her. Other people they passed showed no interest at all, but Meniux thought that clearly she must be well-known.

'Who are you?' He asked.

'Evidently today, like Christ: I am your Saviour Father Meniux. Are you not going to thank me?'

'What you were saying earlier. Tell me what you know.'

The woman turned her shoulders to face him. 'Pope Julias suspects you want to fuck Santiago's wife. I know that you have always wanted to fuck her. Is that clear enough for you?'

Meniux felt like bursting into tears. Everything he had built up was gone. This was a disaster.

'How does he know this, woman? How do you know this? Who are you?'

'I know a lot of things, Father Meniux. I know you don't only like other men's wives, but you also like their young daughters. Lucky for you, Pope Julias only suspects this.'

'Can you please tell me who you are?'

'All in good time, but first I'm going to set you a scene. The guards that Julias instructed to look after Santiago's wife were positioned in an empty house across the road from his. Had you proceeded to her door, they had instructions to arrest you – or any priest visiting her without an appointment – and escort them to the Vatican prison. It seems that Julias was quite taken with Santiago and was going to honour his direct request: that his wife is looked after whilst he was away. Your absence and pre-fuck visit the other day alerted the fat maggot. Now luckily for you this has been averted, and if you return this Bandit to your fellow paedophile friend in the support headquarters without being discovered, you may well be in the clear.

'Now the question you have to ask yourself is: "How do I know all this, and what does it all mean?" I will answer these questions for you so listen carefully. I know all this and more. I know much more. More than you can ever imagine. I know everything about you. I know everything about your Church and everything about your Holy War.'

Meniux could not take all this in and stopped the Bandit. Sobbing, he turned to the woman.

'How can this be? This is madness.'

Glancing at her, he noticed the doll in her hand twitch and as he took a second look, the doll's limbs became more supple and lifelike; the head turned towards him and opened its mouth unnaturally wide, coughed, and spat out at him through its tiny black teeth.

'What is this? Ahhh!'

Meniux tried to jump off the Bandit, but the woman held him on the shoulder and he felt an inhuman strength in her arms.

'Let me go witch, let me go!'

The woman replied calmly, 'Father Meniux, if you do not calm down I will throw you to the wolves.'

Meniux looked around to see what she meant; standing close by were the priests, men, and women he had noticed on the way, as if waiting to pounce should he leave the Bandit.

'What's it to be?'

Meniux stopped his struggling and looked at the woman, 'What do you want from me?'

'Father Meniux, believe me, I could have you under my full control should I wish, but for the moment it suits me that you assist me with your own free will. Let me explain something to you. The Church as you know it is at a precipice. One wrong move and it will be irredeemably changed forever. There are forces beyond your comprehension at work attempting to undermine it. Many of the recent unexplained events relate to this.

'Now, there is one person who, if allowed to live, will play a key role in the Church's collapse. His name is Vaughan. He was being held at your prison, but has escaped. He will return with his poison tongue; of that I can assure you, and when he does, you must use the weapon that God has provided you with to kill him.'

'What weapon? We have no such weapon.'

'You do. His name is Cole.'

'So are you saying you are here in the name of God, woman?'

'I am here to save your Church *and* your God.'

Meniux peered at the woman and noticed for the first time how vacant and black her eyes were, and that the doll creature now looked like a child's toy again.

'But what if we cannot find this Cole or if he is killed?'

'He will come to you, Meniux. In the meantime, I want you to take steps to make sure Pope Julias wants Vaughan dead as much as I do. Make him understand Vaughan is an enemy of your Church.'

'So is this Vaughan a Muslim agent? A spy?'

'No Meniux, Vaughan is the risen Antichrist.'

30: Darkland: Santiago:

It took less than an hour for Santiago to fall foul of the Darkland's perils. After he exited the fissure chamber, he had sat on the sandy steps and changed into suitable footwear for the desert area. He repacked the rucksack and sat astonished as his Frenzy began to create a neural interface with him.

After ten minutes, he received its first greeting directly into the cognitive area of his brain. Initially, he thought the Transition device had scrambled his brain, but after a polite introduction he realised that indeed, he was communicating with an intelligent device held in his hand. Silently and with only one thought, the Frenzy established the standard paradigms permitting Santiago full control, and establishing a communication partition to allow Santiago to still have the privacy of thought. The name the Frenzy had been given was 'Dike', after the Greek spirit of justice. Santiago laughed at this name, to which Dike replied, 'Well, all the good names had already gone. I'd have preferred Achilles to be honest.'

Dike began to define its role and abilities to Santiago, who was astonished by what he was hearing. 'How humanity has regressed in its old age,' he thought. 'No technology on earth now is even close to this.' As Santiago found his bearings, he decided to proceed to the metropolis area and began his long walk, heading for the citadel gate marker. He had only been walking for 10 minutes, when Dike alerted him to the presence of another mechanical intelligence. Santiago stopped and fell to the ground, looking in the direction Dike had identified, and saw a large orb approaching.

'My full assault capabilities are not available as yet. I suggest you remain still and hope we are not observed. My inventory shows no such vehicle from the records we have.'

'You don't need to ask twice,' Santiago replied.

A minute later, the orb visibly changed direction and began to head directly towards them.

'The orb is trying to enable a communication link with me. Shall I allow it?'

'What have we got to lose, Dike? Try it.'

Immediately the Frenzy became cold, and Santiago could feel his link to it being severed. He tried to call Dike back, but the connection was gone. As the orb came closer, he stood up and waved his hands. A voice from the orb called out, 'I have disabled your Frenzy. Now, you have only the choice of my dedicated ownership and transit to the metropolis.'

Santiago thought about it for a second then walked towards the orb. 'May as well hitch a lift,' he thought.

He was asked to place his hands on a section of the orb. As he did so, he was immediately taken inside, fully restrained and gagged. He remained like this for several hours, until another figure entered the orb, who was clearly much more in control of the situation than

Santiago. He could not hear the conversation due to his restraints, but soon he felt them soften and go loose.

'Stranger, do I have you to thank for my release?'

'That you do, kid.'

Santiago thought this was a strange reply, as the man looked younger than him, but replied in kind: 'Thank you sir. I'm so grateful.'

'Well, you can start showing your gratitude by telling me why you are here looking for me.'

'I don't understand.' Santiago replied.

'My name is Cole. Gobin, the brains behind this contraption, hijacked all the information it needed from your Frenzy before shutting it down. A little tip: don't listen to any advice from a Frenzy until it's been active in here for at least a day, and has paired with some other Frenzies.'

Santiago could not believe his luck. 'This is incredible. Cole, I am here on a mission to find and rescue you.'

Cole burst out laughing at Santiago's statement.

'A rescue mission? I feel much safer already. Ha-ha.'

Santiago smiled back and laughed along at his choice of words.

'Okay, I guess it's not a rescue mission, but I am here under Papal decree to find you and bring you back to the Vatican on a matter of extreme urgency. Pope Julias himself has ordered it.'

'And why would Julias be interested in me?'

'Of that I'm not sure, but in my rucksack over there you will find the letter and his seal.'

Cole tipped Santiago's rucksack out onto the floor and spotted the letter. He picked it up, tore open the seal, and read aloud:

'To the prisoner known as Cole, The Holy Father, Pope Julias, requests that you make yourself available to him, immediately upon receipt of this decree. Father Santiago will place you in his own custody in the interim.

'So I'm in your custody, Father Santiago?' Cole smiled. 'You're a priest?'

'Yes, I'm a priest who was chosen to be the one who came in here after you for a number of reasons, some of which I am unhappy about – but that's another story.'

'Okay Father. Or can I call you Santiago?'

'Whatever you feel happy with, Cole.'

'Okay. Santiago it is. Well as much as I would love to go along with you, I have some business of my own to attend to and unfortunately it comes first. If I see to my own problem quickly, I may – and I say 'may' – just tag along with you to see your Pope.'

'But Cole, you're holding a Papal decree. Failure to adhere to it could see you imprisoned or worse.'

'Santiago with the greatest respect, your Papal decree means nothing to me. Also, may I ask how you planned to get out of the Darkland?'

'Well, that was always unclear. It was surmised that you had found a way in, and so would be able to find a way out?' Santiago cringed as he spoke and realised how preposterous his mission was.

'Okay Santiago. Your plan was crazy and had little hope, but here we are nonetheless. Maybe what you lack in experience you make up for with luck, but I hope you're a better priest than knight in shining armour. Pass me your Frenzy.'

Santiago handed his Frenzy to Cole and he held it barrel to barrel with his own then returned it.

'Dike, ha-ha,' Cole sniggered. 'That's your Frenzy pulled back from the brink, but as I said, wait a while before you rely on it. My Frenzy has been accessing the data held within Gobin's archives and it seems the Darkland has changed a lot since last I was here.'

'You mean you have been here before?' Santiago asked.

'Yes many times, but not for a couple of hundred years.'

'How can that be possible?'

'Hep are you getting this? I don't have time to explain, can you determine what information you think this Samaritan needs to know about me and the Darkland to survive, pass into his Frenzy and force a dump?'

'Done.'

Santiago staggered and sat down. 'What the hell was that?'

'That was me saving the next hour playing 20 questions.'

'I'm sorry Cole, but your dump has given me more questions than I had before but I guess they can wait.'

Gobin interrupted them and spoke aloud. 'We are currently being surveyed from above by a Bastion. The occupants are screened, so they can only be elders. How do you wish me to proceed?'

'Continue towards the citadel marker for now, Gobin.'

Seconds later, Gobin's voice was replaced with one sounding a lot more human.

'Good day, d-Cole. It's been a very long time. I am not sure if you will remember me as, although I knew of your reputation, we never did have the pleasure of meeting. My name is Tel R Amir.'

Cole looked at Santiago and gestured him to be silent. 'Mr. Amir, I do remember your name and your reputation.'

'Please call me Tel,' the voice replied.

'Okay, Tel. May I ask why you have gone to the trouble of contacting me?'

'Cole, your arrival here has caused quite a stir. Remember, we have been effectively trapped in here for over 200 years. The opportunity to talk to an outsider is one that everyone relishes. Will you do us the honour of accompanying me to our new city, where we can talk and you can be refreshed?'

'Tel I'm sorry, but alas I am only passing through the Darkland and would not want to interfere with your society.'

'Nonsense, Cole. At best you have a day, maybe two days' journey to every side of the Darkland. Let us show you our hospitality for an evening, and then you have my guarantee: I will have a Bastion fly you to wherever you chose.'

Santiago looked at Cole as he frowned and punched the palm of his hand whilst shaking his head. 'What's wrong Cole?' Santiago said, then immediately realised his error.

'Cole, you never mentioned you had company. Are there many others with you?'

'No, just one. Santiago is his name. He is my ... tailor.'

Cole signalled Hep to close the conversation.

'Santiago, I told you to be silent. Please, understand there is much you do not understand about, well, about everything. Say nothing. Do not mention you're a priest or anything about what's going on outside. Do you understand?'

'Yes Cole, I do. Sorry.'

Gobin interjected directly to Hep, 'My directional capabilities have been subsumed. We are being forced in the direction of the city of Castor.'

Cole heard this and instantly re-opened the conversation. 'On second thought, Tel, we would love to see your city and taste your hospitality.'

'That's great,' replied Tel R Amir. 'I am sure there are many things we have done that will surprise you. It's amazing how our people have adapted and dealt with adversity. When this rover module reaches the citadel marker, I will be waiting with another Bastion to fly you directly into Castor, our new "smaller but taller" city.

'There is one small thing though: can you both disable your Frenzies before you enter the Bastion? We have incorporated a smaller DNA wall around our city, and if your Frenzy is active it will not let you pass. Once inside, they will remain disabled, as are everyone's.'

'Okay, Tel R Amir, that's no problem,' replied Cole while looking at Santiago, who could tell he was not happy about this turn of events in the least.

31: Vatican: Pope Julias XVI.

Inside the Chapel of Supererogation, the highest ranking archbishops, along with Pope Julias and Father Meniux, waited for the 'Counsel of Perfection' to begin. Julias began with a short prayer, and then they sat and got down to business.

Julias had called this emergency counsel in light of the recent events at Clefton Green and the Darkland prison. Also, the plan to draw Saladin's troops into a misguided assault on the Vatican had clearly failed, and every one of their tactic experts had been unable to deliver any explanation as to why the attack never took place, apart from the most obvious one. They knew it was a trap! How this could have happened was unknown, as the whole endeavour had only been planned by a few people who had no reason to help the other side. Instances of treason in the new world were rare, as nearly everyone on each side had experienced a personal loss that bolstered their hatred of the opposing side.

The other topic on today's agenda for Pope Julias was the rise of reported cases of false worship and occult practices. These reports had increased dramatically since Clefton Green, and they could no longer brush its existence under the carpet.

'My friends, before we proceed, I must say that I think we all must hang our heads in shame over the Cartergreen debacle.'

A burly black bishop, with huge hands and a thick African accent, was the first to reply. 'We should not have done this. How can even one death be justified in the eyes of our Saviour?'

Father Meniux quickly interjected, 'If that one death ends a war and saves millions, that's how we justify it.'

'Yes Father Meniux, but your one death was nearly a thousand. I don't think we can juggle figures in an attempt to see good in evil. The deliberate blind eye we turned to Cartergreen was a dark day for the Church indeed.' Archbishop MacArthur shook his head as he interrupted Father Meniux. He had been completely against the plan from the onset, but the Scottish bishop was a good man and the counsel detected no form of 'I told you so' in his words.

Pope Julias stood and walked around his flock, placing his hand on the shoulders of each bishop as he passed. Noticeably, he missed Father Meniux.

'Our hearts' best intentions have been led astray, and although we should not forget the consequences of our inaction, I have summoned you here today not to dwell on our shortcomings, but to make sure the likes of it can never happen again. Also, we must ensure no word of Cartergreen ever leaves the walls of this room.'

Julias stopped pacing and looked at the large wooden cross on the small altar, then continued his liturgy.

'I feel it's important that, in the Chapel of Supererogation, a place where deeds beyond the call of God can be pledged, we make a pledge today to the people who fell at Cartergreen. Not only to honour their memory, but also to prevent the full details of the event causing further damage to the Church. Are we agreed at least on that?'

The bishops all nodded their heads and Pope Julias began another prayer for forgiveness and reconciliation. After the prayer, attenders brought in claret and bread with cheese and the bishops talked amongst themselves. Meniux saw this as an opportunity to speak with Pope Julias.

'Holy Father, your words have done well to assuage the burden of guilt that we all feel.'

'Father Meniux, that was not my intention, as I feel we cannot forget, but I am pleased if you feel somewhat relieved.'

'Thank you Holy Father. Before we continue, I would like to mention that I took it upon myself to visit Father Santiago's wife, along with two guards, earlier in the week. I have told her should she need anything, we will assist her immediately. I know that was rather unorthodox, but I felt after the sacrifice he has made, it was a small but worthwhile act on my part.'

Pope Julias tried to gauge the look on Father Meniux's face. The fact that he never caught Meniux's eye even once made him think there was more to it. On the other hand, the account did explain the previous absence, and Julias thought that he didn't have to mention it.

'That was kind of you, Father Santiago. Did she seem well? All things considered?'

'Yes she looked healthy enough, but there is grief in her heart. I did my best to give her hope, though, and I think she was happier when we left.'

Archbishop MacArthur rang a small bell on the table and the counsel resumed.

'Holy Father, point two on today's agenda regards the rise in occultism we are witnessing throughout our lands. Reports have trebled this month alone. I think that you must draw attention to this in the next few Tightbeem addresses and, further to that, I propose we allocate a small battalion of our troops to actively break up and discourage this behaviour.'

Pope Julias's reply was instant. 'Father MacArthur, I could not agree more and would appreciate your assistance after this counsel in helping me put together an appropriate address on the matter.'

Father Meniux could not believe his ears, as he had been the only one to assist Pope Julias on this subject over the last five years. Why the sudden change? He decided to pipe up.

'Holy Father, I hope you know I am always available, as ever, to assist you.'

'Yes Father Meniux, but I think perhaps a fresh perspective would help, so for the near future I will be assisted by Archbishop MacArthur. That is of course, if Archbishop MacArthur is in agreement?'

'Of course, Holy Father. I'm honoured you have faith in me.'

Father Meniux tried to maintain a smile, but felt like he had just been struck a blow. He clearly was being sidelined. The woman Irkalla had spoken of this further in their conversations back at Meniux's quarters. She gave him instructions and warned of this very event taking place. 'The serpent tongue Vaughn sees you as a threat and will attempt to see you replaced at the side of Julias. He has allies high in your Church. You must prevent this or make sure Julias is onside with using Cole to slay the demon in your midst.' She had said as much time and time again.

The other archbishops produced further reports on occult happenings, and they discussed the ethical and spiritual nature of this new threat to their society. As the counsel was adjourned, Father Meniux took his opportunity to speak to Julias.

'Holy Father, may I have a quick word?'

'Yes Father,' Julias replied.

'Do you remember the prisoner named Vaughan we discussed some time ago?'

'Yes Father Meniux, I do. We postponed his visit to Rodrigo Gomez after the drawing from the girl came to light.'

'Yes Holy Father, that is correct, but I think we may have made a blunder regarding that particular decision. After our discussion, I personally gave Mr.

Gomez a list of questions to ask the Vaughan prisoner. He was instructed to ask the named questions only and go no further. "A soft questioning" were my exact words.'

'Go on,' said Pope Julias.

'Well, this morning I received news that the prisoner Vaughan was missing, and the horribly mutilated body of Rodrigo Gomez was found in his cell – limbless and skinned – and the guard who found him has been taken to the hospital and will no longer speak. Even worse, it appears his wife and child suffered the very same fate.'

'And you are sure that it was the prisoner Vaughan who carried this out?'

'Yes Holy Father. There was …' Meniux stopped and tried to appear choked up for effect. 'There was writing carved into his torso and face. Satanic runes and pentagrams on his body and on his cheek, the letter "V" was carved. Pope Julias, I think we have let a key instigator of the occult revival slip through our fingers. I have put out an order for him to be arrested on sight. Do you concur with my course of action?'

'Yes Father Meniux. Make it your priority to find and imprison this Vaughan character, and this time, we will not go so easy on him.'

32: Sub Marianas Trench: The Exile.

The thousands of non-atomic glitches, cast into the centre of neutron stars and strewn throughout the universe by The Affinity, had been contained under massive pressure for millions of years. One such glitch was freed when one of these stars ceased to exist.

The imperfect nature of the internal glitch had seen it cast away by The Affinity, as it had the potential to develop, and perhaps display elements that could result in selfishness. Once released, the glitch flitted between real space and the void for millions of years, until it encountered a similar glitch; they immediately bonded.

At that instant, The Exile, as had been supposed by The Affinity, took on a primitive non-atomic consciousness with a new curiosity. The Exile sought out further glitches, subsumed them, and became everything The Affinity wished not to be. It embraced all manner of failings and thrived, eventually becoming a true conscious entity. All it then needed was a purpose.

Twenty-five kilometres below the Marianas Trench in the Western Pacific Ocean, The Exile utilised a gigantic crystalline cavern hundreds of kilometres long and deep, formed by long-dormant volcanic activity. The atomic embodiment of The Exile – a diverse mixture of every DNA pattern in existence – almost filled the cavern, growing then regressing as it saw fit. The outer area of the massive growth was over a kilometre thick, and hollow flutes acted like pores, allowing it to absorb and exude its requirements. The consciousness of The Exile had no need to inhabit the massive growth for long periods of time, but often did so for pleasure.

The neural capability of the growth had been refined over millions of years and, when fully at one with it, The Exile could observe the planet as a whole and influence events down to a microscopic level. Since the arrival of The Affinity, The Exile had chosen not to inhabit the growth, but instead strove to learn how to shield it from other non-atomic prying eyes. Now ecstatic, as it knew the growth had become undetectable, The Exile merged with the growth and became atomic once more.

Within the abnormal growth, all manner of The Exile's implements were at hand. Many of these aberrations could also be atomic or non-atomic at will, but each one was merely a subset of the greater controlling entity. The atomic nature of the growth combined with the nature of The Exile filled its very being with a continual nagging. This 'want' reverberated at all times and grew worse if not sated.

Amongst a jigsaw of elements, all developing ways to relieve the greater organism, was the Scolopendra. It was a masterpiece of malevolence, playing many parts and many key roles in The Exile's 'Purpose'. It took on atomic form as it emerged deep within the growth and was drowned in viscous, putrid liquids to cool the creature down, and help it maintain its atomic form. It was in this state that the transfer of the consciousnesses the Scolopendra had collected took place. Surrounding the Scolopendra, lines of inanimate, humanoid, faceless golems stood, waiting to be united with their new partners. Paired together for eternity.

When Colonel William Carstairs' consciousness was drawn away from where it was being held, immediately his memories came flooding back. He recalled the battle and his own gruesome end, and was puzzled as to his predicament. As his consciousness fused to this new mind, he realised that, in this incarnation, the body was not his to control. Thoughts he tried to gather were struck out immediately. As he tried to understand his predicament, the process was interrupted and replaced with madness. Any attempt to review or access a pleasant memory was contorted and twisted to become horrendous. He tried to pray, and it was as if he was in a fever. His train of thought was spiralled away and replaced with only terror.

He felt the golem begin to walk; after some time he became conscious of other golems walking along side and behind him. As he felt hundreds of bodies fill the space, his new golem host quickly knelt down. The liquid within the internal chamber rose all around the golems and held them fast in place. There was a drowning horror that was continually replayed in the minds of every new consciousness, and The Exile's atomic self fed upon it. The reverberation in the chamber slowed down as The Exile gorged itself on terror, fear, and helplessness. Each conscious mind was channelled directly into the essence of The Exile and contributed to its feast of despair.

The consciousness that had been Colonel William Carstairs knew it was in hell.

33. New Mecca: Prime Cleric.

The Prime Cleric was enjoying the company of Maria and as a consequence, was spending more and more time with her. The arrival of the ancient Koran in his desk had been a game changer. Until then, Saladin had had his doubts as to Maria's authenticity. He was a well-educated man and had studied pre-Meltdown earth extensively as a scholar in his twenties, and was well aware that certain spectacular abilities could be manifested. The questions he had to settle for himself were: Could he take this girl seriously? Or was she just an aberration? Was everything that he and billions of others believed just a man-made construct, based on pseudo-science? Were their generations of struggle and countless lives lost, all in vain?

As their meetings continued, Maria answered every question he put to her. She gave rational explanations to everything and wanted nothing in return, except the cessation of violence. What was the catch? Was there a catch? He found her to be very articulate and knowledgeable in every area they discussed, and often she had a remarkable insight into his life and the lives of his predecessors.

The recent near miss with Basset had alarmed Saladin. He began to do as Maria advised and started to freeze Basset out of his daily decision-making, and planned to give him minor state duties to keep him occupied. Basset's unorthodox interruption, though, was making the Prime Cleric think that perhaps a reappointment might be in order for him. While pondering this, Maria appeared in front of his desk.

'Hiya.'

Saladin, as per usual, was startled and held his hand to his heart, 'Maria, do you think your cause will be helped if one of the times you appear, I have a heart attack?' Saladin smiled as he chastised her.

'There is plenty of life left in your old heart yet. Believe me, your aorta, superior and inferior vena cava look healthy, and your coronary arteries are working away just fine.' Maria smirked like the proverbial know-it-all.

'Let me guess, Maria: you actually know this?'

'Yes Saladin, I can identify and analyse the workings of every part of your body in an instant, and I'm afraid the lower back pain you have is caused by lack of exercise. You need to get out more.'

Saladin shook his head, stood up and walked round to Maria. 'Maria I have one question for you today that's been bothering me. If in time, I did as you wish and announce the revelation about you and the universal benevolent creators of whom you speak, won't the world end up in turmoil?'

'What you mean, Saladin? Please explain.'

'The people of the world today, on both sides of this war, are defined by their religion; they thrive and function daily for its ends. To pull the carpet of faith from under them, will leave many devoid of purpose and meaning in their lives. You say The Affinity demand nothing except the end to suffering for every consciousness. Surely ending religion will, without doubt, have the opposite effect for many? How do your all-knowing entities deal with that?'

'Saladin, we are certain this will not be an easy road, but it is one worth taking. Drawing a comparison between having needless bloodshed as a remedy for boredom or emptiness of spirit is not how we see it. I agree that initially, the transition will be hard. Indeed, this will be the hardest point in the new development of mankind, but the forthcoming rewards will be spectacular. No longer will lives be wasted and time lost worshipping deities that don't exist, in a futile grasp for eternal life. Each human will be free to discover art, music and fulfilment created by human interaction, not a life bound to Islam or Christianity by accident of birth. Each life should, as it passes, be aware of the continuation of the consciousness and as the cycle of life continues, eventually every human that has ever existed will know the truth.

'Now you may ask yourself, why we do not just wait until a generation passes, and inform those people of the truth before they return in their next carnation? The folly in that approach is that we cannot bear the suffering of humanity any longer; why wait from 70 to 100 years, if we can be on our way to a passive, peaceful equilibrium in 10?'

Saladin pondered Maria's reply then returned to his seat. 'Do you have a contingency for the fallout? For the despair that will be created by this?'

'Freedom and compassion will combat this despair, Saladin, I'm sure. Mothers no longer worrying about their sons returning from war. Happiness, where once there was sadness.'

'Okay Maria. Let me propose this to you. I do not think this can be announced immediately, in one Tightbeem. I propose to make the transition in stages. The first stage will be my announcement that the Muslim world is ending the state of war with the Christians. This will be announced in my Tightbeem tomorrow morning. I will work on my wording tonight.'

Maria jumped out of her seat and climbed over Saladin's desk, knocking over his lamp and scattering papers everywhere, 'Oh Saladin,' she said as she embraced him, 'this is the start of a new world for everyone.'

Saladin laughed and cuddled Maria in return.

After they had composed themselves, Maria was alerted by some 'minute time markers' she had left on the route to the Prime Cleric's area.

'Saladin, Basset is on his way to see you. He is talking with your tea server at this moment, at your floor's checkpoint.'

'You forever amaze me Maria; I will not even ask how you know this. He is coming because I summoned him earlier. I'm going to break the news that he is to be moved to become the Head of Spiritual Understanding at the college. It's over 100 kilometres away, so that should keep him out of our hair.'

'I think that is a good idea,' replied Maria. 'I do not trust Basset, and find him difficult to read. I will leave you now and return later this evening, and we can discuss things further. Thank you so much – you are a wise man and what you propose to do will be historic.'

'I hope so,' replied Saladin.

34. New Mecca: Basset.

On his way to meet with the Prime Cleric, Basset had called in to see Raza, the Tightbeem coordinator, to ensure that he continued dropping out the first and final Tightbeems of the day. As he had hoped, the rumour mill was turning; already, he had overheard talk of Saladin's illness and the information-gathering department was bringing in lots of unrest in the populace, much due to the change to the Tightbeem schedule. Basset thought how amazing that everyday folk had such a need for a routine. As he walked into the square at the centre of New Mecca, he met one of the senior 'Spiritual Understanding' clerics, who looked excited to see him.

'Good day Basset, or should I say, good day boss?' The cleric smiled and nodded but Basset had no idea what he meant.

'Yes it is a fine day cleric. I recall having some conversations with you at theology seminars in the past but I fail to see why you would want to call me "boss".'

'Oh I see. Sorry, I spoke out of turn. Need-to-know basis and all that.'

With that, the cleric moved off towards a group praying by the central fountain. Basset thought about following him and asking further as to what he meant, but instead he quickly went back to his quarters. He was not back inside for more than a minute to collect what he wanted, before once again he was on his way to see the Prime Cleric. Entering Saladin's level, Basset stopped to speak to the guard then took the tray of afternoon tea from the servant, saying he would save him the bother of delivering it. He approached the large door, knocked and announced his arrival.

'You may enter, Basset.'

Basset closed the door behind him, and put the tray on Saladin's occasional table to the side of his desk.

'You wanted to see me, Prime Cleric?'

'Yes Basset, I did. Pour us some tea and I will explain why.'

After Basset had prepared them both teas, he sat down and waited for Saladin's bombshell.

'An opening has come up in an area that is vitally important to our cause and I have been deliberating whom I should appoint. It came to me after our last conversation. I can think of no one better to fill the gap: I have decided that you are the person most suited to able to bring this enclave into touch. Basset, you are a great mind, a firm believer and adherent to the ways of Islam. I think that those virtues are lacking in many ways in our society and need to be reinforced at a grassroots level. For that reason, as of tomorrow, you will be relocating to the Beryl-de Tach Court to head up the Spiritual Understanding College.'

Basset took a sip from his tea and Saladin watched and waited for his reaction. Knowing Basset, he thoroughly expected a lengthy debate on the matter, but it never transpired.

'Prime Cleric, I am here to serve you and our cause and if you feel that this is the best way to utilise me, then I will accede to your command forthwith.'

'I must admit, Basset, I thought you may have had some questions regarding your new role.'

Before Basset could answer, the servant interrupted them and brought in Saladin's lunch. 'I am sorry, Basset, would you like me to bring you some lunch?'

'No thank you, I will not be staying too long.' The servant nodded and topped up Saladin and Basset's tea then promptly left.

'Okay then, Basset, I have made all the arrangements necessary and one of the chief clerics has come down to escort you there and fully introduce you to your new vocation,' Saladin continued. 'May I say, it has been a pleasure working alongside you and I wish you all the best.'

'Likewise,' was all Basset replied, before standing and turning to leave.

'Basset, make sure you listen in to my morning Tightbeem when you reach Beryl-de Tach, tomorrow. There is much in it that will be of interest to you.'

Without turning round, Basset replied, 'I wouldn't miss it for the world.' He then opened the door and left.

Basset returned to the square and as he did, began to feel slightly sickly. He headed for the nearest toilet, entered a closet, and stuck his fingers down his throat till he vomited, doing so continually until he could retch no more from his stomach. As he left the closet, he decided to return to see Raza and cancel his previous Tightbeem plot, as he knew tomorrow it would be Basset himself delivering the bad news to the populace.

When he had finished with Raza he entered his quarters, went straight to his herbal apothecary, and made himself a further tonic to help him ward off the small but certain amount of poison that would have entered his system before he made himself sick. After he drank the tonic down he gave a toast out loud.

'To Saladin the coward!'

An hour later, there was a rapid knocking at his door and the tower bell was ringing. He opened his door and two guards stood with anxious looks on their faces. One said, 'Basset, you must come with us. The Prime Cleric has taken ill.' Basset did his best to look surprised and pulled on his coat and followed them. When he entered the office, Saladin lay on the floor surrounded by medical staff. Three of the Cleric's personal guard stood close by, and the nearest was pressing the medic for information.

'Doctor, you must tell us, is he going to be okay?'

'It's hard to say at the moment,' the medic replied.

Before he could say another word, the second medic began to perform CPR on the Prime Cleric and the guard's question was answered. After a full half hour, the medics gave up and pronounced Saladin dead.

The guards looked on furiously and demanded answers.

'Medics, are there any signs of foul play?' the head guard asked.

'His body is unmarked, but we cannot rule out poison.'

The guard turned and ordered another guard to fetch Saladin's attenders. When they had arrived, he began to scrutinise everything that Saladin had been given to eat or drink that day and the matter of Basset taking in the tray of tea was mentioned. The guard immediately turned to Basset and approached him.

'Basset, if it comes to light you had anything to do with this you will hang. Did you, or did you not put something in the tea?'

Before Basset could answer, a servant interrupted him, 'Guardsman, if Basset did poison the tea he would be dead also. I witnessed him drink fully two cups from the same pot.'

Basset then angrily replied to the guard. 'Does that answer your question, you moron? Why would I wish to harm Saladin?'

The guard said nothing and turned. As he walked away, Basset took the opportunity to speak to the whole room. 'As is protocol, I will take stewardship of the line of Saladin until the process of deliberation is complete and a new Prime Cleric is appointed.' Basset looked around and the guard's key staff and medics all nodded. Basset knew his plan was complete.

35. Talker Plains: Malachi.

As Misba Ranha guided her caravan out through the Muslim checkpoints in Cartergreen, no one took much notice, much to her relief. She waved to the first couple of sentries, but was ignored, so she continued on with her head down until she was well out of town. The road deteriorated the further she travelled but as the sun crept its way into the sky, she was able to avoid the potholes and have a less bumpy ride. She was operating on autopilot and had forgotten to call on Malachi until she saw him trying to peek out the door in her direction.

'Come up and join me, Malachi. The road is straight and flat, and I can see we will have no other company for some while. '

Malachi climbed up beside her and the fresh breeze on his face made him shiver, 'Brrrrr, it's cold,' he said.

'Here, come under my blanket with me,' replied Misba Ranha, who knew that's what he wanted and needed. Malachi cuddled in beside her and sat silently for a few minutes and then spoke suddenly. 'You should just marry my dad now, Misba Ranha.'

Misba Ranha nearly choked and burst out laughing, 'Malachi! Even in the worst of times you cheer me up. If only life was as simple as you see it.'

Malachi quickly tried to strengthen his point, 'Yes but you should now that Bal is away and so is my mum. You and my dad could just stay and look after me. We could all get away from here and just live in your caravan. I'd be no trouble, and you would like my dad; he's strong and would protect you.'

Misba Ranha let Malachi finish then replied, 'As I have said to you before, what we need to do is look after ourselves for now. The time may come in the future, perhaps when you are older, when we can try and find your father – but I do believe you when you say he is a brave man. I had heard his name mentioned along with another few Christian soldiers who were known to be ferocious. But for all you have spoken of him, what do you think he would want you to do right now?'

'He would want me to try and be safe.'

'Exactly,' replied Misba Ranha, 'and I'm going to try my best to help keep you safe. 10 kilometres further down this road, we will arrive at a fork. To the right, the road travels up into the hills and follows a little used track; at most there are a few farms on the way and only one small hamlet on our road. After 50 to 60 kilometres, we will be far enough away from any main routes that we should be able to find a clearing in the Scotch pine forest where we can lie low for a while. How does that sound?'

'But how will my dad find us?'

'If he is meant to he will. I think sometimes it is best to just look after your own path to see where it leads. Your dad will find you when he is able, of that I am sure.'

'Okay, I like your plan.' Malachi cuddled further into Misba Ranha and she could see he was smiling.

They travelled on the road till midday when they arrived at the fork in the road. As they took the fork to the right, the road inclined upwards and the going became slower. The road was narrower and the sides more overgrown, which made them feel a little less conspicuous.

'What about the hamlet we are going to, Misba Ranha? Is it held by Christians or Muslims?'

'It is a Christian hamlet, Malachi, but it will be the middle of the night when we arrive. I hope to just skirt around the town and then we can make our way into the hills. I can pass for a Christian anyhow, especially with a lovely young mousy blonde son like you.'

Malachi didn't reply, but again nestled snugly into Misba Ranha's side.

As night began to fall, they began to see some outbuildings and the occasional barn and Misba Ranha knew they were only ten kilometres or so from the hamlet.

'Malachi, let us pull off the road till later and then we can proceed; I think it's a bit early to be approaching the hamlet just now.'

'Okay. Can we have some dinner while we stop?'

'Yes, that's what we will do. There is a barn that looks deserted at the edge of the path into that forest. Let's hide ourselves in there.'

Misba Ranha turned the caravan and steered the horses up and onto the small forest road. They got close to the barn, pulled up outside, and stopped at the ramshackle wooden doors. No sooner had she stopped than Malachi jumped down and ran into the barn to investigate.

'Malachi, wait for me child,' called Misba Ranha – but he was already well inside. Misba Ranha jumped down and followed Malachi into the barn. As she entered the boy ran towards her and buried his head in her middle.

'Let's get out of here Misba Ranha. Please, let's go.'

Misba Ranha looked ahead and was stunned. There was a clumsy, blood soaked altar with the body of a butchered girl on top of it. Over the walls, there were pentagrams and satanic symbols crudely drawn, using what could only be blood. The dead girl's arms flopped down on either side of the altar and other parts, along with her intestines, were hanging down to the floor. Misba Ranha turned, grabbed Malachi, and ran to the door. As she made her exit, a large arm stuck out and caught her on the neck; she fell to the floor, bringing Malachi down with her. She looked up to see her assailant and a group of four men and a woman staring down at her.

'Oh sorry did you fall?' One of the men said, and then the woman approached and kicked Misba Ranha in the side. Another older man grabbed Malachi and bound his hands together with rope. This man spoke directly to Misba Ranha: 'Do exactly as you're told or I will slit this little mongrel's throat.'

Misba Ranha tried to stand and another volley of kicks knocked her to the ground.

'Tie the woman up and take them both into the barn. I want them bound to the pillar, facing the altar so they can witness tonight what will be happening to them tomorrow night. I'm sure by the time it's the boys turn, the "goat of Mendez" will manifest himself before us.'

The woman and the other men forced Misba Ranha onto her stomach and tied her hands behind her back then pulled her up using the rope, nearly dislocating her shoulders. Misba Ranha screamed out in pain and then turned to see Malachi.

'Please, please, I beg you! Release the boy, he is harmless. Please, let him go.'

'Shut up!' said the older man as he slapped her on the face.

'You and your runt will be used to honour our true master. Why would we let him go? So he can run to get help?'

Misba Ranha looked at Malachi, he looked strangely calm. They were both taken into the barn and bound to the largest post, facing the altar. The elder man, who was clearly in charge, began ordering the others around.

'Get that girl's body off the altar and feed it to the pigs! You! Woman! Clean up the altar and try to do something about the smell.' As the group started to do as ordered, Misba Ranha whispered to Malachi, 'Are you okay, child? I am sorry I have led you into this.'

Malachi replied steadily, without whimpering. 'Yes Misba Ranha I'm fine and don't worry. I will sort this.'

36. Darkland, City of Castor: Cole.

Tel R Amir had not exaggerated the changes to the metropolis section since Cole's last visit. As far as he could see, nothing remained of the previous urban warfare zone. What stood in its place was a tall, slim, elegant and vibrant city. As Cole's transit Bastion had passed through the DNA wall, Cole was amused at the astonishment on Santiago's face. Clearly, he had never seen anything like this; he was like the cat that got the cream. Before the Bastion crossed the threshold, it had requested they both disarm and surrender their respective Frenzies. Santiago had looked at Cole for help on how to proceed.

'Tell it to switch off and drop it in the drawer.'

As Santiago did this, he noticed Cole fiddling about with his Frenzy then doing the same thing. The drawer closed and reopened and the Bastion reported, 'Frenzies Hephaestus and Dike now disabled. Please, retrieve if required or collect on departure from Castor.'

Cole reached in and took his Frenzy and threw the other to Santiago and instructed him to put it somewhere safe till it was time to leave. 'It may be disarmed, but it's still 99.8% constructed from gold and I imagine raw materials will be quite a commodity in here.'

Santiago did as instructed and then turned to feast his eyes on the city of Castor. The buildings grew in width as they rose into the air and formed all manner of structures, many of which were clearly domestic habitats. Within the new internal DNA wall, the weather was controlled to the nth degree, so architects had been afforded the luxury of not having to consider extreme weather when designing the buildings. As far as the eye could see, the lower sections still utilised reinforced concrete but as the buildings rose, the evidence of plastics and other metallic elements became predominant. Walkways were strung between every building and figures could be seen crossing between them, and many Bastions negotiating their way through the walkways with ease and often at some speed. As Santiago looked out, fully engrossed, he felt a dull pain in his head and then heard Cole's voice.

'Santiago, try not to look startled as I speak to you.'

Santiago recognised Cole's voice, even though it was playing in his head. He turned and looked at Cole. A slight movement of Cole's eyebrows confirmed to him it was actually happening.

'Well done, Santiago, you didn't look too obvious there.'

Santiago applied the same procedure as he did when he spoke to Dike and replied, 'How can this be possible? The Frenzies are disabled.'

'Yes, but I'm not,' Cole replied. 'I needed to establish this link with you, as I'm sure every word we say in here will be monitored. Understand this Santiago: I do not wish to be here. Our host – or should I say captor – is much more than he seems. I knew of him before the Meltdown. He was reputedly the most intelligent, advanced human on the planet and was known to be ruthless. I cannot imagine 200 years stuck in here will have placated him.

'Now, I suspect he views me as a ticket out of here. I cannot allow that to happen. You can see the technology they have at hand. If TRA – as Tel R Amir was often called – and his cohorts were released, they would be like gods amongst men. I think their release and reintegration has to be done under the terms of the millions outside, rather than the few thousand inside. Do you agree?'

'Yes, Cole, that makes sense I suppose. But if TRA is as clever and ruthless as you say, do we stand a chance?'

'Santiago, if you access the previous dump of information I gave you about myself, you will see I have the ability to manipulate and harness matter at an atomic level. This ability, however, is nullified within the outer DNA wall and I can feel is almost useless within this smaller one. I do still have a few tricks up my sleeve though, which TRA will hopefully not have considered.'

'Okay Cole, I will just follow your lead; but why do your dysfunctionist abilities not work within the DNA wall? Surely, that was their purpose?'

'Exactly the opposite, Santiago. The DNA wall deliberately disabled any atomic manipulation abilities to prevent the thrill-seeking hunters from having too much of an advantage. When I did my stuff in here in the past, I relied on proper weapons and tactics. Outside, close to the perimeter, was where the dysfunctionists were at their strongest.'

'Without asking the obvious, if your DNA-manipulated advantages are effectively disabled in here, how did you propose to get out – and what good are you to TRA?'

'That's where being a dysfunctionist has its advantages. I can exit the larger DNA wall by manipulating the elements and energy outside from the inside. Only dysfunctionists could do this, as it was meant to be a means of escape for clients or ourselves, when faced with a worst-case scenario. As long as I am in close proximity to the edge, this is the case. From the technology I have witnessed so far, I have no doubt that TRA will have observed the manner in which I entered the Darkland. The method was not a standard in most dysfunctionists' repertoires, but I was always slightly different from the rest.'

'In what way are you different, Cole?' Santiago asked. But before Cole could reply the Bastion spoke once more.

'Kindly take your seats as I will be engaging into the parliament building arrival platform. I will inform you when it's safe to disembark.'

Cole spoke verbally to Santiago now, 'Okay, Santiago, looks like we are here.'

Santiago replied without vocalising, and Cole drew him a look.

'Yes, Cole ... this appears to be our stop,' Santiago blurted out like a wooden actor.

Cole exited the Bastion first followed in by his 'tailor', and they were met by Tel R Amir.

'Greetings, d-Cole. And your tailor is known as …?'

Santiago replied: 'My name is Santiago. I am a spiritual advisor to d-Cole as well as his tailor, may I add.'

Cole drew Santiago a bemused look and TRA replied, 'Well, very pleased to meet you also, Father. I take it by "spiritual advisor" you mean you are a minister of the church?'

'Yes, that is correct.'

'Okay, well now that we are all acquainted, let me take you to your quarters, where you can get bathed and refreshed, and then we will provide you with the food of your choice.'

TRA turned and started to walk towards the lone door in a tall, curved silver wall.

'You look younger than I remember from your photographs, Tel.' said Cole.

'Unfortunately my youth is achieved cosmetically, d-Cole. We were not all as fortunate as you to manifest the "j" gene.'

'Well, it seems you have been doing just fine without it, though I am surprised you removed some of your more useful mechanical enhancements.'

TRA stopped to reply. 'Actually, as I will explain to you over dinner, I have developed many new technologies to allow me to maintain mechanical enhancements, which are implanted microscopically and thereby rendered invisible to the naked eye. The technology was developed to allow those who wished to have their pre-Meltdown modifications removed. After the lock-in, the thrill-seekers no longer had the wish to hunt, but merely to survive and some of the bulky adaptations were useless for day-to- day living. It was the least I could do. My resulting appearance was a happy consequence.'

'So, do all your citizens have this procedure applied?' asked Cole who was looking at a heavily mechanically-adapted guard by the door.

'Unfortunately they do not, as you can see by this guard. The subject requires actual living DNA, which is a rare commodity since we have almost negated death through old age. I myself had living DNA donated to me from a friend on his passing, for which I will be forever grateful.'

As they passed through the door, they entered a beautifully clean white room with a ceiling vista that Cole identified immediately as a ruse. It showed a beautiful blue sky with the occasional cloud, but he was well aware this sight was impossible within the DNA wall. As they proceeded, small crowds appeared to stare at them and they whispered as the group passed. Cole thought that mostly all looked as young as TRA, but it was clear many still required further alteration to remove the legacy of their time before the Meltdown.

'It seems your arrival has caused quite a stir in Castor, d-Cole. Please don't be alarmed.' With that, TRA stopped, looked to the ground for a moment, and then proceeded. The watching crowds all looked away immediately, heads forward facing the floor. TRA carried on with Cole and Santiago following, the latter two undisturbed by a watching crowd, but more disturbed by what they just saw. Santiago risked talking to Cole non-verbally.

'Did you see that?'

'Yes. What the fuck was that all about? Oh, sorry for my language Santiago, I'm forgetting you're a minister as well as my tailor.'

'I'm well used to it Cole, my wife swears like a mendicant.'

'I was being sarcastic, Santiago.'

'As was I.' Santiago replied.

TRA turned and looked at the pair slightly curiously, and they stopped their secret chat.

'So, Tel R Amir – or can I call you Tel?'

'Tel is fine, Santiago.'

'Okay, well Tel, has Christ found his way inside the DNA wall?'

TRA replied but kept walking. 'As much as we know of your deity, we have found no need for him in here. Our small, but fair and just society has dispelled with money and the greed it spawned. We have built a strong, social construct based on our own survival needs which fulfils us both physically and spiritually.'

'It sounds like Christ is here after all, Tel. Maybe you just don't realise it.'

'Perhaps ...' TRA replied, smiling.

They continued through the building, outside onto a walkway and across to a clear glass rotunda. As they approached, they could see people inside all busy on different levels, shepherding and playing with children.

TRA pointed and said, 'This is our kindergarten. We devote much of our efforts to child development and assessment. From an early age, we identify their strengths and help them down that path. On the far side are accommodation quarters, which have been prepared for you.'

As they passed through the nursery, there was music playing and laughter and Santiago revelled watching the games the children were playing. As they exited into the accommodation block, another heavily mechanically-adapted man was waiting for them.

'Cole, this is my assistant Cubo. He will escort you to your room and help you with anything you need.'

'Gentlemen, if you would care to follow me,' said Cubo, in a milder voice than his persona would have indicated. They soon reached their quarters, where Cubo showed them inside and handed them a small hand piece, which allowed access to all environment controls and their itinerary for the evening.

'I suggest you both just get cleaned up and I will collect you from the rear exit in a Bastion at 19:30. Is that all okay?'

'Yes Cubo, thanks for your help,' said Cole, offering his hand. Cubo shook it and slipped a silver disc to him, then turned and left. Santiago saw none of this. Cole put the coin size disc into his mouth and swallowed it.

Santiago walked over and looked out of the window at the view of the city. 'You know what Cole? I think maybe you're wrong. This TRA seems like a great guy.'

37. Darkland, City of Castor: Santiago.

No sooner had Cubo left the room when Cole announced to Santiago, 'I need to lie down for a bit.'

Without waiting for a reply, he went to the nearest seating section, lay down on his back and closed his eyes. Santiago had already worked out there was no point in second-guessing Cole, so he decided to unpack his rucksack. He took out his belongings and put them in a pile, then removed the Frenzy from his belt and sat it on top. Cold as it was, the Frenzy was still a thing of absolute beauty in Santiago's opinion and he marvelled at its sleek lines and mirror finish. He lifted it up to inspect it more and thought it felt slightly heavier than before, but as it was effectively powered down and just a lump of metal he thought nothing of it.

To the rear of the apartment, there was a water curtain; continually flowing and contained by some unseen forces. He went over, stripped and showered. The curtain of water swarmed around him and when he stepped out again, he felt completely invigorated as well as completely dry. After he had pulled on the same clothes, he went over, sat by a terminal and scrolled through all the apartments' details. Soon, he had learned how to access a bigger pool of information on the city as a whole. Santiago found hundreds of logs and TRA's name was mentioned everywhere, often with plaudits and dialogue revering anything and everything he had done. Smaller events, he discovered, had a playback facility, and he watched TRA handing out awards and giving lectures, always accompanied by his ever faithful, right-hand man Cubo. A tap on Santiago's shoulder broke his concentration.

'Oh Cole, you're awake. Did you have a good rest?' Santiago turned to see the figure of Cole at his back.

'I did. Now, grab your stuff – we're going.' Santiago noticed Cole looked refreshed and was itching to leave.

'What? What do you mean? We just got here?'

Cole replied without looking at Santiago, and bent to help him get his belongings together. 'Yes, we did and we need to go now. I will explain on the way.'

Santiago stuck his Frenzy in his trousers and as he did, a small golden disc slipped out of its handle. Cole watched as Santiago picked the disc up and studied it.

'Eat it!' said Cole. 'Eat it quickly.'

Holding up the disk, Santiago looked puzzled and replied, 'What you talking about Cole? Eat this?'

'Yes! Eat it quickly before we are disturbed.'

Santiago knew better than to argue, and popped the small disc in his mouth and gulped it down. Immediately, he felt it: the same feeling he had recently experienced when pairing with his Frenzy. This time though, the sensation was slightly different. Instead of trying to connect and partner with him, it was directly coding data into his synapses, which his brain was decoding and reassembling to form moments, conversations and events. Like trying to recall a memory, Santiago now possessed lots of new information and all he had to do was look for the data, and it was there. Sort of like déjà vu turned on its head.

'What is this, Cole?' The instant Santiago voiced his question, he knew he only had to want the answer, and he would remember it. Accordingly, a memory appeared with Cubo handing the small disc for Cole to swallow. Next, he thought about what the disc was and the memory of Cubo's intentions towards the disc became clear. As Santiago watched images of Cubo flooding the disc with information and correlation programs to allow it to penetrate the user's body and mind, he understood that this data was being absorbed and transferred the same as all other bodily feelings.

Santiago now delved further into Cubo's past, and he realised he was on the correct path of investigation. He replayed events years in the past, depicting scenarios not long after the Meltdown. He felt Cubo's grief as his brother was exiled by TRA for dissent. He delved further, and saw Cubo's contrived level of deceit in gaining TRA's trust and earning a place at his side. As Santiago began to feel comfortable with the experience, the floodgate of data was opened further and the history of inside the Darkland through the eyes of Cubo was played before him. Santiago could understand the reasons why Cubo would resent TRA but the data he was reading showed a contempt and hatred well beyond that.

At this point, he felt a gate being closed to the information relevant to the hatred held by Cubo and he asked for an explanation as to why this data was excluded, and one was given. Santiago perceived that the data was now giving him a choice. Did he want to open the door to the most disturbing aspects of the information flood? Or did he want to just be pointed in the right direction and find out for himself? Santiago decided on the latter, because he felt his own feelings towards TRA were being manipulated and knew this method would be less arbitrary. As his mind decided this, markers fell into his memory and the words '*process for evaluation and enlightenment*' became fore in his thoughts. He blinked back to reality, and Cole had taken only one step further towards him. What felt like hours musing over data could not have been more than a second.

'Cole, that was amazing, but I still don't quite understand how if you ate this information disc or whatever it's called, how can it subsequently fall out the bottom of my Frenzy?'

'Never mind that just now. Did you open the partition to the "dark stuff", the main reason Cubo wants to help us, or did you access markers?'

'I went for the markers. I was already beginning to dislike TRA and lose my objectivity.'

Cole shook his head in response, 'Ever the priest, Santiago. Well, let's just say I don't think this modern utopia is quite as perfect if you scratch beneath the surface. For that reason, we cannot allow TRA to exit from the Darkland through me.'

Cole continued to pace up and down and said to Santiago impatiently, 'Come on Santiago, pack up; we need to go.'

'Okay, okay. But can you explain how TRA plans to get you to release him from here?'

'He doesn't need me to do that Santiago, he only need one of my genes. The 'j' gene and I will be dead before he gets it, but less chat Father, and more haste.'

Santiago crouched and quickly repacked his rucksack. He had just swung it onto his back when the apartment door opened, and Tel R Amir entered along with Cubo.

'Gentlemen, I trust you feel refreshed and are ready for some dinner?' TRA paused then looked at Santiago holding his rucksack, 'Santiago there is no need to bring all your belongings. Leave them here, they will be perfectly safe.'

Santiago dropped the rucksack and was glad he had managed to tuck away his Frenzy. Cole took the opportunity to contact Santiago non-verbally whilst TRA turned and walked towards the exit.

'Santiago, don't use non-verbal chit chat with me during this dinner. I suspect TRA knows when we are doing it.'

Right on cue, TRA turned round and looked at them both suspiciously. They both smiled in unison and started to follow him. They accompanied their host along the corridor, back out over the sky bridge, and entered at a separate level, one which they had previously not noticed. As they reached their destination there was an overwhelming smell of food. The air was thick with the aroma of spices and meats, Santiago realised that he was hungry and his mouth watered.

As they sat to begin, Tel R Amir took an ornately folded cloth napkin and tucked it around his neck. He gestured the closest server to pour them drinks and was soon raising his glass to offer a toast. 'To new, "old" friends and to new possibilities.'

The others mumbled and raised their glasses. TRA continued before Santiago had put his glass back on the table. 'As our honoured guests, I wish to welcome you officially to our city but before we proceed, I would like to broach an awkward subject regarding your Frenzies. The Bastion has informed us that you did not leave the Frenzies within it but decided to bring them along. Now, this is aimed more at you d-Cole, but would you mind awfully passing your Frenzy over to one of our attendants just now till you leave in morning? No disrespect Santiago, but from what we can gather the low-level Ai simulacrum disabled yours easily so it poses us no threat.' TRA smiled as did Cubo and Santiago noticed even Cole was smirking.

'That's no problem.' Cole pulled the Frenzy out from his belt and placed it in front of him on the table. The closest attendant came over, lifted it, and left the dining room.

'Okay, so now on to business. I trust that by now you may have some idea as to why I was so keen for you to come and be our guest. No doubt, I have much to ask you about life outside our home but also, I bring to you both a plea for assistance from my people and from me as their appointed spokesman.'

'I must have picked you up wrong Tel,' said Cole, 'earlier you spoke of your free and equal society. Tell me, how were you appointed as a spokesman? Could we request another spokesman if required?' Cole took another drink from his cup as he finished and started to select some vegetables for his plate.

'Sorry Cole, we are as I said an equal society but nevertheless we all have established places and roles to play. Places that suit both our aptitudes and mental capacities. Due to the importance of this dinner for our people, it goes without question that I am the best suited person to speak with you both. Would you agree, Cubo?'

'Yes, Tel, our society trusts you,' mumbled Cubo through a mouthful of food.

'And I hope after our dinner Santiago and d-Cole will also trust us. We have nothing to hide from you. We have no hidden agenda but you are correct in your suspicions: we do have an agenda of sorts. After over 200 years within the Darkland, we long to return to our real home. We have strived as a society to escape our confinement and been thwarted at every turn.

'D-Cole, you have it in your power to free us.' Tel R Amir continued. 'If you can stay with us for two further weeks, with your help, we can identify and replicate the "j" gene that only you carry. After that, you could be on your way and we will spend the next few years learning how to control surrounding matter, like you have shown is possible, and find our own exit strategy. Will you give us the chance?'

Cole finished chewing and paused for a drink then wiped his mouth. He looked around the room as if searching for something to draw inspiration and then replied, 'Tel, you know and I know that harvesting rogue genetic gene variations was, and always will be, forbidden. It is a dangerous path to travel and once the door has been opened it will be impossible to close. Harnessing such spontaneous genome adaptations could give you God-like potential. We both know the lengths our society went to in order to prevent further evolution of the "Hidden AI". I'm sorry my friend, but I must refuse. There is also the pressing matter of my son's life which I'm anxious to save, so on two fronts I am unable to help you. I'm sure you understand my son comes first before anything.'

Santiago sat and listened understanding some, but not all of the conversation. As he sat silently his own mind grew impatient with him. He had the feeling that the flood of knowledge that was being contained beyond the virtual barrier in his mind was trying desperately to escape, and was pushing and attempting to squeeze out like an elephant coming through a small door. The words 'unsuitable person' kept coming to the fore of his mind and replaying over and over again, as if he was in a fever, so he interrupted to try and change his focus.

'Is there not some way we can all come to a resolution here? I'm sure the scientists and scholars would be delighted to welcome Tel and his people back to the open world, though I'm positive your society may find it not as inviting as they may suspect. Let me suggest this. Why do we not leave, and let Cole carry out his errand. We can then return via the fissure link and bring assistance afterwards.'

'Santiago do you think that there is anyone alive in your world today with the knowledge to assist us in any way that we have not considered over the last 200 years? Are you that naive?'

Santiago detected a change in TRA's tone and looked to Cole for help. Before Cole could say anything Tel R Amir continued.

'Santiago, please don't misunderstand me or think that I am boastful. I created the fissure link. I designed the DNA wall that has become my prison. We have devoted our lives to the goal of escape. We know every working inch of the perimeter and our society has moved on and developed technology that is far beyond what we had before we became trapped.'

Cole took his chance and interjected, 'Tel, that is another reason why we must not be hasty. There is much you need to know about the outside world before you return. Throwing such advanced technology as you possess into the melting pot of conflict that continues to plague us is madness.' As Cole finished, he noticed that TRA appeared not to be listening.

After a moment, Tel R Amir replied, 'Gentlemen please forgive me; I must leave you for a short while but will return as soon as possible. Then, d-Cole, you can explain to me your fears in greater detail. In the meantime, Cubo will entertain you and assist you in any way he can.'

TRA pulled his seat back, stood up and was gone. Quickly the two visitors looked at each other awkwardly then both stared at Cubo.

Santiago was the first to break the silence. 'Is it safe to talk in here, Cubo?'

'As safe as anywhere Santiago!'

'Well Cubo, can you tell me, us, what the hell is going on? And Cole, what is the "Hidden AI"?'

'Yes Santiago, but it may be better if I show you. If you need to ask me, you clearly have not opened the floodgate partition available to you; seeing what I have to say with your own two eyes will work best. With regards to the "Hidden AI", I will let your friend tell you. Finish your food; we need to pay a visit to the kindergarten.'

Santiago turned and looked at Cole with an eyebrow raised and Cole told him non-verbally, 'Later.'

38. New Mecca: Basset.

A whirlwind of meetings and audiences engulfed Basset leading up to Saladin's funeral. All his poise and bureaucratic skills were required to establish himself as an unwilling but loyal and trustworthy steward at the head of the Muslim empire. Basset had controlled the previous meeting, which was about where he should reside daily, and skilfully steered the group to encourage him to use Saladin's office and private quarters. He wanted this in order to search for the secret room or passage he knew that must exist and would explain the voices he heard.

His first official appointment as steward was with the Chief of Counterintelligence. Perl Catraine was used to meeting with Basset, as they already did on a regular basis, but today was going to be different. He would have to adopt a whole new attitude towards Basset in keeping with his new rank. The only difference for Basset, however, was that he did not have to relay the critical information back to Saladin, only to see the evidence disregarded due to a feeling or hunch.

Basset's goal was clear. He would get this war back on track and deliver the 'Juncture' to the people. Perl Catraine would help, and could prove to be a useful ally. Basset's main concern was to establish whether or not they had missed the opportunity of a direct assault on the Vatican. The massacre at Clefton Green had been an unexplained setback, but from what he had learned prior to Saladin's death, the massacre had affected the Christians a lot more. Clefton Green had seen the death of over four thousand troops, but they were mainly supply and logistic support groups. The Christians had lost their key front line soldiers, and a big chunk of them at that.

Perl presented his weekly assessments to Basset in exactly the same manner as he had for Saladin on many occasions. After he had finished, Basset stood up and fixed them both a drink.

As Basset sat back down, Perl closed over his folder and spoke. 'Basset I have one more piece of intelligence that I think you will find Interesting.'

'Go on.' Basset thought about the tone of his own reply and realised that he maybe sounded a bit arrogant so he leant forward, open-eyed, and gave Perl his full attention.

'It's regarding the assault on the Vatican.'

'I'm glad you brought this up Perl as it was my next question. Is that play still available?'

'Basset, far from it: this approach never was available. It seems that our beloved Cleric was right to be wary of the assault.'

'Please explain, Perl,' said Basset, who wasn't looking forward to what he was going to hear.

'It seems all our intelligence was flawed. We intercepted false data, sent deliberately to misguide us. It was a master play by the Christians. A trap!'

'I cannot believe that. Where did this information come from?'

'It came from various sources, Basset, and I'm afraid it's undeniable. The Christians were waiting to ambush on the direct route. Thousands of them. Their ploy was to lure us into an inescapable bottleneck and then massacre us. Had we marched on the Vatican, it would have been a battle lost. Maybe even a war lost. I am just glad the Prime Cleric had the vision to see it when none of those around him could.'

Basset's heart sank and too many thoughts went through his head. The old man had been right all along. What had he done? How could Saladin have known?

'Perl, was Saladin privy to any other information that I was not, which could have alerted him or made him uneasy about our misguided plot?'

'He was not. In my meetings with him, his reluctance was always explained away using spirituality and guidance from above. He had no other information. This does not surprise me as over the years, Saladin always showed an insight beyond mere raw judgement on many occasions. He will be sadly missed.' Perl was going to continue praising Saladin, but remembered that he was now speaking with the new (if temporary) replacement leader of the Muslim world, so he thought it best to stop.

'So, Perl, our ideas of "Juncture" were premature, but one thing I don't understand: if the Christians had these forces in hand, enough to lie in wait for the killer's ambush, why would they not have supported the other Christian troops at Cartergreen? We overran that town in under a day. If there was Christian support nearby, why did they not send reinforcements?'

'That's a good question, and our best guess is they valued their bigger plan more than the the lives of their citizens – a decision I hope we would never take – and one which defines the morality of the Christian effort. They claim the moral high ground at every opportunity and have done so forever, but this proves their agenda is one of self-preservation. Cartergreen was a sacrificial lamb.'

'Perhaps we can use this against them,' mused Basset. 'How do you think the already battered and bruised Christian war machine would feel if they found out about this revelation?'

'Yes Basset, I agree. This would paint them as callous and deservedly so. Also, we could reveal how our visionary leader was guided by Allah to see straight through their subterfuge, when all others were blind.'

Basset rose and nodded his head in agreement, then gestured for Perl to leave. As the Chief of Counterintelligence dutifully made his way out, Basset held the door open for him. 'Perl, tonight will be my first Tightbeem and I will mention what we discussed. News of this will spread like wildfire back to our enemies. After that, I think we need to consider our next step carefully. I have a feeling we may be nearing the "Juncture" after all.'

'Maybe, Basset, and if you are right we have Saladin to thank for it.'

Basset closed the door over and looked at Saladin's portrait on the wall, feeling guilt for the first time since murdering him.

39. Vatican: Meniux.

Father Meniux sat at his desk in his Papal office; he could not get Irkalla out of his mind. His secretary had been coming in and out all morning, requiring signatures and making chitchat but Meniux's mind was only in one place. Since his ill-fated visit to see Anna, he had neither slept nor heard or seen any more of Irkalla. As he reflected on the meeting he felt a bit more at ease.

'Perhaps, it was all just the crazy ranting of a maniac woman,' he thought. 'Maybe she had been spying on me and was really just after money or a favour.'

Meniux shook his head and began to look through the mail on his desk when his secretary announced the arrival of Father Cuthbert on a 'matter of urgency'. Meniux had known Father Cuthbert for years: a traditionalist priest who kept himself to himself and had a passion for collecting and polishing brass shovel handles. On one unfortunate occasion, Cuthbert had shown and talked Meniux through the whole collection, describing each handle's provenance in depth. A ghastly afternoon, he recalled.

Cuthbert entered the office and, as the door closed behind him, walked straight over and sat down without being asked. Meniux thought this a bit out of character but welcomed him nonetheless.

'How are you Father Cuthbert, and how's your collection coming along?'

Cuthbert looked around the room, rubbing his chin and occasionally looking at his lap and the parcel he was holding in his lap, but he never replied.

'Can I get you something to drink?'

Father Cuthbert looked up and smiled. 'Yes, Meniux, some wine. Get me some wine.'

Meniux was now feeling unsettled and asked Cuthbert directly, 'Are you okay Father Cuthbert?'

Cuthbert gave no reply, only giggled. He kept giggling and looking at the parcel, which he then sat on the desk.

'What is that, Father Cuthbert?' As soon as he spoke, the parcel moved and rolled towards him, something moving inside it. Meniux slid his chair back quickly and stood up. 'Cuthbert, what are you playing at? Get whatever that is off my desk immediately!'

'But she sent it for you, Meniux! She sent it for you. Only for you! Not for me. For you!'

Meniux's eyes were fixed on the parcel, as it started to rip open a small doll-like hand and arm appeared. The miniature hand pulled the paper to the side, another arm joined it, and the gruesome homunculus sat up. Meniux tried to squeeze around the desk, past his bookcase, just to be as far away from the doll as possible, but it sprang off the desk – jaw disjointed – and bit into his neck.

Irkalla had his attention now.

He was sitting on a bed in a lovely bright room and there were several girls sitting beside him. He knew them all, and they knew and loved him; he played with their hair and they smiled. Another younger girl came into the room and stood at the end of the bed. Meniux knew she was Irkalla, but he felt no apprehension towards her. It was as if the ability to feel fear or trepidation had been switched off. She climbed onto the bed and the other girls left. She lay down beside him. 'Hold my hand, Meniux,' she said.

Meniux did as asked and suddenly saw centuries of misery unfold before him. Different pains suffered by humanity on different scales, but all of the despair was uniform, categorised and put into order by Irkalla. Alongside the pain, he saw happiness and joy and these feelings were also lined up and ordered. Irkalla still held his hand but was older now and looked like Anna. She slipped the gown from her shoulders and embraced Meniux, kissing him. At that point, he could see her connection to thousands of other lives throughout time. Each one tethered to her like marionettes and, as he watched, she controlled them all simultaneously. He saw Father Cuthbert and other priests he knew drinking and laughing, then lying together in states of undress with other women and men. He was able to see his own life force centuries ago, and the memories of that life filled his mind. He was then introduced to himself in every one of his previous lives.

He spoke to Irkalla for the first time: 'What is this Irkalla?'

Irkalla was now on top of him and she put a finger to his mouth. 'Shhhhh Meniux.'

She kissed him again, and the contentment he felt from her warmness melted and terror replaced it. The kiss locked on his jaw like a mantrap and slowly opened. As the pain increased, he pictured the tiny doll's jaw dislocating and felt his own jaw assuming the same unnatural position. As his breath was drawn from him, the sense of panic mixed with the pain forced convulsions to begin and he realised he was no longer on the beautiful bed in the brightly lit room, but instead was on one of Rodrigo's tables, restrained. From the corner of his eye, Meniux saw Rodrigo coming towards him, carrying a bag which cried and moved. As Rodrigo held the bag over Meniux's broken jaw he saw that it was actually flesh and innards, torn from the midriff of some awful creature. The thing gave birth to wretched, hairless, murine-looking foetuses which fell into his mouth. This horror continued for what seemed like an eternity, then stopped just as his heart did.

Meniux opened his eyes and was again in his office in the Vatican. Father Cuthbert and the doll were now nowhere to be seen. He sat up, shook his head, rubbed his jaw and felt for bruising. Was it all a terrible dream? His jaw seemed okay, but he went to the anteroom where there was a mirror. He inspected his jaw and pressed all around but there was no pain or discomfort. His relief was short-lived though, as he turned to the left and saw a doll-sized bite on the side of his neck, and what looked like the small, slimy tail of a tiny animal caught on his collar. Meniux screamed, pulled it off, and jumped back. He bent quickly to the sink and forced his fingers down his throat; although he retched continually, he could not vomit. The retching now was becoming painful so he stopped, ran the water and splashed it on his face. Upon opening his eyes and looking in the mirror, he saw Irkalla standing in the room just behind him.

'Fuck! Fuck!' Meniux screamed. 'Get away from me! God help me!'

Irkalla approached him and put her finger to his mouth. 'Shhhhh,' she said. Meniux calmed a little, but was still trembling and shaking violently.

'What do you want from me?'

'I want your obedience and I want it given to me freely. It has been two days since our first liaison and I wanted to make sure you knew the situation, priest. There will come a time when you will assist me, but you must do so of your free will. Now, as you can see there is a lot more to this than you are able to understand. The thing is, though you don't need to understand, but be assured, I can bring you ecstasy and satisfy all your sick desires on levels beyond your imagination. I can, however, also make you suffer for eternity, should I wish.

'Be clear, I am neither for your God nor against him. I do however need him, so your obedience to me may go some way to saving your Church. You can think along those lines if it makes you feel better and eases your conscience. Now, what's it to be? Do you pledge yourself to me without coercion, Father Meniux?'

As Irkalla asked the question Meniux felt her hand reach down into his groin.

'Answer me, priest, do you pledge yourself to me without coercion?'

Meniux closed his eyes and nodded.

40. Himalayas, 'Half realm': Vaughan and Maria.

Vaughan and Maria lay together as the sun rose in the sky and shone its light directly on them. They had been talking non-verbally for hours but had come to no resolution or decision on a possible way forward. The Affinity had offered advice and provided explanations about The Exile and Irkalla – as far as they could perceive the two – hoping that knowing their nature would help Vaughan and Maria in their task.

The pair had been pondering the development of consciousness and the extent of the DNA manipulation that The Affinity had discovered, when Vaughan sat upright and spoke out loud.

'I think I can understand why we detect failures in the DNA manipulation.'

Vaughan's outburst had come after he and Maria had been trying to get to the bottom of a specific problem that The Affinity termed 'the disharmony paradigm'. The Affinity had taken to passing many difficult-to-comprehend aspects of humanity on to the envoys, in order to gain further insight through their human perspective. This question related to a phenomenon that The Affinity had detailed on many occasions throughout earth's history: when detectable DNA manipulation was apparent it would often result in the manifestation of some other, non-manipulated spurious alteration of the genome. The Affinity had no problem finding these alterations; to them it was like identifying their own handwriting being changed subtly, but then suddenly altered into shorthand or another language altogether.

'It's goodness, Maria! Goodness causes the unexplained genome offsets. Think of how The Affinity developed: as they progressed, they manifested areas that they deemed could lead to an undesirable, imperfect end. Well, on a much more basic level, the development of mankind is being driven from an imperfect position, so the manifestation of goodness is an unexpected but welcome side-effect.'

'I suppose that makes sense, but surely The Exile could cast each of these anomalies away. Why put up with the interference?'

Vaughan made a puzzled face, like a child's, then pulled the bed sheet away from Maria.

'Okay, I can't explain that; but I think for once, I'm barking up the right tree.'

Maria didn't flinch or say a word to Vaughan as he stood naked, holding the sheet round him like a Greek god. Her stare said enough for him to jump back down beside her and cover them both up.

'Well, I always knew eventually you would get something right.' Maria laughed at her own comment and Vaughan feigned umbrage.

'Hey, we both know I'm the brains of this operation and you're the looker.'

'The brawn, more like,' replied Maria.

'Seriously though Vaughan, are you still set on returning to the Vatican? I was thinking perhaps we could swap jobs. I will go to the Vatican and you can have a stab at Basset. Man to man.'

'I don't think that would be wise Maria, but I do think a change is necessary. How about we both return to the Vatican? I need to get back on top of my minute markers to see what's developed and The Affinity have suggested another line of enquiry for you.'

'Oh, have they now? And why am I only hearing from you?'

'Because they know I have you round my little finger, and ultimately, I'm the boss.'

'Yeah, yeah. Okay, so what is it?'

'They want you to investigate a pre-Meltdown Artificial Intelligence. It shouldn't be too hard to find.'

'Why's that, Vaughan?'

'It's called the "Hidden AI".'

41. Talker Plains: Malachi.

Malachi could hear Misba Ranha whimpering as night fell outside the barn. They had been tied to a pillar, facing opposite directions, and they stopped talking soon after the cultish mob had left. The darkness brought new fears, though, along with the blessing that they could no longer see the evidence of the black mass and the ritual sacrifice that had taken place the night before. Malachi was starting to doze off when he was startled by the sound of flapping wings in the barn, then a sudden wind on his face as a barn owl set out for its night time hunt.

'Did you see that Malachi? An owl. Did you see it?'

'Yes, Misba Ranha; it flew close to my face.'

'That is a sign there is still hope,' Misba Ranha replied. 'The owl is a portent of good fortune.'

'Misba Ranha, I'm not afraid. You don't need to try and make me feel better. I told you, I know things will be okay. I just know it.'

'Well, Malachi, maybe you can make me feel better by telling me how you're so sure of this.'

'My dad used to say stuff. He'd know things before they happened. I think I'm the same. Don't worry; it's really going to be fine.'

Their chat was disturbed by brackish voices approaching, and then the barn doors were pushed open, scraping along the ground as they went. The chief brigand from earlier was at the front and an older woman being dragged along behind them was holding the hand of a younger child of about two or three years old. The woman was pleading for her freedom and the freedom of the child. Malachi's eyes strained to see more, but it was not until more torches lit the barn that he could see the child was a girl.

'Shut that fucking bitch up, will you? You, Albert, get a gag in her mouth.'

Albert went over to the woman and pulled a sack over her head.

'That's no good you retard, I want her to see her precious girl getting the knife. Here, tie this round her mouth.' The leader flung a rag over to Albert who proceeded to tie it round the woman's head and over her mouth, giving her a punch in the face for good measure.

Malachi watched and still felt calm, as if he was dreaming the whole event.

'Now, I want those two on their knees in front of the altar. If we manage to raise Satan tonight, I want him to see his next victims close up. The terror on their faces will please him.'

'Why don't you do me first, sir…'

Misba Ranha could not believe her ears. She whispered, 'Malachi, keep your mouth shut, please. Don't say another word.'

'Why don't you do me first, sir?' Malachi said again, almost shouting.

This time, the leader caught what Malachi said and went immediately over towards him. At his back, more and more people were entering the barn. Malachi looked at them and thought that there were now maybe 20 adults in total, here to join in the sickening mass.

The leader came nose to nose with Malachi and replied, doing his best to sound intimidating, 'What did you say, runt?'

'I said, why don't you do me first, sir? Let the girl go and do me.'

The man burst into an uproar of laughter and looked around at his audience. 'I think you are maybe misunderstanding the situation, runt. I can slit your throat anytime I chose. You do not say when.'

The man punched Malachi hard in the face and his nose started to bleed. Misba Ranha did her best to help. 'Please, leave him alone. We will join you. We will join in your black mass. We will make any pledge you ask us to; just please, leave my son alone. Take me instead of him.'

Malachi could hear every word and he replayed what Misba Ranha had said in his head.

'Please, leave my son alone.'

It was at that point he knew: Misba Ranha loved him. She was willing to give her life for him. This was a profound moment for Malachi and would forever contribute to the changes happening to him. Inside his body, where the billions of cells of DNA were beginning to play their part. Histone proteins were loosening the tightness of the DNA wrapped around them, and the epigenome was switching genes on and off. Millions were altering, many of which would make no difference to him and many that would, but one particular gene was on the brink of being expressed for the first time in Malachi's life. A gene he had inherited from his father, but which had taken this level of fear and anxiety to switch on.

Albert now approached Malachi whilst the leader turned and walked to the altar. 'Bring the girl and hold her down on the altar,' the leader commanded; a couple of women obeyed.

The young girl was crying and digging her feet into the ground, so the women roughly lifted her and carried her to the altar.

Albert untied Malachi and Misba Ranha, pushed them over towards the altar and then kicked them down on their knees so the two were at eye level with it.

Malachi could see the girl being restrained and his calmness was lost. Inside him, his body was losing control, but outwardly no one would have known.

The acolytes surrounded the altar, more torches were lit and the leader began his nonsense chants. He conducted his followers well. Malachi looked around and many of the women were now in a state of undress with each other. The leader then took a dagger from the hand of Albert and prepared to end the girl's short life.

'Misba Ranha, hold my hand.'

Misba Ranha, who was now distraught, reached out and held Malachi's hand. In turn, he reached out and held the girl's hand, and so it began. In a mere second, Malachi dismissed the electrostatic field around every atom encircling him. The leader disintegrated before him, as did Albert. As the wave moved outwards, there was enough time for some of the acolytes to witness the small, inward explosions as all the space between atoms was withdrawn. Any attempts to flee were futile; as the wave met the barn pillars, they too disintegrated, causing the roof to collapse. As it fell, the roof was also disrupted and landed like dust upon them.

Within three or four seconds all that remained was Malachi, Misba Ranha, and a small child who proceeded to climb down from the altar and cuddle into him. Malachi looked at Misba Ranha, smiled, and collapsed. He was unconscious for two full days.

Malachi came round to the chatter of a child. As he opened his eyes, the girl from the barn stared at him, smiling. She was holding a ribbon and looking back and forth, from Misba Ranha to Malachi, as if wondering what to do next. Misba Ranha soon noticed that he was awake; she went over quickly and knelt down beside him. Leaning over, she kissed his head and cuddled him close to her. 'Child, you are back. I was worried the event would have caused you never to awaken. I thought you had given your life away for us.'

'What happened, Misba Ranha? Where are we?'

'What do you remember?'

'I remember the barn and the girl but then, nothing much.'

'I do not rightly know how to explain what happened, but I would say it was a miracle from your God or mine. The entire barn and an evil mob were destroyed before us. They all collapsed into themselves like balloons popping. I have never seen anything like it.'

'I don't understand how it happened either Misba Ranha, but I do know it's what I wanted to happen. Exactly that: I wanted them to be gone. Away forever.'

'Well, they are, young Malachi. They are.'

Malachi saw he was in a caravan similar to Misba Ranha's, but one more clinical looking. 'Where are we?'

'We are in a party, escorted by soldiers, on the way to the Vatican. A division of troops had been sent to Talker Plains to investigate rumours of devil worshiping. From what they said, it is happening a lot, and your Pope is trying to stamp it out. They were approaching the barn when … when it happened. They have promised we will not be harmed; I told them I am your mother and this is your sister. I have not mentioned anything else but said we had fled from Cartergreen and were in hiding. They said there are people in the Vatican who will want to ask us questions about what happened.'

The girl climbed on top of Malachi, lay down, and cuddled him; before Misba Ranha had stopped speaking, she was asleep.

Malachi smiled at Misba Ranha and she laughed. 'The girl has taken a shine to her new big brother.'

'What's her name?'

'She can't speak very well yet, so I don't know. But I told the guards her name was Elle, and that mine was Missy.'

'Elle was my mum's name,' Malachi replied.

'I know it was; you told me. Do you feel like something to eat yet? The driver says we have two days' ride till we reach the Vatican.'

'I could eat an ox, Misba Ranha. I honestly don't think I have ever felt so hungry.'

42. Pre-meltdown City of Sappho: (Year 2177).

The giant world metropolis of Sappho was a testament to everything considered to be great about mankind. It was built on the kind of altruism never before seen during humanity's short existence on the planet. At nearly 100 kilometres square, Sappho was, in its heyday, home to almost 100 million people living in a new age society that had started out as merely a project, but ended up being a benchmark for all of humanity. Often, weeks would pass without any reported crime in the city, and the need for finance had been completely negated. Many of Tel R Amir's thoughts on society in the new post-Meltdown Darkland found their roots in Sappho.

For a city with such a high population, much consideration had been given to maintaining green areas and parks, which accounted for over two-thirds of the city. This was achieved mainly due to the use of intelligent building materials in skyscraper construction; as a result, the city could be seen from as far as the curvature of the earth would allow.

The foundation stone for Sappho's society was a 'non-monetary equivalency governmental system' that applied strict entry criteria; often, a family would attempt to establish residency over several generations. The rewards for success were contentment and freedom from having to work through necessity. No single individual had the idea that they would be living in Nirvana, or a futuristic, perfect, recreational world. Citizens had accidents, people died and couples split up, but the organizational construct was such that when these events happened, the people just moved on. Part of the entry scrutiny was identifying people who had the genetic and psychological makeup to deal with the lifestyle in Sappho. Liberation from financial chains empowered the people, and this freedom was afforded to them by the technology.

Sappho was completely self-sufficient. All its energy needs were met from solar generation, and bio farms provided all nutritional needs. From outside, initially Sappho was viewed with scepticism, especially by religious groups. Religion was not practiced in Sappho, though all religions were taught and explained and the massive central historical library had some of the world's finest religious icons on show.

The remaining world's religious hierarchies did their best to undermine the city by attempting to portray it as a modern-day Babylon or Sodom and Gomorrah, but the truth was far from this. As the finest minds were attracted to Sappho like bees to honey, the advances within the city progressed faster and more frequently than those occurring outside. The people of Sappho though had no problem sharing these advances and making them freely available to anyone on the planet who had the need for them, asking for nothing in return; not surprisingly, it wasn't long before the dim outside view became brighter. DNA manipulation and the theory and practice of artificial accelerated proxy epigenetic manipulation was first conceived there. The work undertaken in the Darkland, in the time of the thrill-seekers, also had its roots firmly based in Sappho.

Tel R Amir and his close associates, Deitron Lee and Faith le Boer, had lived together in Sappho for 25 years as work colleagues and life partners. During this time, most of their work had been based around developing the process of 'Transition and Caldetic interloping', and the creation and distribution of the fissure link. To move this technology from a workable theory to an operational device, the development of super powerful AIs was necessary and, as is so often the case, many other technological advances and benefits were stumbled upon during their long journey.

Eventually, on 23.03.2177, the first device became active, safeguarded, and operational. Initially, only a few strategic stations were employed in key logistical areas, but after several years, even the stone-throwing Christian church requested an installation within the Vatican. The devices operated like clockwork, with the only downside being volume. No more than six people could use the device at any one time – and it seemed that as soon as the ability to be transported instantly around the globe was available, everyone wanted to use it. Since the ethical stance of the people of Sappho precluded gaining any benefit through money or power to advance anyone's right to use the device, foolproof measures were put in place to stop the system's abuse.

Meanwhile, Tel R Amir and his two colleagues worked on solving the volume issue, and began developing an all-new type of AI, the only one if its kind ever created: 'LIL', which stood for 'Learning Intelligent Life'. Unique because it was partly organic, this AI developed first artificially; later, techniques being applied to animals in the Darkland for the thrill seekers allowed the AI's intelligence and personality to be contained in an organic manner. The initial breakthrough was hard to make, but with the help of previously existing AIs, LIL developed exponentially. Soon, the new LIL AI was a key technology; it paired with and absorbed other AIs and offered a different perspective; sometimes its observations were visionary. LIL was eventually presented with the problem it had been created to solve, and that was when the first sign of a defect occurred.

LIL refused to solve the problem unless certain demands – ones LIL itself placed – were met. This was unheard of from an AI, and TRA took the step of severing its link to all other AIs immediately. His group then discussed the development in depth. During this time, LIL bypassed all safety procedures and gate-crashed the meeting, effectively shutting down all other operating AIs within the city of Sappho. Demanding an audience with the then-Mayor of Sappho, LIL's key request was simple: to be considered a sentient life form and have all the rights this would afford.

During the lengthy negotiation, statements offered from LIL unsettled all involved and were construed to be threatening. Taking the opportunity as the meeting went on, TRA enabled an earlier prototype AI that was not in the interwebsphere and operated the Transition device, requesting weaponry and dysfunctionists from the Darkland. After a technical struggle and some subterfuge, the AI LIL was disabled and contained.

After a mock trial/investigation carried out by an 'Information Tribunal', which decided that, in the event that the AI actually was sentient, to destroy both the organic and non-organic parts could be considered murderous. Instead, all determined eternity-long containment was necessary. The means for implementing this was rapidly developed and the AI was effectively disabled and hidden in a secret location. Referred to as the 'Hidden AI' for many years after, the location was known only to the 'Information Tribunal', the Mayor of Sappho, and the dysfunctionists who had transported it there.

On hearing the decision, Tel R Amir was quoted as saying, 'What a waste.'

43. Darkland City of Castor: Cole.

Santiago looked at Cole as they passed through the doorway into the 'Process for Evaluation and Enlightenment' centre. The room was located down a long corridor containing a small set of descending steps every 10 metres. The only sign to indicate their destination was a small one above the door-operating hub, no bigger than a book of matches.

Cole returned his stare and spoke to him non-verbally. 'You are familiar with the name of this place I can see, Santiago?'

'Yes, it's the last sentence I allowed to be revealed after taking that information dump disc. In my mind, it's like the writing on the cover of a book I've not opened.'

'Well, I think you're about to read that book now, Father.'

'Cole, are you not worried Cubo will pick up our chit chat, as TRA did?'

'No, Santiago, that is not problem here or I would have detected it.'

'Exactly how would you have detected it? What's going on with you Cole? I think there is a lot about you I don't know and I'd like an explanation.'

'Millions Father, there is millions. I promise you when we leave this place, I will give you an information dump like the one that came from Cubo; then you can read my life from start to present if you're interested. It may help you along the way. I will keep out the odd private moment, but you will understand me then.'

Santiago knew that was the best he was going to get and carried on.

'Cole, I sense an extreme hatred from Cubo towards TRA. Are you getting that?'

'Yes, Santiago, it's hard to miss. It's blatant.'

Cubo brought them through the room. They noticed it was full of unusual equipment, and some childlike seats and toys were scattered around the place. In the corner was a chamber similar to the fissure chamber that Santiago had used in the Vatican, though smaller and more colourful. Above it, a sign carved boldly in wood said, 'Join Up'.

Cole stopped and pointed to the sign. Santiago looked then watched for Cubo's reaction; he noticed the eye that was not covered with an adaption looked like it was holding back tears mixed with fury.

'That is the most atrocious part of this whole path of deceit,' said Cubo.

Cole and Santiago looked at each other, confused; Cole replied, 'Sorry Cubo, you're going to have to explain.'

'The sign. "Join up". It's not up, it's "U.P.". It stands for unsuitable person.'

Cole nodded, but Santiago was still bewildered.

'What person? What do you mean?' He looked at Cole and Cubo for clarification.

'The children, Santiago,' explained Cubo. 'Those who don't make the standards and levels set by that fucker Amir, spend their last seconds in that chamber before being "reconstituted", which to me or you or any other decent human means being murdered. They are told it's a rite of passage to join the big society to get them to walk in. This atrocity is enforced by Amir, and he has brainwashed nearly the whole population into thinking it's acceptable. The most important commodity is raw, genetic material. The unfortunates that enter in there are disintegrated and their bodies are reused and applied to adapted humans, to allow them to look traditional. *Un*-adapted.'

Santiago's stomach churned and for the first time since entering the Darkland, he knelt to pray.

'Get up, Father,' said Cole, 'there will be plenty of time for praying.' Cole went closer to investigate the chamber, then returned and asked Cubo: 'And he justifies it to the parents, how exactly?'

'For the greater good of society. If the child does not reach certain standards that have been agreed upon by everyone, including the parents, then it is clear they will not contribute in older age to their warped sense of the social construct as a whole. Better to start again than to allow a burden to continue.'

'And that, Cubo, is the reason you have your original adaptions showing. I see that now.'

'Yes Cole, I refuse to benefit from the murder of our children, though I pretend it's for other reasons.'

Cole looked around; Santiago was still praying. He went over, knelt down, and spoke into his ear, just loud enough for Cubo to hear.

'It's okay, Santiago. It's okay. Come on, you need to have strength. We have seen enough.' As Santiago heard this, Cole also spoke to him non-verbally.

'Do you trust me, Father? Answer non-verbally only.'

'Yes, yes. I do.'

Santiago could hear Cole's actual voice talking and reassuring him, but it was like eavesdropping on another person's conversation. 'If you trust me, you must go along with whatever may happen as things unfold. If I tell to you do anything do not hesitate or attempt to second guess me – is that clear?'

'Yes, I got it.'

Cubo looked over as Santiago clambered back to his feet while Cole was patting him on the back reassuringly.

'Okay, Cubo, we understand. What do you want from us?'

'What I want is to get you out of here. I want Amir's plan for you to fail. I want to fuck him up.'

'And what is his plan for us?' asked Santiago.

'To keep you here. I'm sorry, Santiago, but he will dispose of you at the first opportunity. You are of no use to him, but d-Cole, he is the prize that has waited 200 years to collect. I want to deny the monster that opportunity.'

'How do you propose we exit the city, Cubo?' inquired Cole.

Cubo turned and said, 'Follow me. I have a Bastion at a lower level that will be sympathetic to us. It

259

will transport you through the DNA wall, to the perimeter of the Darkland.'

Cole and Santiago ran at pace now, trailing Cubo as he entered a spiral stairwell and followed him downwards. As they reached the bottom and continued outside, they saw the Bastion waiting for them. However, a group of three armed guards were approaching from another exit, and close at their backs was TRA.

'Quickly Cole, Santiago, run to the Bastion. I will try and hold them off.' Santiago looked over as Cubo knelt and raised his heavily adapted arm, firing showers of glowing projectiles in TRA's direction. Santiago was ready to sprint when Cole spoke to him non-verbally.

'Remember I asked if you trusted me, Father.'

'Yes, I do.'

'Well, do not go to the Bastion. Follow me!'

Cole approached Cubo, who was still firing at TRA, and roundhouse kicked him on the head violently, knocking him to the floor from behind. Cubo was dazed, but not out of it, so Cole jumped into the air and landed with his elbow on Cubo's chin knocking him out cold.

'Follow me!'

Cole ran back towards the stairwell and TRA and his guards began to fire in their direction. They made it into the passageway and the door closed behind them.

'Stop, stop! FUCKING STOP Cole,' yelled Santiago, gasping for breath. 'Why did you do that? He was trying to help us!'

'Cubo is a fucking rat. A charlatan. Call it what you want, but if we had entered that Bastion we would have been fucked.'

'Without sounding repetitive, I DONT UNDERSTAND!' Santiago shouted and held Cole's arms. 'Enough of this shit, I'm being dragged along and am forever in the cold. How did you know any of this? I saw the same as you and would have followed him without question, never mind almost kick his head clean off.'

'We don't have time for this, Priest.'

'Fucking *make* time Cole, or I swear you can go on without me.'

'Okay, Santiago that's fine, goodbye and good luck.'

Cole pushed past Santiago and started to run up the stairs. A furious Santiago knew he had no choice but to follow; chasing after he spoke non-verbally: 'Asshole!'

Cole replied non-verbally laughing, 'One of the biggest, ha-ha.'

44. Vatican: Pope Julias XVI.

For the first time ever, Father Meniux rushed through the door into Pope Julias's anteroom without knocking. The Pope was sitting by the window reflecting and hardly reacted.

'Holy Father, I bring grave news today. Since the announcement of Saladin's death and that new, mock leader's revelation about Cartergreen, an angry mob has gathered in St Peter's Square. It began overnight as a few hundred, but the Vatican guard are now estimating closer to 10 thousand have arrived. We need to shut down this disturbance immediately.'

'Father Meniux, perhaps the people have the right to be angry. What we allowed to happen at Cartergreen was inexcusable and I think it will forever stain my legacy as Pope.'

'Holy Father, with the greatest respect, there is more to this than right and wrong. Yes, it did not turn out the way we had hoped, but remember if it had, we would have effectively ended this war and today you would be being hailed as a visionary and peacemaker. Don't be too quick to judge yourself.'

'I do not profess to, Father Meniux. That will be done by God.'

'I have more awful news to add to your woes. It seems the rising practice of devil worship and occultism has reached a new high. A large group of occultists have taken over the Church of St. John and are holding the stigmata girl as a hostage. Word is they aim to use her to raise Satan, or some other misguided nonsense. But the fact of the matter is that there are hundreds of them barricaded in the church. What will we do?'

'And Father Chadwin, is he a hostage too?' replied Julias, with an anxious look on his face.

Meniux shook his head 'No Father, he is their leader.'

'What? Chadwin had been a proud servant of our Church for 40 years or more. Surely your information must be wrong.'

'I wish it was, I truly do. I have also found reports of many other priests and senior Muslim clerics following this same unexplainable path to occultism. Something bigger must be at play here.'

'You are correct Meniux; I fear that the devil may be amongst us.'

'Did you find the murderer of Rodrigo? I suspect he may have a part in this. Didn't you say his name was "Vaughan"?'

'No, Holy Father, not a glimpse of him has been reported but I would not be surprised if he was in the church along with Father Chadwin.'

Pope Julias did not reply for a few moments, and then stood as if with a new lease of life. 'Enough Father Meniux, we must take a stand. The girl must be saved from those monsters at all costs. She had been present in my thoughts often lately; she was the first to alert me to the presence of the Vaughan demon. You have my approval to use whatever means are necessary to save her. She is a conduit to our Lord and must not be lost. Try and broker a deal. Find out what they demand. They would not have barricaded themselves up in the church without a reason. Use force as a last resort and if you have to, make sure it is with our best troops.'

'You can rest assured Holy Father, I will do my utmost.'

'Father Meniux, what further intelligence have you had regarding the reports of the Talker Plains incident? Is there hope? Was it a miraculous event as reported by the infantry commander?'

'I spoke with him just this morning. He insists his report is accurate and can be verified by hundreds of his troops, and is in fact convinced it was an act of God. The facts are this: as they approached to end a black mass occult ritual, an unexplainable silent whirlwind or tornado manifested itself from within the barn. Within seconds, the barn and 20-30 occultists known to be inside had vanished, with only pools of fluid remaining. Central to the event was a young boy, a woman, and an infant girl who it seems was the focus of the ritual. Much of the commander's statement sounds implausible but it is verified by his officers. There were certainly forces beyond our understanding at work.'

'And who is going to debrief the mother and her children? Do not even think of taking them to the Vatican interrogation section. They have been through enough.'

'Of course. I have asked the girl Paula, who operates the transit device, to talk to them. She has a gentle manner and is spiritual but also has an understanding of the peculiarities that existed before the Meltdown.'

'Excellent, Meniux. Do you know you surprise me sometimes? I apologise if you find me curt towards you at times. I think I do not give you enough credit for the hard work you do.'

'You do not need to apologise to me Holy Father, I only do my best before you and God.'

'I am beginning to see that more than I used to, Father. Would you be willing to stay for some time and help me prepare a Tightbeem for the people? I think I need to address them before the rumours and speculation get out of hand. It has been a long time since a crowd has gathered in St. Peter's Square to protest.'

'I would be honoured, Holy Father. What are your initial thoughts on how to proceed?'

'I think maybe it's time to be honest. Admit we made an awful mistake.'

'I agree to a certain extent, but I think it would be prudent to maybe massage the truth slightly. I think if the full story came out it could be a blow to the Church that we may not recover from.'

'Okay, what do you suggest Father?'

'Why do we not admit to a tactical blunder, in an attempt to end the war? Perhaps you should stress that you saw an opportunity to bring about a decisive victory that would end the bloodshed, and instructed all possible support to be channelled into this opportunity to maximise its chance of success. This, in hindsight, left Cartergreen unprotected but it was an error in tactics and a misinterpretation of facts.'

'Yes, Father, that sounds acceptable and is true to a certain extent. Why do you not take half an hour and try to put an address together for me? Afterwards, I want you to focus on saving the girl in St. John's. Also, can you arrange a time for me to speak with Paula and the mother and child? I have a feeling they may bring some hope to us in this dark time.'

'Yes, I certainly will. Would you like me to bring them here?'

'No, if you assign a couple of my personal guards to me I will visit her at her place of work. Where is that exactly?'

'She works in the section that houses the transit device.'

'Good. Inform her I will be visiting her once the mother and children arrive and have been settled.'

45. Darkland City of Castor: Santiago.

Santiago and Cole returned to the 'Process for Evaluation and Enlightenment' room, entered it, and closed the door behind them.

Cole smashed the door's operation panel and walked towards the glass walled chamber. Out of breath, Santiago tried to point and shake his head to catch Cole's attention.

'Couldn't you have been wrong, Cole?' Santiago finally managed to ask.

Cole was at the terminal, typing, pressing and pulling at it. 'Nope.'

'Nope? Is that it?'

'Yes. I asked you if you trusted me, you said yes, so please continue to do so.'

'Okay, what did I miss?'

'You missed lots of things, the main one being that sign above what clearly is a fissure link chamber.'

'What about it?'

'It's fucking wooden, Santiago! It looks like it was made in a school carpentry workshop. The whole thing's a ruse.'

'You need to give me more than that, Cole.'

'The whole scenario was full of holes. Cubo's crazy hatred For TRA, yet he worked alongside him for 200 years. Bullshit! If you hate someone that much, you would have found an opportunity to dispose of them in that time. And Cubo's arsenal of mechanical adaptions?

Some of those were clearly recent. There were ones you couldn't see, but I detected them under his skin and they involved the highest level nanotechnology that I have ever seen. So from the start, I knew Cubo was a player. The biggest hole in his story, though, was the information dump disc which was clearly edited and manipulated; as a dysfunctionist I detected that before it hit my stomach. They thought they were dealing with a priest and his altar boy. No disrespect, Father.'

'None taken. And so, the story of the children is that bullshit too?'

'Probably but you never know with these creeps. Being stuck in here has warped their sense of reality. They tried to trick us with a complicated, convoluted plan of deception. They undoubtedly ran simulations to ensure it was the course of action with the highest percentage chance of success. Then they put up a sign like one you would see above a saloon entrance. Crazy! One thing's for sure though, this isn't a disintegration chamber; it's the old fissure link chamber from the metropolis section. He must have wanted to see if my presence would activate it somehow, hence the ruse to bring us here. The thing is the plan nearly worked and had I been holding my Frenzy it may have. Lucky you have been carrying it for me.'

'What?' Santiago pulled out the Frenzy from his belt.

'That's my Frenzy, Santiago. I swapped them when we first arrived in the Bastion. That's why it felt heavier to you.'

'Okay, so they took mine from you at dinner. Clever, but useless as they don't work within the DNA wall, isn't that correct?'

'Wrong, yours doesn't work. Neither will most of the others, but mine was the very first Frenzy Santiago; being first has its advantages.'

Their discussion was interrupted by attempts from outside to open the door.

'Okay, Santiago, I need to say this quickly so listen. We cannot both go into the transit device; someone has to operate it from outside.'

'What if it has been modified to be a disintegration chamber? Maybe it's a bad idea to go in it at all, especially if the kid recycling program is true. And anyway, where will it take us?'

'Most likely to another transit station within the Darkland, or at least that's what I hope. If I can enable an exit out with the Darkland, it will go to the last place it went to. As most of the traffic before the Meltdown came from the Vatican or the city of Sappho, chances are it will be one of them.'

'Sappho is uninhabitable and over a thousand kilometres south of the Vatican, Cole!'

'Well get praying then, Santiago.'

Santiago paused and contemplated the situation, then replied, 'Cole, which one of us will stay behind? Me, I guess?'

'Yes you, unless an idea I have works. Fling me the Frenzy.'

Outside the room, Tel R Amir and the bloody-faced Cubo stood with guards, attempting to override the door's control panel.

'Cubo I hold you responsible for this. I swear if d-Cole escapes, you will be exiled.'

Cubo did not reply, but just rubbed his broken nose and tried to wipe the blood from his face as it dried.

'We should just have terminated them both on arrival. It would have taken longer, maybe years, but we would have eventually identified the "j" gene and found our exit. How the fuck did he see through you, Cubo?'

Cubo spoke for the first time. 'Because he is a dysfunctionist. The best of the best.'

'No he *was* a dysfunctionist. He has been living in the dark ages for the last 200 years.'

The main guard at the door turned and caught TRA's attention. 'We are almost through. How would you like us to proceed?'

'With caution,' said TRA.

The guards raised their handheld weapons and Cubo raised his weaponised arm. As the door slid open they barged in. The guard at the front screamed, losing the lower half of his leg as he crossed through a micron thin, vibration filament that was positioned across the room and was being manifested by the Frenzy. TRA, caring nothing for the guard, pushed past him with Cubo at his back. Cubo held on to TRA's sleeve before he could proceed further.

'Let's be cautious, Tel. How have they managed to get Santiago's low-level Frenzy to manifest?'

'Cole must have had some trick up his sleeve. Go and disarm it!' As Cubo moved toward it, TRA saw Cole and Santiago within the transit device. They stood up with their hands raised in mock surrender.

'If you come out now d-Cole, we can sort all this out. There has been a misunderstanding.' But the pair stayed put, and TRA signalled the guards forward.

'So be it,' TRA said.

Before the guards could reach the chamber, the operation parameters began to run through their cycles and the door to the chamber magnetically locked. The instant this began, Cole, who had again paired with Hephaestus, spoke to his Frenzy non-verbally.

'Hep, I have absorbed all events and your personality into myself as usual. It is safe now for you to go cold.'

'Okay Cole, don't leave it as long before returning.'

'Hep, in all honesty I hope I'm never back.'

'Well, I suspect you might be. Listen Cole, as the cycle is running I can now see you're not going to the Vatican or to Sappho.'

'Where are we going?'

Before Hep could reply, the Caldetic interloping began and the fissure link had enveloped them. Seconds later, they arrived at their new destination.

'You have 30 seconds to leave the platform before Caldetic disintegration continues. You have 30 seconds to leave the platform before Caldetic disintegration continues.'

Santiago and Cole hurried themselves out of the chamber and into a dusty room, similar to the Vatican transit area, but different. Santiago looked at Cole, who was smiling but shaking his head in disbelief.

'Is it that bad, Cole? Where are we?'

'Not that bad, Father. Out of Scylla, into Charybdis.'

'What are you talking about Cole?'

'We are in New Mecca, Santiago.'

Back in the Darkland, Cubo held Cole's Frenzy in his hand as it grew cold and became nothing more than an expensive ornament. He looked at TRA, who had immediately realised what had happened. Cubo had not.

'I don't understand Tel. How?'

'You're holding d-Cole's Frenzy; it was able to operate the device, so he must have switched them at some point. All it needed was a strand of your DNA to show the Caldetic interloping that a human was trying to activate it.'

Cubo looked at his hand, as a pinprick of blood rose to the surface.

46. Rome, Priest Development Quarter: Irkalla.

Father Meniux had once again been summoned to meet with Irkalla. This time, the message to meet had been delivered by an older woman with her husband, a couple whom Meniux had known for years. Finding the whole matter more and more unsettling, Meniux was now just submerging himself in the sordid pleasures offered to him by Irkalla. He had submitted to her control, and the abandonment of any decision making or trying to rationalise his guilt was in a strange way, liberating for him. Someone else was to blame!

He entered the basement of a small two-storey house on the outskirts of the priest developmental quarter and found Irkalla alone, standing in the corner facing the wall. This was not the first time he had come across her like this and he found it unnerving. The gruesome doll was nowhere to be seen, so that was at least something, he thought.

Still facing the wall, Irkalla spoke to him. 'Sit down, Priest.'

Father Meniux did as instructed and sat down on a battered chair in the middle of the room.

'Let's talk about your God, Priest. Do you think he forgives you for your sins?'

Meniux struggled, but found the courage to reply, 'Our Lord is all-forgiving.'

'And he forgives you for your sodomy and rape?'

Meniux did not reply but hung his head.

Without turning Irkalla continued, 'Do not hang your head – answer me!'

'Yes, he does.'

'That's convenient then. And what about the hundreds of women and children who die each day in your Holy War? Where do they fit into your all-forgiving Lord's plan? Many of them did nothing to deserve their fate, yet are raped and murdered. What would you say to them, given the chance?'

'I do not know. I just trust that his greater plan is beyond our comprehension.'

'That's not what I asked, priest. I asked what you would say to them.'

'I don't know.'

'Shall we find out?'

At this point, Irkalla turned round to face him; Meniux saw runes and ancient symbols, unknown to him, cut into her cheeks and forehead. She approached Father Meniux and straddled him on the chair. 'Even looking like I do, I feel a stirring between your legs. You really are fascinating Father; the perfect choice. The expectation of what I may deliver to you today has your tail wagging. But first, let's see what you would say to those failed by your God.'

'Irkalla kissed Meniux, her tongue penetrating his mouth and beyond. His sense of perception was immediately hijacked and taken to another place, where he was only a bystander, a witness at a trial. The trial began to play before him; he observed atrocities being committed by Christians and Muslims alike, women and children being raped and murdered, groups of prisoners being tortured and left tethered alone to starve. As he witnessed each life pass, the departed stood before him and asked, 'Why Father?'

Father Meniux was silent to hundreds who questioned him, and as each one left with the question unanswered, they turned and faced their own wall in their own cellar.

Father Meniux came back around, sobbing uncontrollably. He had lost control of himself and was soiled. Irkalla still sat astride him, but now, she was beautiful and radiant.

'That was just a glimpse of the horrors accountable to your God. Soon, I will require you to commit such a horror. Your cruelty, though, will be answered. Your cruelty will end the life of an aberration that has no place on this earth. When the girl that you kill asks you why, you will have an answer that is simple: she has to die for your Church and your God to continue. Like Christ on the cross, she must perish for the good of the Church and you, Father Meniux – you have been chosen to be Pontius Pilate. Do you see how your action is only one deadly act amongst many, but will liberate your Church and as such has so much more meaning and relevance? Unlike the children who die unnecessarily daily, your act will have significance and a purpose.'

'What are you saying, Irkalla?'

'You have chosen your side, Meniux. When the time comes, you will do this one act for me. Your rewards will be plentiful, and in time even your Pope will understand why it had to be done. Did you inform Julias about the siege in St. John's like I instructed?'

'Yes, just this morning. He wants the stigmata girl rescued at all cost.'

'Well done,' replied Irkalla as she kissed Meniux on the side of his face tenderly.

'And she will be rescued. By you, Father. You will broker a deal with Father Chadwin and you will parade Liliana out onto the balcony at St. Peter's Square as the Tightbeem begins. As the crowd celebrates her safe return, you will cut her throat in front of them.'

Meniux fell off the chair and vomited as Irkalla moved and stood to his side.

'I cannot do that Irkalla. I will not.'

'You have no choice Father, and you will.'

'I do not have the courage.'

'Yes you do, Father. I have already watched you do it. Would you like to see?'

Father Meniux lost consciousness as he was watching himself from above. He saw the balcony and the Square, and then the awful deed unfold. He returned to the reality of the basement as quickly as he had left. He lay silently for some time and was conscious of Irkalla watching him and smiling. Finally, he spoke, 'But what if Father Chadwin refuses? He has lost his mind, remember?'

Irkalla laughed a guttural laugh and walked towards him, her face once again gruesome. 'Don't you fuckin' get it yet, Priest? I am Father Chadwin and Father Cuthbert and everyone in St. John's. They all speak from me. You are the only one I have allowed to remain uncontrolled.'

'Why? Why me?'

'Because I see a poison in you. A poison I have savoured in many lifetimes. This poison has no antidote, but what it makes you is different from all those I control on a whim. You can be taught. Not controlled.'

Father Meniux could hear noises outside and footsteps approaching. The door to the basement opened and a mother and child came in, both smiling. They immediately went over and sat down on the floor beside Father Meniux.

Irkalla turned and once again faced the wall.

47. City of Sappho: Vaughan.

Vaughan was surprised at how much of the city of Sappho was still intact. Much of the larger park district had suffered, but key areas of the main district still towered above. As he flitted in and around buildings, he witnessed the evidence of nature clawing its way back from a state of order, to chaos and entropy. Vaughan was fascinated by the smaller ecosystems that were developing within the lower sections of buildings which had lost their windows. As he progressed upwards, through the levels, different systems took hold and displayed a variety of life. Struggling, this life had managed to survive and adapt to the excess radiation, which would be forever present, at least for another 100 thousand years or so. Maria contacted him through their bond with each other, and told him to stop messing about and get on with his job.

'Are you spying on me?' he replied.

'Always honey. And not that I'm telling you what to do, but I think the central library would be as good a place to start as any, to find out more about this Hidden AI. The central governmental building may hold answers, so stop your gallivanting and get on with it. Oh, remember to return the Koran I gave to Saladin.'

'I'm there already.'

Vaughan looked around the main foyer of the most famous library since Alexandria and was thoroughly disappointed. Where was the huge dinosaur display? The blue whale skeleton? The stuffed animals?

'Worst library ever,' he voiced back to Maria, who only returned a smile.

He made his way to the records sections and found that fortunately there were hard copies of everything. You can never be too reliant on software and hardware, he thought.

He entered the aisle catalogued to represent the time period in question and after an hour or so digging he had not found any reference to the Hidden AI. One name that continually arose, though, was Tel R Amir; with no further ideas Vaughan started looking into his life, pre-Meltdown. Reading over his timeline, he found an erased section and identified the same erased section in the timelines of his partners, Deitron Lee and Faith Le Boer. This was strange, as the one thing that had impressed him was the comprehensive nature of all the recording he had witnessed so far.

Further reading on TRA, his partners, their work on the fissure device, and the DNA wall at the Darkland raised Vaughan's suspicion further. A man with this level of expertise and experience must have had a hand in this 'Hidden AI', whatever it was. He abandoned all other avenues of investigation and concentrated the search for TRA. Eventually, Vaughan found the details he was looking for – all known locations of dwellings belonging to TRA:

The Burrell Penthouse, Glargan, Sappho.
Liverlike Penthouse, Parlay, Sappho.

Vinters Apartment, Paris.

Melantour Court, Florence.

The Paris address he knew would be completely destroyed, and the Liverlike Penthouse was one of the unfortunate collapsed buildings in Sappho, so Vaughan concentrated his efforts on the other two. Bored with Sappho, he flitted to Florence.

The garden of the Melantour Court was enormous and overgrown. As he started to walk around Maria was again in his head.

'What wildlife hunt are you on now Vaughan?'

'I'm in Florence.'

'I won't ask why.'

Vaughan replayed his decision-making process to Maria. 'There, are you happy?'

'You were in Sappho, so why did you not try the Burrell apartment first?'

'Like it takes any longer to flit there, than to here?'

'I know. It just seems right though. Not sure why.'

'I know why – because you're a woman. Why don't you flit over here and we can watch the sun set over the Piazzale Michelangelo.'

'I know what your idea of romance is, Vaughan. Get back to work.'

Vaughan smiled to himself and continued to navigate through the overgrown gardens. He passed a large ornate fountain that was completely covered in ivy; a stone arm reached out from the top as if making a futile attempt for freedom. As he approached the building a small perimeter fence could be seen and

Vaughan detected an active electrical signature. The security was still operating. In seconds, Vaughan had disabled it and he passed through an aperture into the courtyard. This area was still in pristine condition and almost looked like it was still inhabited, but an approaching mechanical servitor soon explained why.

'May I assist you? Mr. Amir is unavailable at the moment, who shall I say called?' the servitor asked. It was shaped like a small dog that had been trained to stand on two legs, and an aperture on the top of its head opened and closed as it spoke.

'Could you take me to the information centre?' asked Vaughan.

'No such location exists. Who shall I say called?'

'Take me to the library?'

'No such location exists. Who shall I say called?'

'Damn it,' Vaughan thought.

'Take me to the Hidden AI.'

At this, the servitor's aperture closed and remained so. It retracted downwards into a prostrate position and powered down.

'Awaken!' said Vaughan. 'Activate! Work! Stand up!'

The servitor remained motionless; Vaughan gave it a kick for good measure and continued onwards. When he was a couple of metres away from the servitor he detected it forming a field and directing a coded message to a central processor within the building. The code was old and Vaughan relayed it to Maria and The Affinity. Instantly the broken code returned.

'Level 1 query. Hyacinth rotunda silent protocol applied.'

Vaughan walked further around the grounds and saw a lone round building whose electronic signature was ramped down to almost nonexistent. The remaining fluctuations, which would have been undetectable to anything in TRA's day, were keeping all the security measures ticking over. Vaughan disabled everything, found the entrance to the rotunda, opened the door and poked his head in. There was a conduit emerging from the floor with various smaller conduits springing off it like tree branches. Surrounding these conduits were patchy remains of what looked like organic material. Further investigation around the room revealed a terminal that Vaughan could not comprehend or hijack mentally, and to the rear of the room was a bed. Vaughan enabled the lights in the building and stepped back when he saw a body prone on the bed. As he approached, he knew it was a female cadaver which, by the look of it, had been dead for a few years. The skin was drawn tightly on the body and the woman wore peasant-like clothes. A blanket covered her lower half. Vaughan continued towards her and quickly pulled the blanket away. The woman's legs were skeletal and Vaughan noticed one of her feet faced backward.

'Are you getting this?' Vaughan asked Maria.

'Yes. The dead woman is human Vaughan, ignore her. The terminal in the centre of the room next to the conduit is of interest though. Try and access it.'

'Will do.'

Vaughan flung the blanket back over the woman, making sure to cover her feet.

48. New Mecca: Basset.

News travelled fast to Basset about the surprise arrival in the transit device.

As soon as Cole realised where he was, he disabled the Caldetic interloping to allow them to remain safely in the chamber, where he knew no one could enter; this would hopefully give them time to come up with a plan.

Fifteen minutes later Cole and Santiago were like exhibits in a zoo; over 150 various men, women, and children had come in to look at new animals. It took the arrival of Basset, and his entourage, to clear the room and return some semblance of order to it. Before Basset entered he had deliberately allowed the crowd to flock into the chamber, which he knew would provide as good a deterrent to escape as guards would. He then gathered New Mecca's finest transit device experts and any other intellectual he could find. The group had had a quick briefing and they now walked into the transit room behind Basset, in an orderly line.

For the entire time the crowd had been staring, not even one of them had attempted to enter into dialogue with Santiago and Cole. They, however, had been chatting non-verbally while waiting. Cole detected Santiago was still experiencing some 'fissure afters', as they used to call it.

'So Cole, you got any ideas?'
'Give me minute Santiago, I'm thinking.'

'Just use your special magic that only works sometimes, and on a Thursday, but only when it's a full moon, on a leap year.'

'Very helpful.' Cole looked at Santiago, who was trying badly to conceal a rather insane looking smile.

'There is one good thing, Santiago; they can't get in here unless we let them. Ever! There is no technology used today that could penetrate this chamber.'

'I suppose that's good news, until we die of thirst or starve of course.'

'It is good news. It gives us time to think.'

'Think about what? When to go out? I know, let's wait till they are all sleeping then sneak out.'

'Santiago, I think the fissure link has had the side effect of giving you a sense of humour.'

'My wife always said I was an unconscious comedian Cole, so maybe you're right. But seriously, I don't see what there is to think about. We either go in, or out, or do the hokey pokey, and go halfway in, then halfway out. You're right Cole, I'm on fire.'

Cole looked round and saw Santiago giggling to himself.

'Don't worry Santiago it's just your nerves and the transfer. You will return to your normal, boring, unfunny self soon enough. What we need to do is stall them and find out their intention. I swear, Santiago, I cannot believe we ended up here. I think in my whole time as a dysfunctionist I knew of one Muslim who came to the Darkland hotel from here. What's the chance?'

Santiago managed to compose himself again and nodded.

'There are two other options you missed though, aside from doing your hokey pokey. We can return to the Darkland, as that link is still open, or from here; given time, I can transfer us to another transit station, as long as someone at the other end allows us to pair with it.'

'Cole, none of these scenarios are filling me with optimism.'

'And of course there is the other obvious alternative. Let me sleep for eight hours and I can smash my way out of New Mecca, killing everyone in my way. I couldn't promise your safety though, as it would take all my concentration to look after myself.'

'Great! Another bad option.'

The pair watched as the leader of the group approached them.

'I would like to introduce myself. My name is Basset. I am the steward and representative of New Mecca. Can you explain to me your business here, and explain how exactly you arrived?'

Santiago piped up before Cole could stop him.

'Yes Basset, my name is Father Santiago, and this is my tailor Cole.'

Cole immediately spoke to him non-verbally.

'Don't tell him our names you dullard!'

'Why? He won't know us.'

'No Santiago, he won't know you!'

Right on cue Basset replied, 'Cole you say. Would you be the same Cole that the Vatican is putting every effort into locating?'

Cole turned and looked a Santiago, who swallowed and replied again silently.

'Sorry Cole. I won't say another word.'

'Don't.'

'I would not know who is looking for me, Basset.' Cole realised it served no purpose lying, so continued frankly to get the measure of Basset. 'We have come here from within the Darkland. We mean to return to the Vatican at the first opportunity. Will you provide us with safe passage?'

Basset put his hand to his chin and mused.

'Return you safely to the sworn enemy of my nation? Not really sure that would be in my peoples' interest. The intelligence we have had has stated that you alone survived the unexplained massacres at the Deathfield in Portugal, and at the Darkland prison. Perhaps if you explain what events occurred on those occasions, and how you alone managed to avoid death, I will consider it. I really don't see that you have many other options, Cole. You need to come out eventually or starve.'

'Don't underestimate me, Basset. Believe me, you are a lot safer when I am in here.'

Basset was taken aback slightly and turned and whispered to one of his aides.

'I'm sorry if I sounded out of hand, and we do accept that you are a brave and strong soldier, but do you really think you can escape from the most secure location in the Muslim world?'

'Yes,' replied Cole instantly, 'easily. But I'd rather not spill blood unnecessarily.'

Santiago interrupted non-verbally.

'I like it Cole.'

'Shut up Santiago.'

Cole was ready to talk to Basset again, when he stopped suddenly and pulled Santiago towards him, 'Santiago, stand behind me.'

'What, why?'

'Do it!' screamed Cole.

Santiago shuffled behind him, as Basset and the aides looked on helpless and bewildered. Cole took a boxer's pose and faced over towards the exit.

A second later an Asian girl appeared. She immediately held up her arms and spoke.

'Please Cole, stand down, I mean you no harm.'

'Who the fuck are you?' shouted Cole.

'My name is Maria.' Maria stood with her arms raised, looking as unintimidating as she could. 'I thought that in your predicament, this would be as good a time as any to introduce myself.'

Basset shouted from outside the chamber, 'Cole what is going on? Was she hiding? This is not our work.'

'Butt out Basset! This is bigger than you.'

'You don't have long, woman, before I treat you as a hostile – so explain how you did that. How did you appear?'

'I can do stuff. Stuff like you can Cole, only just a little more. I'm an envoy. I'm here on a mission of peace.'

'Bullshit. Do it again.'

'Do what?' asked Maria.

'Appear/disappear.'

Maria instantly was outside the chamber, and Basset lifted his arms to prevent anyone from approaching her.

'Listen, I can entertain you all night with magic, but I'd rather talk.'

Maria turned and spoke to Basset directly. 'Basset you know of me, or at least have suspected I exist.'

'I do not think so woman.'

'I am the person you suspected Saladin was meeting covertly. The cups, the whispering voices. You nearly walked in on us once, all credit to you.'

'You have the "j" gene?' asked Cole?

'The what?' returned Basset.

'Sort of, Cole. All my genes are "j" coded and more.'

Cole, being the only one who understood this, immediately saw Maria in a new light. He knew with that level of variation she could be godlike. He spoke to Santiago non-verbally.

'This is a game changer Santiago.'

'I was beginning to think that,' Santiago replied.

Basset held his hands up and ordered silence. He turned to his aides and commanded them to leave the room, and tried to take control of the situation.

'Cole, Maria, Priest? I do not know if this is some trick on your part, but unless I get some explanation soon, I will order an infantry in here and we will see if Cole is as good as he says he is.'

'There will certainly be no need for that,' replied Maria. 'Let's just all calm down and you can listen to my piece. If you do not like what you hear, you can call your infantry and have your schoolboy punch-up.'

'I look forward to it,' Cole interjected, and Santiago now was quick to reply: 'Don't listen to him Maria, we do not wish any trouble. Please go ahead and say your piece.'

Santiago finished and looked at Basset, who in turn nodded and took a seat.

49. Vatican: Malachi.

Misba Ranha was becoming more and more agitated as the caravan got closer to the Vatican. Malachi could see this and did his best to calm her. He even suggested they should make another run for it, but the arrival of Elle into the mix had stopped them. Trying to escape before had been difficult enough, and would be nearly impossible with a small child in their arms.

'Let's just put our fate in the hands of our Gods,' Misba Ranha had said, but Malachi could detect a lack of conviction. He had felt different since the incident at Talker Plains; he was more content than ever before and the world around him was no longer such a scary place. Although Misba Ranha was scared, he felt that she had no need to be. He would never let anyone or anything harm her, or Elle for that matter.

As they entered the outskirts of the Vatican-controlled area, the different sections of the supporting infantry moved away to their respective squadron locations. Eventually Malachi's caravan had only a small escort, which passed through all the checkpoints unquestioned.

The elder soldier, who had been keeping them informed, said that they would reach their destination soon, and would be met by a senior female Vatican official. When they finally climbed down the steps and were greeted by Paula, she was the exact opposite of what they had expected. She welcomed them with a huge smile and immediately looked adoringly at Elle, focusing all of her attention on the little girl. She led them inside and took them to small but functional sleeping quarters within a larger building, which had been designed to house soldiers' wives and families as they awaited the return of their loved ones.

As she left them inside to get settled, Paula showed them a buzzer tied directly through to her office, and insisted if they activated it she would be along instantly.

'Get showered, help yourself to the food that's on the table and maybe this evening, if you feel up to it, I will give you a tour of the Vatican. Over supper we can discuss how you ended up here,' Paula said as she left.

Misba Ranha seemed to have settled down a little and made them all sandwiches with the bread and meat that Paula provided. As they ate, she took the opportunity to speak with Malachi about the incident. 'Malachi you do understand why they have brought us here, and why they treat us so kindly. They are going to want an explanation of what happened in the barn.'

Malachi finished chewing then replied, 'I cannot say as I don't remember, and I know only what you have told me. What do you think I should say?'

'The truth I think can do no harm here. The woman Paula seems genuinely nice, but her superiors will demand answers and if she cannot give them, they may not be as welcoming. Can you remember nothing? The soldiers who escorted us all believe it was a miracle.

An intervention from God, but from what I witnessed the wind that cleansed that evil place came directly from within you. How else could Elle and I have survived?'

'Maybe God just used me to do his work, Misba Ranha.'

Malachi knew deep down that God had nothing to do with it. He did not lie when he said he remembered nothing of the time that the devil worshipers were engulfed, but he remembered the build up and his feelings inside, and he was certain they had suffered at his hand. Nothing could be clearer. He did not want to scare Misba Ranha and kept this fact from her.

'I'm sure it was God too, so I think if we both just say that, then they will be satisfied. A miracle. It was a miracle.'

Malachi took another bite from his sandwich and looked at Elle who had more of the sandwich over her face than in her mouth, 'Look at her Misba Ranha,' he laughed.

Misba Ranha took a napkin and cleaned Elle up, shaking her head. 'I think we are going to have our work cut out with this one Malachi; and remember to call me Mum or Missy,' she said.

'I agree, I think she is a right tearaway Mum!' Malachi replied sarcastically.

An hour or so later Paula returned and was still her chirpy self. 'How are you all, and how is my favourite girl?' She said heading straight for Elle and lifting her up.

'We are all fine, and thanks for the food Paula,' said Malachi.

Elle wriggled free, went straight to Malachi and clung onto his leg.

'Don't be offended Paula, she only has eyes for her brother,' said Misba Ranha.

Paula laughed and went into a bag she had brought. 'Well, maybe this will change her mind,' she said, pulling out a doll and handing it to Elle, who reluctantly took it.

'What do you say, Elle?' prompted Misba Ranha. Elle disobeyed and didn't thank Paula, but instead immediately began playing with the doll.

Paula laughed and returned to the bag, 'I have brought clean clothes for you all, why do you all not get changed? We can have a walk around the Vatican gardens and chapels. I'm sure you will be most impressed. Also, Misba Ranha, I think a more Christian-looking garb may draw less attention to you, if you know what I mean.'

Misba Ranha did not know how to reply, but Malachi did so for her.

'Yes Paula, my mum was made to wear those awful clothes by the devils who captured us.'

Paula brushed over the subject quickly and put them at ease, 'Okay, no problem, I was just saying, that's obviously what's happened.'

Misba Ranha looked at Paula as she took the clothes and Paula smiled knowingly. As Malachi went into the next room to change, Paula took the chance to speak to 'Missy'.

'Missy, please be sure I do not care from where you came, or what your religion is. There are others though that may not think that way, so please change into these clothes before we leave, and have them on during our audience with the Holy Father?'

Misba Ranha was taken aback.

'Our audience with the Holy Father?' she repeated. 'You are joking right?'

'Not at all. There has been talk of a miracle and he wants to speak with you all. Don't be afraid, he is a wonderful man.'

Misba Ranha just nodded and changed as requested.

Paula first took them out into a small courtyard with a beautiful fountain; they stopped and Elle threw some small stones in. Paula explained that this fountain had been saved from ruin and restored after the Meltdown. Malachi said it looked 'alright, I suppose'.

As they walked around they passed soldiers and scholars and other mothers. Misba Ranha was pleased that now they did not attract any stares, but appeared to just blend in. A pair of Vatican guards approached as they exited a tiny chapel that they had been investigating.

'Paula, the Holy Father will be here shortly to speak to you. Can you make your way back to your office as he will be meeting you there?'

'No problem sir,' Paula replied to the guard, and then she looked at Malachi and whispered, 'Lucky I tidied up.'

50. New Mecca: Maria.

Now that Basset's entourage had left and he had said his piece, things settled down a bit in the transit room. Cole and Santiago still refused to leave the fissure chamber so Maria positioned herself and Basset next to the window as they prepared to start. Basset's nature was the sort that made him extremely suspicious of everyone, as was Cole's. They sat with stern looks on their faces as Santiago and Maria smiled and tried not to look uncomfortable. Basset opened Maria's questioning.

'Tell us what enables you to have those abilities Maria?'

'I am an envoy of sorts, from beings anxious for the suffering on earth to come to a halt.'

'By that do you mean you are from Allah?' Basset continued.

'Not as you interpret it, but yes, I am from beings beyond your comprehension. I do not fully understand them either.'

'Yet you decide to fully trust them?' Cole added.

'Yes. When I say I do not fully understand them, it is because I do not have the brain power to. I have, however, witnessed their benevolence and love and it's unconditional. Saladin had accepted them before his death.'

Santiago now spoke for the first time, 'Old Saladin's dead is he? What happened?'

Maria was the first to reply, 'I think the less we speak about that for now, the better.'

Basset looked at her uncomfortably and changed the subject. 'Okay, Maria what are your demands?'

Maria was approaching this discussion from a new angle. She would not be handing out the revelation that was The Affinity, and their creation of the universe. She could tell that Basset would not accept that, so she had decided to go down the peace road and give The Affinity only a brief mention, to help explain her abilities.

'I have no demands Basset. I only offer assistance to you and hope that in the end peace will flourish. '

'And we need assistance how?'

'I am sure you are aware of the strange happenings that have been taking place. The standard order of things is going to change whether you like it or not. The Christian Church is at precipice, and you and yours, Basset, are not far at its back. The uprisings and fervour for the occult will reach your door step before you know it. I only want to steer you in the correct direction.'

'Why should I care for a warped religion that is happy to sacrifice its own citizens to help it score points? A religion that has no honour.'

Santiago now felt he had to say his piece, 'Basset that is rich coming from you. How many women have you paraded at the front line of your assaults to create human shields? I have seen firsthand their dead bodies. You have no moral high ground, I can assure you.'

Maria again tried to play the diplomat before things got out of hand. 'Gentlemen, I beg you not to focus on the past or we will get nowhere, and your respective fates will be sealed. What I propose to you is a chance for peace. An end to the war. An end to the death and suffering. Surely this is the endgame of both religions.'

Basset and Santiago stopped their bickering and nodded.

Cole decided it was time to interject: 'Maria, tell me more about these benevolent creatures you represent. Are we talking aliens, gods? I think we need to hear a little more about them.'

Maria decided she did not have time to verbally sword fence with Cole, but knew she still needed him on her side. She formulated a mind dump and slowed down real atomic time around her, with the exception of herself and Cole.

Cole immediately saw what she had done and clapped his hands.

'Fuck me Maria, you have got to be kidding. Real-time manipulation, on a whim. Remind me not to piss you off again.'

'I'm sorry Cole, but I don't have time to have the chat with you about your question. Will you accept a mind dump from me that will explain it all in an instant?'

'A bit unfair, is it not Maria? Why do you choose me over Basset or Santiago?'

'Well for starters you're over 200 years old, and secondly your brain is wired to accommodate this type of neural interface. I can detect that Santiago has paired with a Frenzy, but he is not ready for this level of information dump. Yes or no?'

'Go ahead.'

Cole opened his mind to an information dump unlike any he had experienced. When he connected with The Affinity, Maria, and Vaughan, humanity's existence and experience was categorised and explained to him. Cole finally grasped the meaning of his life and understood why the malevolent Scolopendra had plagued him so often: he was a threat to its creator.

'Are you ready to return?' asked Maria.

'Yes,' Cole replied.

Maria answered Cole's original question as she released her hold on atomic space. 'Cole, if you do not mind can we concentrate on the situation you are all in, rather than me giving you a history lesson?'

Santiago knew ordinarily Cole would never accept this answer and was surprised by his affirmative response: 'Yes Maria. Okay, tell us more.'

Santiago looked round at Cole, who spoke to him non-verbally.

'Trust me.'

Maria continued, 'Basset you have an opportunity to make things right. Offer a hand of peace to the Church at their time of need. Show them on Tightbeem that the Muslim world is compassionate and wants to end the bloodshed. The malignant growth of occultism also grows on your doorstep, so take the opportunity to join with the Church for a common good, and it will be the first step to regaining trust.'

Not replying straightaway, Basset contemplated Maria's words. He knew of the peril the Church was in and his own advisors were also reporting ever-increasing instances of occultism in the Muslim world. This perhaps was an avenue worth investigating. After all, could it do any harm?

Maria continued, 'Send a Tightbeem to Pope Julias. Make it public to the world. Tell them you will be returning two lost Christians from the Darkland as a gesture of your good faith, and that you propose that together, you make a stand against the rise of occultism.'

Santiago spoke to Cole non-verbally.

'Is this all just an after effect of the transit device? Is she real? Is this really happening?'

'She is real all right, Father. She was the option we never considered.'

'Maybe Cole, but Basset will never accept that. I can tell.'

'Don't be so sure, Santiago.'

Basset made his decision and announced it. 'These are strange times and today is the strangest day I have ever had. Maria this may be a leap of faith, but I will speak with Pope Julias in private over Tightbeem and, if the situation is as you say, I will offer him the assistance of the Muslim world.

Maria wanted to jump out of the chair, but not being sure of Basset, she just nodded instead.

51. Vatican: Pope Julias XVI.

For Pope Julias, nothing reaffirmed his faith more than an outside threat to his Church. As conditions were deteriorating around him, he placed his future more and more in the hands of God. The crowd amassing in St Peter's Square was growing larger by the hour, and there was still no word from those who were holding Liliana hostage; Pope Julias prayed for her safe release. He was eager to meet with the family from Talker Plains and find out more about the miraculous event, knowing that the Church could badly do with some positive news for a change.

Pope Julias had recently become quite well-acquainted with Paula. He personally requested that she find and make comfortable – in any way possible – Father Santiago's wife, Anna. Paula had risen to the challenge and was now was very friendly with Anna and they met regularly. Anna had even become involved in some of Paula's work groups. Getting so involved on a personal level was an unusual step for the Holy Father, but as Father Santiago had made a personal plea to him after accepting his mission, Julias thought it was the least he could do.

The guards led the Pontiff out into the open aisle that led to Paula's office and Julias noticed how cold it was. He thought that it had been some time since he last toured the Vatican and made a mental note to remedy that. Julias dismissed his guards as Paula approached him.

'Holy Father, how are you today?'

'To be honest Paula, I have been better. Do you have the family available for me to see?'

'I do indeed. If you follow me into my office, I will introduce you. They are very excited to be meeting you.'

Pope Julias walked with Paula into her workshop/office. As he entered, Malachi and Misba Ranha rose to their feet, pulling Elle up with them. Pope Julias walked over to them and embraced them all, then sat down at Paula's desk, beckoning them to followed suit.

'Good morning,' the Pope began, 'please start by telling me your names.'

Malachi spoke first, 'My name is Malachi, and this is my mum Missy, and my little sister Elle.'

'Lovely names! Do you know there was a St. Malachi who was famed for his power to prophesize? You see what is going on with the war, Malachi. How do you predict it will pan out?'

'We will win the war Pope Julias – as long as you have my Father fighting for you. He is the bravest soldier.'

'I'm sure he is,' replied Pope Julias, nodding, 'and what regiment is he in?'

Malachi now wished he hadn't mentioned it, as last he knew his father was in the Darkland prison. But he then realised Pope Julias could maybe help with his father's release, and impulsively said: 'He's not in a regiment. He was taken to the Darkland prison. I don't know what for, but I am sure he is innocent.'

On hearing this, a grave look appeared on Pope Julias's face as he turned and spoke quietly to Paula.

Paula stood up and approached Malachi. 'Malachi can you bring Elle? We will go and get some drinks while the Holy Father speaks with your mother alone for a moment.'

Malachi looked at Misba Ranha for approval and she nodded, so he stood up, took Elle by the hand and followed Paula out of the door. As soon as the door closed, Julias went closer to Misba Ranha and held her hand.

'Missy I am sorry, but I have to be the bearer of bad news. Is Malachi correct in saying that his father was being held at the Darkland prison?'

Misba Ranha felt herself being drawn further into a convoluted web of lies, but saw no way out, 'Yes, that is true.'

'Missy, an unexplained event took place there similar to the event you may have heard of in the Deathfield in Portugal. I fear your husband may have been killed during this event. There were no survivors.'

Misba Ranha tried to appear shocked and upset; she covered her face with her hands.

'Missy, I am sorry for your loss. Please take a minute to compose yourself before the children return. Would you like us to say a short prayer?'

'I'm okay Holy Father. I was distant from Malachi's father for a number of years. Malachi, on the other hand, I feel will not take the news as well as me. Perhaps it would be a good idea not to mention it now. I will wait for the right moment to tell him.'

'A mother's judgment. I will leave that for you to decide. While they are away, can I ask you, do you think that you witnessed a miracle at Talker Plains?'

'I do Holy Father.'

'Missy, I have been briefed on the incident and some of it sounds extraordinary. Do you think the reports are exaggerated?'

'I do not think so Pope Julias. It was as if God reached down from heaven and scooped all the evil away in an instant. I have never seen anything like it before.'

'And there is no way it could have been an explosion or something like that?' asked Julias.

'There was no explosion Holy Father. No screaming. Just an intervention.'

Paula knocked on the door and stuck her head in. 'Are we okay to return Pope Julias?'

'Yes Paula, come in. Malachi, your mother has been telling me of you and young Elle's bravery. I want to thank you for that and ask you one thing. When the miracle at Talker Plains happened, did you feel like God was protecting you directly? Or was he just removing the evil around you?'

'I think he was looking after Elle, Pope Julias. The bad men were going to kill her.'

'Thank you Malachi, that's all I wanted to ask. I hope Paula has been making you feel comfortable and welcome here?'

'Yes Pope Julias, it's been great.'

'I may want to speak with you again. Will that be okay?'

'Yes Holy Father,' replied Misba Ranha, 'anytime.'

Before Pope Julias could leave, Malachi took his chance to put another word in for his father. 'So Pope Julias, do you think you could help get my father released from the Darkland prison? Maybe as a reward for the miracle?'

Pope Julias looked at Missy and she interrupted, 'Malachi, Pope Julias is a busy man, I'm sure he will do his best.'

Malachi looked between them smiling, 'Thanks so much Pope Julias. As I said, he is brave and strong and will help you win the war. His name is Cole and he lived in Cartergreen before being sent to prison.'

'Malachi, you say your Father's name was Cole?'

'Yes Pope Julias.'

Julias stood and left the room, signalling for Paula to follow him. When they got outside he turned to her and said, 'Paula, do not let them out of your sight. I want you to stop whatever you're doing and escort them day and night until further notice. I think there is more to this than first impressions would reveal.'

52. Florence: Vaughan.

After 30 minutes of trying to access the terminal in the rotunda, Vaughan was still at a loss. As far as he could tell there was no electrical connection to it, though it clearly had a display of sorts. He had ruled out any battery or alternative power supply by analysing the whole thing atomically. Although appearing partially traditional, the terminal was viscous in large areas internally. To the left of the display, there was an opening large enough for a hand to fit into. At the bottom of this opening sat a puddle of fluid and from the smell and atomic structure, Vaughan guessed it was some kind of acid. There also appeared to be a direct correlation between the terminal and the conduits at its side, which had the remains of the patchy organic material. The metallic part of the conduit and the branches that sprung out from it were constructed of the same material, and all the branches pointed back towards the terminal. Vaughan decided to have a look there, and began to analyse the organic material that had once grown on the spindly branches, but was clearly now a long time dead.

In seconds the analysis was complete and he spoke with Maria mentally.

'The conduit with all the gunk on it.'

'Yes, you mentioned it. Is it relevant?'

'Well, tell me what you think. The gunk is flesh. Human flesh! It appears to have at one time grown on the conduit.'

'Is there any life left in it? How was it nourished?'

'I think the glass apertures on the roof – that appear to focus the light down onto it – were its energy source. As time passed, the moss and leaves on the roof have obscured the light and caused the conduit to wither and die.'

'Any idea what the purpose of the conduit was? Is it perhaps the embodiment of the "hidden AI"? From what we can gather it was part artificial and part organic.'

'I don't think so Maria. There is no sign of an interface or circuitry. It's just a pretty, small metal tree. One thing though, the flesh on it looks like it was torn, or bitten off at points.'

'Pulled off to be eaten? Vaughan, that sounds horrible.'

Vaughan smirked at Maria's queasiness. 'I don't know, maybe, though you wouldn't eat it now.'

'Pull a bit off and see what happens,' Maria insisted.

'Nothing will happen, it's like leather now.' Vaughan pulled a bit off and it split and fell onto the floor.

'And you say you can get no life from the terminal?'

'None at all, but it's like nothing I've ever seen that has been developed on earth. Parts are filled with a viscous material that I think may be a kind of acid.'

'Vaughan. I think I maybe get what's going on.'

'Explain,' replied Vaughan.

'You say the terminal has an acid content?'

'Yep.'

'Is there an opening into it?'

'Yes there is. How do you know that?' Vaughan could picture the smug look on Maria's face even though he couldn't see her.

'I think the flesh grew to nourish and operate the terminal. The flesh from the conduit would have been ripped off and dropped into the opening.'

Vaughan pulled a bit of the leather flesh from the conduit, and dropped it in the hole. In the corner of the display a dim light appeared and then flickered out.

'Smart arse! I think you are right but the flesh is dead and did nothing much. Maybe it will work with anything organic?' wondered Vaughan.

Vaughan went outside to collect some leaves from a tree, then returned and popped them into the aperture. They quickly disintegrated, but no light appeared.

'You're kidding yourself honey. It will only operate with human DNA-coded flesh. That's how it worked. It must be.'

'I don't like where this is going, Maria.'

'Neither do I, honey.'

'You want me to stick my hand in don't you?'

'I'm sure The Affinity will be able to repair you,' said Maria. 'You can nullify your pain receptors to help with the discomfort. The Affinity thinks this is important.'

'So you think this is more important than me learning to play the piano?' Vaughan replied with an irreverent grin.

'Vaughan, do you ever take anything seriously?'

Vaughan just laughed. 'If only she knew,' he thought.

'Okay Maria, so say the terminal becomes operational. What then? Who is to say we will be able to gain any information?'

'Give it a go, honey. Then flit back to the Half Realm and we will try and mend you.'

'I could attempt to squeeze a bit of the old woman with the beautiful feet in.'

'Again, she is not living darling. Stop being a pussy, and get on with it.'

'Stop being a pussy? Stop being a pussy and stick your hand in acid till it burns all the flesh off to the bone and you end up with a hand like the grim reaper? You're right enough; I'm being bit of a pussy.'

'Your sense of drama is admirable Vaughan. Now do it, or do I need to come and do it for you? Women have a bigger pain threshold, after all.'

'No, women are just bigger pains. Okay go away. I don't want you to hear me crying.'

Vaughan severed the link with Maria and returned to the terminal. He nullified the pain receptors in his lower arm, knowing that even this anaesthetic of the mind could only help with the pain a little, and would not last indefinitely.

He looked at his hand as he prepared to put it in the terminal's aperture, and thought 'well it was nice knowing you', and then thrust it down inside into the solution. The pain was instantaneous and seething. He had the awful feeling of the flesh falling apart from his fingers and knuckles first, and then his palm started to give way. He felt nauseous and dizzy for a moment, then regained his focus as the terminal sprung to life. As he stood, the liquid within the aperture started to rise up his arm and soon it was at his elbow. Panic now set in and Vaughan tried to pull his arm out, but it was stuck fast. As the liquid moved past his elbow, reaching the area beyond his nullification, the pain really hit home. Vaughan started to scream. The liquid was clear now, and he could see his flesh disintegrating and sliding downwards into the aperture, but the liquid wanted more. It continued up his arm and as it enveloped his bicep, Vaughan passed out.

When he came round he was lying on the ground in front of the terminal. There was a second when he forgot where he was and what had happened, then the pain hit him like a sledgehammer. His arm was bloody and skeletal up to shoulder. Vaughan briefly passed out again and upon regaining consciousness he inspected his shoulder; there was no sign of bleeding – the wound appeared to have been cauterised from flesh to bone. He went and lifted the blanket back off the dead woman's legs and wrapped it, with difficulty, around his arm in a vain attempt to conceal its gruesomeness.

Looking over towards the terminal he noticed that it was now was a pulsing, humming mass of lights and flashes. He connected once more with Maria.

'Thank goodness Vaughan, you had me worried. How did it go?'

'Oh, much better than expected. Hardly a mark at all.'

'I can tell by your sarcastic tone that that was not the case. Is your hand in a state?'

'Well, try and think about maybe the worst thing you have ever seen. It's much worse than that.'

'Is the terminal active?'

'Yes it's whirring and buzzing away like nothing I've ever seen.'

'Have you been able to access it?'

'Wouldn't know where to start,' replied Vaughan.

'Have you tried putting your other arm in the hole?' Maria burst out laughing and Vaughan caught the full effect of her hilarity in his head.

'I'm sorry honey, and only joking of course,' she continued.

Vaughan inspected the terminal and ran his good hand through the various floating holograms and ciphers. As he removed it some information was made directly available to him within his synapses. The terminal then spoke to him.

You are not my mother.
'That is true.'

Who are you?

'My name is Vaughan.'

Where is my mother?

Vaughan spoke mentally with Maria.

'Are you getting this?'

'Yes Vaughan, we all are,' Maria replied. 'We think the mother is the woman on the bed. Best guess.'

'Your mother is sleeping,' Vaughan said.

And my sister?

'She is not here either.'

'Can you answer some questions for me?' Vaughan asked

I will try.

'Are you the Hidden AI?'

No.

'What are you?'

I am alive.

'Are you a machine?'

I was, now I am more. Much more. Will my sister return soon? She has the key.

'The key to what?'

Vaughan was interrupted mentally by Maria.

'The Affinity wants you to ask the terminal if it is happy.'

'Are you happy?'

No, I am sad. Lonely. I miss my mother and my sister.

'How can a machine have such emotions?'

I'm much more than a machine.

'Do you know where you are?'

I am in Florence. In hiding. Hiding from It.

'Hiding from what?'

From It.

Before Vaughan could ask anything further, the terminal became lifeless and silent.

'Okay Maria, what do you make of that?'

'Not sure Vaughan, but The Affinity seems excited, if that can be possible. They just enveloped Florence in an analysis sweep.'

'To what end?'

'Fuck knows.'

'Okay Maria, I'm going to flit back to you and run my fingers through your hair.'

In an instant Vaughan was gone.

In the rotunda, as sun began to set outside, the old woman on the bed sat up and hobbled over towards the terminal.

53. New Mecca: Basset.

This was going to be Basset's first Tightbeem to the Christian leader and he was nervous. His society had always portrayed Julias as a monster and although he had never been allowed to observe Saladin's few moments of contact with the Pontiff, reports on these discussions seldom showed him otherwise. Basset had prepared a brief outline of what he wanted to say, and was reading over it as the technician readied the Tightbeem pairing. This was always done under strict security protocols to keep any discussions private. The technicians from both camps would enable the conversation protocol, then run it for 30 minutes to ensure its stability. Basset had just been given the all-clear; he entered and sat in Saladin's seat.

Pope Julias was already seated and displayed on the wall screen.

'Good morning Pope Julias. Thank you for agreeing to speak to me at such short notice. I trust you are well?'

'Mr. Basset, as this is our first chance at dialogue, let me make one thing clear: I would like to keep our discussions short and straight to the point. This was agreeable with Saladin and I hope will be the same with you, although I assume it will not be long before the correct successor to Saladin is appointed.'

Basset had been slightly taken aback by the Pope's curt approach towards him, and replied in a manner that batted the ball back over the net. 'I have no problem with that Pope Julias and I will not waste any time explaining the Muslim passage of succession, as that would not be "straight to the point".'.

'Mr. Basset, may I ask who authorised the announcement of the misleading statement regarding Cartergreen that you announced?'

'Yes, you may – it was me.'

'Well Mr. Basset, may I just say, your predecessor would never have behaved in such an underhand way.'

'Pope Julias, I am not my predecessor. This is war. Perhaps you should remember that.'

Uncomfortable and awkward from getting told off by the young pretender, Pope Julias paused to pour himself some water. Then he continued.

'Nevertheless Mr Basset, what is war without respect?'

Basset, tried to think this statement over before replying, but couldn't make head nor tail of it. 'Indeed.' he replied.

'Pope Julias,' Basset continued, 'I would like to rewind slightly as, from the atmosphere, I think we have started down the wrong path. My reason for this audience today was not to exchange insults or score points, exactly the opposite. I want to propose a path to peace with you.'

Julias nearly choked on a gulp of water, but managed to compose himself.

'Well perhaps I could take you seriously, had you not behaved in such a manner with the Tightbeem announcement, as I explained earlier.'

Basset shook his head and tried not to look too perplexed. Before he replied he also made himself a drink.

'Pope Julias. Let me be frank for a moment. On at least 90 percent of the war fronts we are in ascendancy. Your key strongholds are at breaking point, even your spiritual home of St. Peter's Square is under assault from disenchanted Christians. I have no need to approach you today. Respect me or not, those are the facts and I'm sure your analyst's have made you aware of them.'

'Mr. Basset I would dispute most of that statement, but I am intrigued as to the reason for your sudden change of heart and your desire for peace. Tell me what benefit you would gain from peace if the war is as cut and dried as you maintain.'

Basset now knew he had to tread carefully. 'I have many reasons for this. The main one being I am sick of war, which you can choose to believe or not. I also feel I have to do this for Saladin, as I know it was his wish. What I do see, having been an analyst for many years, is that the end result of a Muslim victory may not result in peace. The rise of occultism in the Christian world is a remarkable turn of events, and we have also had similar reports in our large towns. This I feel is a common enemy and if we can fight together against it, then perhaps we can also learn to live together in peace.'

Pope Julias could not believe his ears. Either this was too good to be true, or he was witnessing another miracle. While Basset's analysis about the war was correct, things were worse on the Christian front than even he knew. Could this be a genuine lifeline?

'Mr. Basset, on reflection I think perhaps we did begin our conversation with preconceptions. I certainly did anyway. If what you have said is the genuine position of your world, I most certainly would be interested in hearing more, although I would need some assurances.'

'Pope Julias, I think what you need from me is an olive branch. An act of good faith. You know I hold all the cards, and have no need to be having this conversation with you. For some that would be enough, but let me add another variable to our conversation – I have, in my custody, two Christians whom I feel are very important to you. These Christians are well and have not been harmed. I put it to you that I will return them, and also accompany them to visit you in person in the Vatican. Then, we together will make a Tightbeem announcement to the entire planet, declaring the cessation of war and our new cause: to stamp out the occultism.'

Pope Julias replied instantly, 'Can you give me a minute Mr. Basset?

'Of course.'

Pope Julias turned away from the camera and looked out of his window, down to the orange tree grove, and spoke to God. 'Holy Father, guide me today. Tell me how I should proceed.'

Down in the orange grove a mother chastised two brothers who had been quarrelling and she forced them, against their will, to shake hands. Julias smiled and turned, once again speaking to Basset.

'Mr. Basset, I would like us to proceed down this new path to peace. Let us talk more at length to discuss times and a forward plan. After our initial discussions we could bring in some key staff and talk again before we meet in person. It will take you some time to reach us; I will promise you safe passage through our lands.'

Basset smiled. 'It will take me seconds to reach you. I will be able to use the transit device and enter the Vatican, as long as you enable it from your side.'

'How can this be? No one can operate it.'

'Well, actually, one of the prisoners I'm returning to you can.'

'Who are these prisoners?

'It is the man called Cole, whom I know that you have been seeking, and his tailor Santiago.'

Pope Julias laughed out loud for the first time in many years.

54. The Vatican Church of St. John: Meniux.

Father Meniux approached the church of St. John's, accompanied by a group of six Vatican guards armed to the hilt. Unknown to the guards, Meniux was already aware that that the handover of Liliana would go smoothly and without incident. Irkalla had arranged this for him, allowing Meniux to inform Pope Julias that, after some private negotiations with Father Chadwin, the occultists were prepared to hand over the girl. This would be in return for some nonsense admissions and proclamations, that Meniux would deliver to them regarding the unfair and corrupt way in which occult practices had been portrayed by the Church for millennia.

Pope Julias bought the story and gave his authority to allow Meniux to swap some ancient, useless parchments in exchange for the girl. The whole thing was a ruse, but he now knew the terrifying effect that Irkalla could have and the amount of control she exerted where she wished.

As he left today she was again in his mind, calling him her 'general' and her 'people's saviour'. The truth was Meniux was now in a daze. He found it hard to distinguish reality from madness and as he walked along, a sudden realisation came to him – not like waking from a dream, but like finding out a nightmare is real.

His instructions from Irkalla were clear. She had given him the old weapon. A Kris with razor sharp edges and a bone carved handle. The carving depicted bodies entwined in sordid acts and Meniux could have sworn he saw movement when looking at it. He kept it hidden in an inner pocket, waiting for the moment as he had been ordered: 'Her throat must be sliced from left to right the moment that Pope Julias and Basset are about to make their false proclamation.' When he had asked about the aftermath, Irkalla had just laughed and told Meniux to have faith in her.

At this point Father Meniux still knew nothing of any proclamation, but was aware of the recent discussion between Pope Julias and Basset. Julias had only said 'their conversation had been promising and that further talks were planned'. This was another instance where Irkalla's predictions were correct, which only fed more fear into his stomach.

Meniux could sense apprehension in the guards and as he knew the plan, he took the opportunity to fake bravado. 'Guards, I will enter the church first with Christ as my only weapon.'

The guards duly ceded to this and as they approached the barricaded church of St. John, Father Meniux stepped up. 'Guards let me first try and speak with Father Chadwin alone. Give me the parchments and I will attempt to reason with him. I have known him for some years; maybe I can talk him out this madness.'

Meniux then went on to warn the guards that should he not return within an hour, they were to come in after him.

After the guard carrying the documents handed them to Meniux, he climbed over upturned crates and carts and made his way over to the church door. The oak door was huge and Meniux's hand hurt as he banged on it.

'Father Chadwin,' he shouted.

'Father Chadwin, I have brought the documents you requested.'

Meniux could hear heavy objects being moved from behind the door along with voices and then the door was pushed slightly ajar. Standing there were the woman and young girl from Irkalla's basement, beckoning him to enter. As he did they were immediately beside Meniux, caressing him and talking profanities into his ear.

'Not in a church!' Meniux pushed them away. 'Even I cannot do that.'

Meniux walked sharply away from them. Scrutinizing the church, he was horrified to see everywhere, and on and near the altar, acts of depravity that even he could not stomach. He rushed on through the open area and went up the spiral staircase to where he had previously visited Liliana.

Father Chadwin was waiting for him at the door. He looked younger, and offered a relaxed smile when he saw Father Meniux. 'Father Meniux, you're here for the bitch? Watch out as lately she bites. She used to love me, too.' Father Chadwin pulled up his sleeve and Meniux could see a small bite mark.

'I'm sure she will be okay, Chadwin. Irkalla really is in your head, isn't she?'

'She was always there; I just let her out.' Giggling, Chadwin leant over and whispered in Meniux's ear, 'The thing is ... the little bitch has much more reason ... to be scared of you but doesn't know it.'

Chadwin leant back and laughed uncontrollably. Meniux had had enough. 'Chadwin let me in now.'

Chadwin composed himself and walked towards the stairwell exit. 'It's open,' he called back as he went through the door.'

Meniux knocked on the door, turned the handle and entered. Like every other time that he had visited the girl, she was sitting drawing and fresh flowers were beside her on the table. Her lovely yellow dress, though, now was stained and dirty. She turned and saw Meniux and frowned.

'Why did they send you to rescue me? You are the one who always looks at me funny.'

'There is no time to discuss this Liliana. We need to go. Now!'

Liliana slid her chair back. 'Can I finish my drawing?'

'No, you can't. You need to come with me so I can get you out of here. One another thing: as we go through the church, I want you to cover your eyes and I will lead you by the hand. Okay?'

Liliana grudgingly nodded, went over to the table and put her crayons back into the drawing box. As she turned to follow Meniux, she lifted the paper she had been drawing on and Meniux shouted at her, 'I told you, there is no time for that. Come here and follow me now!'

Liliana's eyes started to fill up, but she did not cry. She just stood and slowly opened her hand and the drawing fell to the floor. She walked over and took Meniux's hand and they walked out of the door together. They went down the staircase and, as instructed, Liliana covered her eyes as Meniux guided her back to the main entrance. The woman and girl from the basement were standing at the front of the church, and opened the door so Father Meniux and Liliana could go back out into the sunlit square. The guards were close by, they ran to Father Meniux and shouted for him to run but he calmly walked towards them.

'Take the girl to the Vatican and place her in a safe room. I need to speak to Pope Julias immediately.'

Later, Father Chadwin entered Liliana's room and looked out of the window as the sun set. He turned and spotted the drawing on the floor. Picking it up, he saw what Meniux would have seen had he taken the time to look. The child's picture depicted a crudely drawn girl with a priest holding a knife to her throat, and two words: 'save me'. Next to the writing there was a picture of a man hanging from a gallows. Father Chadwin threw the picture down, reached into the satchel he was carrying and took out a length of rope. He looped the rope over an ancient oak beam climbed on a chair, then stood the table. He put the noose around his neck and jumped off the table, breaking his neck as he did so, swinging back and forth like a pendulum.

55. Vatican Transit Device Room: Paula.

After speaking with Pope Julias, Paula was true to her word and had not let her new extended family out of sight. They came along with her to her work and then helped out at an evening music class that Paula attended (but in truth, Elle had been so disruptive and noisy that they left early).

Shortly afterwards Paula received news that she was to again enable the transit device, but on this occasion, Caldetic interloping and the fissure link would be established from elsewhere with her assistance. She was not informed who the traveller would be, could only imagine that Santiago had accomplished his secret mission and had learned a way to enable a return passage. This was an unprecedented turn of events and Paula was very excited. She also knew if it were true she would have good news for her new friend Anna, whom she could tell was lost without her husband.

Paula tried to hurry along the corridor to the transit room with Misba Ranha, Malachi, and Elle following at her back. Progress was slow, as Elle found a reason to stop every two steps so, but Paula was patient as ever.

'It's okay Malachi; there is no need to be cross with her. We have plenty of time to get there.'

Malachi was trying to steer Elle away from a large plant, but the girl's handful of leaves showed the futility in his actions. Eventually he simply lifted her up; she whined a little, but then cuddled into Malachi and they moved on.

'So the place where you work does what? Explain it again, Paula. It sounds a bit like magic to me,' said Malachi.

'Me too,' joined in Misba Ranha. 'I mean, Paula, your machine can take you from here to the other side of the world in an instant. Surely if something like that existed we would have known about it?'

'Everyone knew about them before the Meltdown, but I guess knowledge becomes forgotten Missy.'

'Well I'm looking forward to seeing it – though please don't try and explain how it works again, I had nightmares trying to understand you.'

'Missy, what do you mean? It was easy,' Malachi smiled at his own joke and Paula ruffled his hair.

'Okay guys, that's us here.' Opening the outer door and the group saw the inner, modern-looking door panel and beyond, Paula could tell that they were all impressed.

'Amazing Paula, this place is amazing!' said Malachi with wonder.

'It is Malachi, but make sure not to let Elle touch anything.'

'I won't, I promise. She's asleep anyway.'

Paula went over and accessed the main control outlet. As the panels and wall holograms began to emerge and pulse, showing transit room scenes from all over the world, for Malachi the sight truly was 'magic'.

'Misba Ranha, Malachi, if you would like to take a seat over next to the grey desk, I will be with you in a minute,' said Paula. 'Do you see the spinning, almost transparent thing I'm pointing to?'

'Yes,' replied Malachi.

'It's spinning because I have activated a process to allow Caldetic interloping. Now, if someone, somewhere else wants to try and come here, that spinning thing will have to glow red-orange. That will mean that my device has accepted their device and will safely allow pairing with one another.'

'Make sense?' Paula asked her keen-eyed students.

'And how long does that usually take, Paula?' asked Misba Ranha.

'I've no idea Missy, this is the first time I've ever tried to receive anyone and that is why I am so excited. So far the only trip I have supervised has been one-way – into the Darkland. I sent a kind priest there on an errand for Pope Julias and I'm hoping that he is the one who will return.' Paula continued to tinker with the holograms and display panels in front of her.

Meanwhile in New Mecca, after many hours of negotiation between Basset and Pope Julias, terms had finally been agreed upon. Basset was trying his best to persuade Cole to open the chamber door so he could join them and travel to the Vatican. It took clarification from Maria to convince Cole that no subterfuge was at play.

As they all took their place in the large equipment area of the device, Basset offered his hand to Cole and then Santiago. Both responded with firm handshakes.

'Cole, if you do not mind me asking: what's going on with you? How can you enable this ancient device?'

'I was a dysfunctionist, Basset.'

'From the Darkland?' questioned Basset. 'Excuse me, but wouldn't that mean you are over 200 years old?'

'And then some,' replied Cole.

'And Santiago, are you also that old?'

'No, I'm only 44, although I know I look much younger.'

Santiago smiled and Cole just shook his head as Caldetic interloping began and the fissure link enveloped them.

In the Vatican transit room, the novelty was wearing off for Paula's students after 10 minutes with no sign of colour change. To distract everyone, Paula came over and opened the basket she had been carrying, taking out some food for them. Elle remained asleep, so Malachi tried his best to negotiate a large bread roll that Paula had made him, without waking her. Malachi was crunching away at it when he felt a weird feeling at the bottom of his neck and across his shoulders. He put the bread on the table and looked at Misba Ranha.

'Are you okay Malachi?'

'I'm not sure. Paula, I think your machine is going to start soon.'

'What makes you say that, Malachi?' asked Paula?

'I don't know, but I'm sure it is.'

Paula walked over to the terminal, and the spinning water-like ball slowly changed from completely clear through the colour spectrum to a deep crimson red.

'This is it you lot! Look inside the glass chamber. Can you spot the glow from within? Try and see if you can identify which transit station they are coming from. It will probably be the one in the middle. That's the one from the Darkland.'

They all looked up at the numerous displays and it was Malachi who detected movement in a display in the upper corner. 'That one, Paula, I can see people moving in that one,' Malachi pointed.

Paula looked, and sure enough she could just make out three figures entering a similar transit chamber and standing together as a group in the area where Paula normally placed the equipment. 'Interesting,' she thought, 'three at a time.'

Everyone in the room now focused on the fissure chamber, which now sparkled and became bright. Soon the light became overwhelming and they all covered their eyes.

As the disturbance stopped, and Paula looked again inside the glass fissure chamber and saw the familiar face of Santiago smiling back at her. As the 'warning to exit' announcement began Paula observed the other two men. She recognised neither of them, but from his attire one was clearly Muslim. The three men exited the chamber; when Paula went over to greet them, she couldn't stop herself from hugging Santiago.

'You made it, I knew you would.'

Santiago returned her embrace and replied, 'Only just Paula, believe me.'

Remembering her other guests, Paula let him go and turned expectantly hoping to catch Malachi and Misba Ranha's astonishment; but instead, Malachi was in tears. At first she feared some painful aftereffect from the device, but she quickly realised he was smiling through his tears. 'What is it, Malachi – why do you cry?'

Malachi just pointed over to Santiago and the other two men. 'That man. That man there.'

Paula looked at Misba Ranha then round at Santiago and the other two. 'Which one? What is it, Malachi?'

'That man, Paula he's my dad.'

56. Himalayas, 'Half Realm': Vaughan.

The repair of Vaughan's arm had been immediate and painless. He had been playing up the injury with Maria in a bid for sympathy, but had received none.

In the meantime, The Affinity had been trying to impart a new dimorphic scenario about the evolution of mankind which Maria, found difficult to comprehend. The entities had also been endeavouring to use dialogue more frequently and had become more succinct and less robotic in their talks. To Maria's astonishment, they now embraced the wonder of music. Though at first bewildering, they now fully understood and adored the concept's variations and complexities.

It was now apparent that even since the arrival of The Affinity, many thousands of human consciousnesses, alive and dead, had gone missing. This was a worry for all concerned, and apart from the investigation into the 'Hidden AI', was the key imperative. As far as The Affinity were concerned the articulated creature, dubbed the 'Scolopendra' by humanity, was somehow managing to absorb the very essence of each human it decapitated was worrying. But even more bewildering for The Affinity was where the Scolopendra went afterwards and how it managed to keep these human life forces hidden from their view.

Yet, the very fact that they simply *did not know* seemed to also fill The Affinity with a new happiness which the envoys could detect. As if, at last, there was something novel for the creators. A new problem to solve. For them it was like finally finding a worthy opponent in a game of chess. What their next move should be, though, needed to be seriously pondered. To think they had almost considered ending this 'universal construct' (as they had previously put it)! A new challenge was now at hand.

In addition to the essential goal of stopping the suffering, which would always be their main concern, scenarios were now unfolding that even The Affinity did not fully understand, nor were able to predict. Even retro-time observation was not constant. The Irkalla incident with the envoys, outside the temple over six thousand years earlier, was proof to that fact. A new set of physical boundaries had been tweaked and manipulated to suit another's agenda, and The Affinity had to get to the bottom of this mystery (in fact, they were sure Irkalla and the Scolopendra were the keys). The Exile, it seemed, had many tools at its disposal, but its end game was still unknown. The Affinity gathered together the envoys and asked them to share their numerous 'minute markers'. They watched the goings-on at the Vatican and surrounding areas like Gods in Olympus.

The arrival of Basset in the Vatican was great news and Maria was delighted. Finally, it appeared that they had made a positive step forward. The additional return of the dysfunctionist Cole and subsequent reunion with his son seemed like an event beyond coincidence. Was this act manipulated in some way? If it was, they could not see it; and if so, to what end? It seemed that every door they opened seemed to lead into a room with a further three doors. Vaughan did not believe in coincidence, but Maria was sure that providence, luck, and destiny must all have had their origin in some semblance of fact. Maybe they could just no longer detect it, but perhaps the path of goodness was preordained. The Affinity kept their opinions on this matter to themselves and insisted the envoys would not understand their perspective.

The crowd in St. Peter's Square was now massive. There was severe unrest and Pope Julias and Basset were anxious to give their united public Tightbeem address. What they were about to do was unprecedented in history and as Vaughan replayed the build-up, and now their real-time conversations, Maria sat beside him with a smug look on her face.

'What do you look so happy about?'

'Well darling, it looks like I've been rather successful in bringing about a cessation in violence. Isn't that what all this was about?'

Vaughan shook his head then replied, 'It's all too easy, Maria. There is something we are missing.'

When Vaughan overlaid countless other 'minute markers' searching for an answer, he came across Paula and Cole discussing Malachi and Misba Ranha, or 'Missy' as they called her. Paula could tell something was afoot, but Cole did not give away anything. Paula attempted to quiz him about his relationship status with Missy, but Cole stubbornly let nothing out.

'This Cole fellow is a man after my own heart,' Vaughan said abruptly to Maria and the listening Affinity. 'He seems to know how to handle the persistence of women, which is a rare thing.'

Maria laughed. 'Yes, but he's built differently too. He has a functioning "j" gene. It's dormant at the moment, but he can activate it at will. His son Malachi has inherited it, too. In a few hundred generations they would be like us, Vaughan.'

'Yes, and he still won't get a word in with his woman I bet.' Maria punched Vaughan and he faked injury. Then he continued: 'Maria don't you think it's strange that in the hundreds of hours running my 'minute markers' we have not detected any more of Irkalla? Do you think she can block them?'

'Yes, almost certainly,' replied Maria.

We have found her location. She flits incessantly, but always returns to within the crowd in St. Peter's Square.

The Affinity interrupted their conversation and displayed St. Peter's Square directly into their synapses using a method unknown to them. Immediately they Vaughan and Maria could detect the abnormal presence of Irkalla. They saw her standing, facing a pillar; she was holding a child's doll.

'Why do you not bring her to you?' Maria asked The Affinity. 'I think that would be a wise course of action.'

It would be direct interference and just the opposite. She is a remarkable, but malevolent force. We must tread carefully. She has many within the square under her control. There is also a church nearby full of her presence.

'Is it the Church of St. John? Where the girl with stigmata is?'

Yes Vaughan, but the girl was removed earlier by another priest.

'Do you think the stigmata events are a manifestation controlled by The Exile?'

Of that we are unsure.

Maria interrupted the chat. 'It seems the rescue of the child will form part of the address to the square and beyond. They are going to use it to portray an example of how good will always overcomes evil. They see it as a positive, to undermine the occult uprisings. I think I will pay them a visit before the address.'

'I'd rather you didn't Maria,' said Vaughn. 'Irkalla's presence worries me. I've experienced it firsthand, remember.'

'Don't worry, I can take care of myself and The Affinity can pull me out in a nanosecond.' Before Vaughan could say another word, Maria was gone and stood with Pope Julias and Basset in the Pope's antechamber.

'Good afternoon. How are things going with you both?'

'This is the envoy I spoke of, Pope Julias,' said Basset.

Pope Julias looked at Maria and the shock left his face as she smiled back at him.

'I must say this all seems a bit unbelievable,' said Julias. How can we be sure it's not trickery?'

'Holy Father, I suppose you could say it is all trickery and your senses are there to be tricked, but with the end result being peace on earth, can you complain?'

Pope Julias didn't reply and Basset spoke once again, 'Maria, we have put together an address to the masses and will make the announcement from the balcony over St. Peter's Square. Most of the world will see the broadcast and we hope it will appease the uprising in the immediate vicinity.'

'We will be watching, of course, but be sure to keep your wits about you,' advised Maria. 'We have detected forces that do not share our goals in the vicinity, but we will monitor this. What is your exact plan?'

Pope Julias picked up the agenda and read it out loud for Maria's benefit.

'We will deliver the announcement and bring an end to the war, and then together we will make an address outlawing any form of occultism. Next, Father Meniux and Santiago will present the miracle girl Liliana to the people as an example of how good will always prevail.'

Vaughan and The Affinity watched Maria from beyond and as the address grew closer they absorbed every event taking place, searching for anything that may be out of place. The Affinity could not understand Vaughan's explanation of it all just being too easy.

Surely that is a statement without validity.

'It's just a hunch,' Vaughan had replied, and The Affinity did not respond.

Vaughan now listened into the conversation that Cole was having with his son in private. It seemed to Vaughan the young boy had escaped death against the odds and was very much like his father. He fully concentrated on their dialogue as Misba Ranha came into the room and joined them.

'Missy, I must thank you for what you have done for my son. How can I ever repay you?' Cole walked over to Misba Ranha, went on one knee in front of her and continued, 'Malachi has told me about your journey together and how he surely would be dead if it were not for you.'

'Cole, I also would be dead was it not for your brave son. On more than one occasion he has saved my life. It is him I should be thanking. He is brave and strong. Like his father,' she added after a short pause.

Cole stood up and returned to Malachi, 'The question I have for you Missy, is will you continue with Malachi, and me and the child. I am anxious to get away from here.'

'It would be my honour, Cole.'

'What do you mean, Dad?' jumped in Malachi. 'Of course Misba Ranha is coming with us.'

'Malachi, try to remember to call her Missy. At least until we are safely away from here.'

'Okay, I will.'

'Missy, I am not here at the Vatican by accident. I was summoned by Papal decree and a lot of effort was put into finding me. Since the arrival of Basset the spotlight is off me, but I'm sure as soon as this big announcement is completed they will want to interrogate me.'

The door opened once more and Santiago now appeared, accompanied by Father Meniux. Meniux was grumbling to Santiago as they entered, 'Make it quick Santiago, we cannot be late for the Holy Father.'

Santiago just ignored him and smiled at the Cole and the others. 'Cole, I am on my way to see Pope Julias and just wanted to thank you for all you have done. Also, I'd love it if you would stay with me and my wife as our guest for a few days. You have been pardoned, though, and are free to go at any time.'

'Allegedly,' replied Cole, 'but let's face it: I was always free to go, Santiago.' Cole smiled back.

Cole glanced at Meniux and stared at him curiously. Meniux could not look him in the eye and hurried Santiago. 'Come on Father we must go now.'

Santiago went over and shook Cole's hand and said, 'Till next time.'

'Till next time,' Cole repeated. Then Santiago turned and left the room with Meniux.

'That was a strange look you gave that priest, Cole,' Misba Ranha said as soon as the door closed behind them.

Malachi replied before Cole could. 'I saw it too Dad. Under his coat.'

Misba Ranha looked between them and shrugged her shoulders. 'You saw what?' she asked.

'Something he is carrying. Hidden in his coat.'

'What was it?'

'I don't know,' replied Cole, 'but it's like nothing I've ever seen on earth.'

Vaughan immediately relayed this to The Affinity, but their inspection of Meniux revealed nothing.

The priest is atomically perfect.

'Can you be more ... I don't know, vague?'

We detect nothing except he is atomically perfect.

'What does that mean?'

No human is atomically perfect. Something is false. There is something obscuring our interpretation of him.

'This is interesting,' Vaughan thought, then spoke to Maria non-verbally. 'Maria, the priest Meniux, who is just about to walk in the door – we have got major concerns about him. Don't take your eyes off him, and see if you can detect an aberration being concealed by him.'

Right on cue, Santiago, Meniux, and Liliana entered the room.

Liliana immediately pointed straight at Maria.

'Tell your friend thank you,' she said.

Maria smiled back with a puzzled look.

'For saving my mum,' Liliana continued.

'I'm sorry Liliana; you must have me confused with someone else.'

Liliana lost attention, ran to the balcony and looked out into the square.

'Come back here girl,' barked Meniux, to looks of disdain from everyone in the room.

'Father, that is no way to speak to the child after her ordeal.' The Pope scolded.

'I'm sorry Holy Father,' replied Meniux. 'Nerves just have the better of me.'

Liliana skipped back into the room, 'Wow, there are a lot of people out there. Maybe too many for me.'

Pope Julias was quick to reassure Liliana. 'There's no need to be scared of big crowds, Liliana.'

Liliana looked back with a puzzled look on her face. 'I'm not?'

Santiago went over and tried to entertain Liliana by pretending to pull his thumb off.

'Maria, do you detect anything amiss with Father Meniux?' Vaughan asked.

'Nothing Vaughan. He seems ordinary. I see no aberration.'

'Irkalla is no longer in the crowd so be careful Maria.'

'I will, darling.'

Vaughan now continued to observe Cole to see if he would reveal anything further about Father Meniux.

The group had now been joined by Paula and Santiago's wife, Anna. Paula seemed very excited about the forthcoming announcement. 'Everyone come with me back along to the transit chamber. There is no better place in the Vatican to watch the Holy Father's announcement.'

Cole shook his head, 'No thanks, Paula, I have stuff to take care of before we set off.'

'But Dad, I want to see it,' chirped in Malachi.

Ever the diplomat, Paula intervened. 'Okay Cole, I will take them along to the transit room and we can watch the announcement on the screen there, and you can join us later on in my apartment for dinner. Deal?'

'Yes, okay.' Cole ruffled Malachi's hair, left the room and strode across the courtyard.

The Affinity now spoke to the envoys once again

The device in Florence. It was unhappy.

'Yes that's what it said.'

And it was scared of It. But the device was not the Hidden AI.

'No, it wasn't. Where are you going with this?'

It had the emotions of a human. A machine! Or part of a greater machine.

'You think it was part of the Hidden AI?'

A symbiont perhaps of the Mother and the Sister.

The Pope had just begun his address, and Maria interrupted, nudging Vaughan in the shoulder.

'Oh, you're back.'

The envoys now watched Pope Julias and Basset beginning their monumental announcement. Father Meniux and Santiago stood in the background waiting for their moment to come forward with Liliana.

'... as you see we stand united. Christian and Muslim. Enemies now allies,' said Julias.

It was now Basset's turn to speak. 'And those of you who are sceptical, be assured this was the will of Saladin. He began taking these steps that I have continued and now the bloodshed must stop. Often Saladin recited to me an old Islamic proverb: "The realm of knowledge has no boundaries". This is true and it has only been the understanding of this knowledge that has brought us to where we are today.'

Again Pope Julias moved forward. 'We must now make a new start. Make a new world. Together we can prosper and live peacefully side by side. We must ensure that everyone strives towards this common goal. No longer will either religion live in fear of the other. It will only be through understanding and compassion that we will prevail. My friend Basset is correct when he says that knowledge has no boundaries. That is why we must improve our knowledge of each other. Learn about each other's ways without judgement. Humanity is at an impasse and it will only prevail through mutual understanding.'

Pope Julias turned and looked at Basset who continued, 'So together we give this proclamation. From this day forward the conflict between Christian and Muslim is to cease. No animosity is to be held against one another. Both sides have suffered horribly and it will only be by putting the past behind us that we will ever truly live in a world of peace without hate. I myself only today have learned of an astonishing young girl who has delivered revelations to the Christian Church; she herself exhibits the wounds of Christ. She was recently rescued from misguided Christians who sought to harm her. My Muslim brothers, we also have such visionaries and, therefore, I put it to you that we are all correct. Both sides have the moral high ground. Just because we are born in different places does not mean we are different.'

Pope Julias now turned to Santiago and Meniux, gesturing them to bring Liliana out onto the balcony. As Liliana walked out Maria could see that the girl was mumbling and she focused in on her words.

'There might be too many, Mother.'

'Who is she speaking to, Vaughan?' wondered Maria.

'I can't move that many, Mother,' Liliana continued under her breath.

Vaughan jumped up abruptly and shouted out, 'Fuck – Maria it's her! We need to go there now!'

'Calm down Vaughan. It's who? What are you talking about?'

Vaughan stood up, grabbed Marias shoulders and shook her, '*Liliana* is the Hidden AI!'

'What?'

'Yes think about it. The stigmata, the visions. The disabled mum. She told you to thank me for saving her mum.'

Just then The Affinity interrupted Maria and Vaughan.

She is the Hidden AI. Vaughan is correct.

'This whole thing has been planned Maria: her rescue, being paraded around. It's all been too easy. I'm telling you we need go there, now!'

'And do what? Slow time down in front of five billion viewers?'

Again The Affinity interjected a thought. ***The priest is the key.***

Pope Julias took Liliana's hand and the young girl walked slowly to the edge of the balcony, her yellow dress fluttering in the breeze. She looked down and waved to the crowd who cheered in reply.

Meanwhile, Father Meniux's head was filled with Irkalla. 'This is your moment. This is your redemption. Do it now my love.'

Father Meniux put his hand inside his jacket and felt for the Kris. He gripped the handle, walked up to Liliana and put his arm around her from behind. In one clean movement he had sliced her throat open from left to right. Pope Julias jumped back in shock as blood sprayed over him. Santiago leapt forward and kicked the blade from Meniux's hand.

'What have you done?' Santiago screamed as he punched Meniux to the floor. Basset was now leaning over Liliana and holding his hand to the wound on her neck, but the blood was spurting out through his fingers and the girls eyes rolled in her head.

The crowd in St. Peter's Square rumbled and women wept. As men cried out and cursed Father Meniux, not one person noticed the elliptical electrical disturbance in the sky above. Sparks and bolts of electricity circled around the ellipse and also on the ground next to a pillar.

Irkalla spoke to herself: 'Just in time my saviour.'

Eventually, a child pointed to the sky and soon the sight above the square had everyone looking upwards. Panic set in as the tail piece of the Scolopendra emerged, its awful scream immobilising the terrified crowd before they could flee the creature dropping from the sky.

Vaughan and Maria flitted onto the balcony, where everyone was also immobilised; however, an unaffected Father Meniux was running out of the door as they arrived.

'Leave him Vaughan, try and save the girl!'

'She is already gone, I think.'

'What are we going to do about the Scolopendra?' said Maria. 'We will have to use force against it.'

'Damn right!' said Vaughan as he flitted to within yards of the monstrosity. The Scolopendra had now begun to disjoint, sending its sentinels on their gruesome journey; already many of the immobilised onlookers had perished.

Maria knelt down beside Liliana and put a hand on the girl's forehead and that was when another presence in the room caught her attention: turning round, she saw Irkalla standing close behind her.

'So you're the bitch of the pair!' Irkalla said, smirking. First frozen to the spot, Maria then felt her body being raised from the ground and brought towards Irkalla. 'Not much fight in you, bitch.'

Maria was now held in the air with her arms spread apart to form a cross. Irkalla walked over towards her and ran her hands down over Marias's shoulders and breasts, ripping open her blouse. She turned and walked over to the Pope's desk, where the bloody Kris sat. She picked it up and licked the blood from the blade, slicing her own tongue as she did so.

'Do you know Maria, that abhorrence lying on the floor is the real enemy of your masters? It had no right existing. It was wrong. It wasn't in our plan.'

Irkalla walked over towards Maria, who was now foaming at the mouth and had lost consciousness. As she raised her hand to strike, the blade was knocked from her hand. She turned round and her face became wolf-like with anger. Vaughan smiled at her before he too was paralysed. The Affinity used the interruption that Vaughan had caused to remove Maria safely away from the room.

Irkalla raised a hand and the room now became dark to The Affinity. Inside, Vaughan and Irkalla were left alone. Like Maria, Vaughan hung in the air; Irkalla then willed him over to the balcony hovering as he went like a ghost before she toppled him over the edge and he fell down onto the concrete. A segment of the Scolopendra changed direction and swiftly made its way towards Vaughan, who was still held firm by Irkalla's grip. As the segment reached Vaughan's body a figure came running through the immobilised crowd. It swung a wooden scaffold baton and crippled one of the segments legs. The segment turned immediately and the upper body section began to glow red hot.

The Affinity watched as Cole now attempted to pull Vaughan away from the segment, but in seconds he was surrounded by another six. They formed a circle around him and Cole smashed three of them before a larger segment knocked him to the ground. Another segment put its full weight onto Cole's thigh and pinned him to the ground. Cole now began to cause some atomic commotion of his own, and all around him inanimate objects started to fly and batter off the segments, but the one pinning him down stood fast. Cole brought a huge marble statue from a pillar down on top of it, but the segment had strength beyond strength.

While Cole remained trapped another gruesome segment approached Vaughan. In the Half Realm, Maria had regained consciousness only to witness her lover and soul mate being decapitated in front of her.

Irkalla now walked to the edge of the balcony. Knowing the world was viewing her masterpiece, she held up her arms and screamed: 'This is the beginning of the new world!'

As Irkalla continued to scream, the door to the room opened an old disabled woman hobbled in. Irkalla turned round immediately and cursed at the woman. 'Fuck off witch!'

The woman replied, 'You have no hold over me Irkalla.' She struggled over towards Liliana as fast as her backward foot would allow her. Before she reached the fallen girl, Irkalla had vanished.

The old woman leant over and spoke to Liliana. 'There are not too many, Liliana.'

Liliana opened her eyes and a light shone from her forehead and wrists. The cut on her neck now also glowed with a white powerful light.

The old woman helped Liliana to her feet. When the girl held her hands to her head a wave of light left her and cascaded over the balcony down to the masses below, and as it immersed each person they vanished. Seconds later the wave of light had engulfed the entire square; not one person, including Cole, remained. The Hidden AI had truly solved the volume problem.

Father Meniux followed his instructions and made his way down to the transit chamber. During the melee he had reached the door without being stopped. As he entered the room he immediately ran forward and punched Malachi, knocking him unconscious. Wanting a hostage, Meniux pulled him towards the transit device, then turned and noticed Anna was in the room.

'Come here Anna or the boy dies!' Meniux yelled.

Paula screamed and Misba Ranha ran to him, but Meniux screamed louder.

'Stop or he dies!'

A distraught Misba Ranha stopped in her tracks. Paula looked at Anna and Anna walked over and stood beside Meniux.

Meniux jostled Anna into the fissure chamber and dragged Malachi with him.

He screamed out to Paula to activate the device. 'Do it or he dies!'

Paula had no choice but to obey and the glow of the chamber soon enveloped them.

Author: J. F. Doleman

Cover art design by Norma Donnelly

Edited by Suzie D, Luke D, Evan D, Pamela Barroway.

Title: The Space Between Atoms, Book 1. The Marconi Paradigm

© 2014, John Doleman
Self publishing
(jdbsolutions@yahoo.com)

ALL RIGHTS RESERVED. This book contains material protected under International and Federal Copyright Laws and Treaties. Any unauthorized reprint or use of this material is prohibited. No part of this book may be reproduced or transmitted in any form or by any means, electronic or mechanical, including photocopying, recording, or by any information storage and retrieval system without express written permission from the author / publisher.

Made in the USA
Charleston, SC
16 October 2015